A
CHRIƧTMAƧ
MURDER
OF
CROWS

A CHRISTMAS MURDER OF CROWS

D.M. AUSTIN

First published in 2022 by D M Austin, in partnership with whitefox publishing

www.wearewhitefox.com

Copyright © D M Austin, 2022

ISBN 9781915036506

Also available as an ebook

Edited, designed and typeset by Jill Sawyer Phypers
Cover design by Dominic Forbes
Project management by whitefox

For AJ

Floor Plans of Crowthwaite Castle

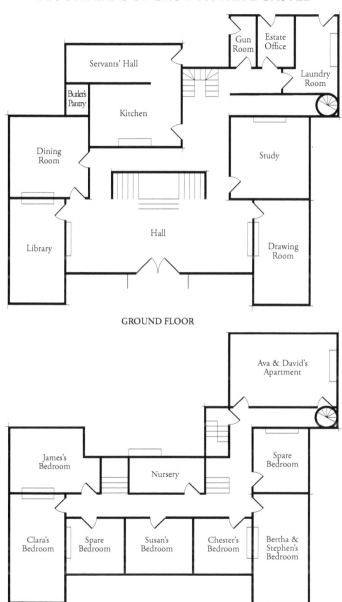

GROUND FLOOR

FIRST FLOOR

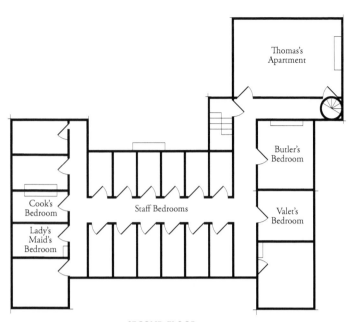

SECOND FLOOR

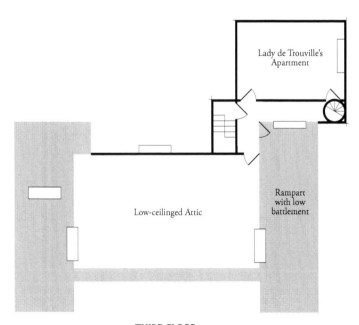

THIRD FLOOR

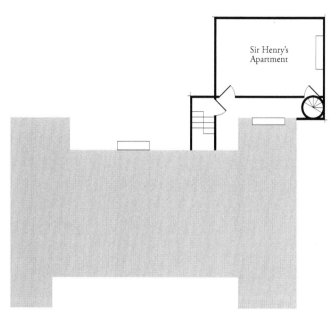

FOURTH FLOOR

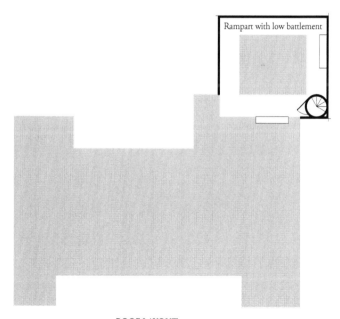

ROOF LAYOUT

Character List

Sir Henry de Trouville, Lord of the Manor of Crowthwaite and Tenth Baronet of Crowthwaite Castle, in the county of Westmorland

Lady Violet de Trouville, his wife

Ava Rickard, Sir Henry's eldest niece

David Rickard, Ava's husband

Bertha Taylor, Sir Henry's second niece

Stephen Taylor, Bertha's husband

Their Children: Betsy – age six

                                 Rose – age four

Clara de Trouville, Sir Henry's youngest niece

Chester Johnson, Clara's guest

Susan Markham, Sir Henry's distant cousin

James Bowes, friend of the family

Thomas (Tom) Atkinson, Sir Henry's private secretary

Fawcett, butler

George Turner, Sir Henry's valet

May Carver, Lady Violet's maid

Ivy Bridges, housemaid

Lizzie 'Silver-Tone', housemaid

Pearl Bell, barmaid at The Black Feather

Kenneth Watson, Chief Constable of Cumberland and Westmorland Constabulary

Gilbert Dunderdale, Detective Inspector of Manchester City Police

Charles Collins, Sergeant of Appleby Police, Westmorland

ERNEST SHAW, Constable of Appleby Police, Westmorland
JOHN DONNELLY, Constable of Appleby Police, Westmorland
JOHN ATKINS, Sir Henry's solicitor
PETER BARNES, Chief Constable Watson's nephew

PROLOGUE

GILBERT DUNDERDALE DIDN'T only wake to Christmas alone but earlier than intended due to the urgent knocks on his mid-terrace front door.

'By Athena!' he protested, not best pleased while looping the belt of his dressing gown into a knot. 'What's the reasoning behind this, Jonesy?'

'The motor's waiting, sir... Chief said you're needed up North.'

'We are *up* North,' the detective inspector of Manchester City Police reminded the constable.

'Pardon, sir, I meant *further* north. Someone from somewhere back of beyond's dead and Chief said, nevertheless, it matters.'

'Hmm,' Dunderdale replied, and, turning around, began to undo the short-lived knot.

ONE

'Do yer know what the collective noun is for a gatherin' o' crows?' the barmaid asked the traveller while pouring his ale.

'Haven't the foggiest.'

'Murder. A murder o' crows. Not many people know it, but ask anyone in Crowthwaite and we'll know it.'

Over the rim of his tankard, the traveller regarded the bonny young woman.

'If heat hadn't taken Grandad this summer, he'd be sittin' in his chair opposite and while he warmed his worn joints – his back legs as he liked to call 'em, he'd be suppin' ale and puffin' away on his pipe and tellin' a story. 'Course, he used to say "word" for a gatherin' o' crows. Sir Henry de Trouville – that's *ninth* not tenth baronet – told him the correct name for it, but Grandad wouldn't have it. *Do yer know what the* word *is for a gatherin' o' crows?* he'd have said... and then, right this minute, he'd be tellin' yer a story.'

'Of a murder of crows? Then why don't you take his place?'

After topping up the traveller's tankard and placing the ceramic pitcher on the table beside him, the barmaid settled down onto the threadbare seat cushion that still held Grandad's imprint. 'Search the history books,' she began, 'and yer'll discover Crowthwaite in't reign o' King John, hidin' in a vast area of huntin' land, but try as yer might to travel back further and yer'll soon see the ink dries out. *You*, if yer divn't mind me sayin', are fortunate to have travelled here in body and mind for now yer'll hear words passed down from afore

Christianity itself reached us lands... From long afore when these parts were thick with forest...' Leaning forward to stoke the fire in the open grate, the storyteller's voice was drawn up the chimney; detangling from heavier particles it was carried away on the cold dusk air. Drifting north-east, her voice followed a gentle rise from where, as time had travelled through millennia, trees had been plucked and the ground gutted to make way for settlement. Barely above roof level the waves mounted the lower contour of Cross Fell, until a magnet from the east altered their course: the manor of Crowthwaite, nestled within the remaining forest like the frog within the horse's shoe. Before the barmaid's words could reach the forest edge they snagged on the thorn of a lonely, bare hawthorn, where a black-and-grey-hooded inquisitor, perched on a gnarled branch, cocked its head to the valley below, its beaded eye picking out two white dots cutting erratically through twilight shadow in perfect parallel.

———

'Yes, the journey's been tiresome, but I was referring to you. Look, you know full well these tracks weren't built for speed never mind motor cars!'

'You promised a quiet Christmas,' David said, 'just the two of us to see in nineteen twenty-four.'

'I never made any such promise.'

'Then you should have.'

'Uncle Henry would never countenance our not joining the family for Christmas.'

'Because, Ava, dear wife, you indulge him – as does everyone else.'

'What was I saying...? Oh, yes, *tiresome*! What I don't

understand is for someone who professes a dislike for family gatherings, you've certainly driven with enthusiasm.'

'I'm fed up of driving, that's what this is,' her husband corrected her while negotiating a few houses clinging to an s-bend. 'I want this journey to end!'

'You were the one who insisted on driving.'

'Because the alternative would have meant being cooped up in a train compartment along with your sister and her husband.'

'David!' Ava cried, her gloved fingers grappling at the blanket tucked round her lap.

'Damn bump! Catches me out every time…' And while David proceeded to mentally redesign the road layout – 'How does a bit of ditch water warrant a bridge, that's what I'd like to know!' – Ava acknowledged she should not allow Uncle Henry to dictate her life.

The obstacle to the Rickards' marriage being a happy one was rooted in Ava having failed to disguise a habitual yearning for the manor, the childhood home provided to his three nieces by Sir Henry de Trouville upon his brother's death. Worse still, without a seed there can be no germination, and Ava knew someone had planted a seed in David's mind early in their acquaintance that Crowthwaite would always hold another draw for the woman whom the young, handsome, wealthy David Rickard had fallen for. A draw which, at this moment, was precipitating a collision of heart and stomach not even the bridge had produced.

David had split their journey down from London into three days, the route planned so they'd incorporated two overnight stays with friends. The first two days she'd found tolerable, with glimpses of her husband's old self, but during today's stage he'd regressed, and Ava had observed a correlation between a reduction in mileage and an increase of criticisms. The bridge had given way to tarmacadam – rather, the lack of – before tarmacadam had laid the foundation for a tirade on Westmorland County Council's reluctance to invest in arterial roads. 'The construction alone would create employment,' he concluded, finally reducing speed as the car entered the village of Crowthwaite. 'God knows the poor souls have need of work.'

Smoke was billowing from one of The Black Feather's chimneys. Outside, under lantern light, the pub landlord was balanced atop a pair of wooden stepladders, clutching one end of a garland. Seeing the black sedan's approach, he inclined his head. Ava returned his greeting and David, misreading her beautiful smile as being for the man holding the garland's other end, slammed his foot down on the pedal. The large motor car surged forward and David, no longer spouting verbal criticism, drove up the main track that split the green in two (the cottages long ago having spilled out to its edges). Where the track diverged at the height of the village, David kept right to trace the Pennines' lower contour to the east. The light now rapidly fading, the headlights alone directed their journey's end and Ava knew it wouldn't be long until two large stone posts would embrace her return to Crowthwaite Castle.

Suddenly, a lonely jackdaw perched on a gnarled branch of an ancient hawthorn took flight, giving a keen 'jack' while its wings displaced the still and silent air. 'And that's another raucous I could well do without,' David said, his voice returned. 'Damn crows!'

———

A few miles back, Sir Henry de Trouville's chauffeur was driving along the same track.

A girl of four broke off from singing and, reaching through the sliding glass window to the front passenger seat, tugged a strand of dark hair. ''Ots and 'ots of toys, Mummy?'

'Of course there'll be lots of toys, silly!' her elder sister by two years answered. 'Father Christmas always brings lots of presents to Uncle Henry's, doesn't he, Daddy?'

The father playfully pinched her plump cheeks. 'He most certainly does, Besty Betsy.'

'There!' Betsy delighted in telling her sister. 'Now sing, Rose... *A day or two ago, The story I must tell / I went out on the snow, And on my back I fell; A gent was riding by / In a one-horse open sleigh, He laughed as there I—?*'

'*He laughed as there I sprawling lie, But quickly drove away...*' her father prompted. 'Come, Rosie Posie... *Jingle bells, jingle bells...*'

Betsy was well into the next verse – '*...Take the girls tonight / And sing this sleighing song...*' – when her mother complained to her husband with an 'Oh, Stephen...!' about teaching the girls 'that' version.

'Look, Betsy!' Stephen exclaimed, disregarding his wife as the motor car cruised up to The Black Feather, where a garland of holly and ivy was bedecked in soft light. Clambering across her father's lap and pushing her sister aside, Betsy planted her hands against the glass and launched into another song: '*The holly and the ivy, Now are both well grown...*'

In the doorway, the bonny barmaid reached up on her tiptoes to kiss her companion on the lips – a bunch of mistletoe hanging above their heads. 'Tom and Pearl?' the mother questioned the chauffeur, who, his eyes on the track ahead, said nothing.

'I told you of my suspicions, old girl,' Stephen said.

'Sing, Daddy, sing! *The rising of the sun, The running of the deer, The playing of the merry groan, Sweet singing in the choir...*' The chauffeur, turning right onto the village green track, gave a *sotto voce* groan at father and daughter's blasphemy.

Crowthwaite Castle and its surrounding forest came into view as one silhouette against a cloudless sky, and Betsy and Rose burst into applause. Upon opening their door, the chauffeur was almost unbalanced in their hurry to get out of the car; then it was Susan Markham's turn. The distant cousin of the de Trouvilles, who'd been standing in the outside porch awaiting their arrival, was likewise unsettled when she became tightly bound in a skirt hug. 'Oh my, Bertha,' she said to their mother, 'what it is to be young!'

'Look at that... The old man's finally gone and done it!' Stephen greeted Susan, referring to the weathered red sand-stone arch and its newly carved coat of arms, whose edges, accentuated by the shadows cast by the lamplight, were as clearly defined as its predecessor, circa 1340.

'Didn't you say,' Susan teased, 'our Creator would be more likely to witness you eat your own tail before that creature ever ate its own again?'

'Really, Susan!' Bertha said.

'Sometimes, Suzie, a man likes to be proved wrong.' Without warning Stephen tickled Rose, then Betsy, under the arms, loosing both from Susan's skirt. Betsy pursued Rose through the vestibule and into the great hall, where four little shoes rapped across the stone-flagged floor. David, already sitting by a roaring fire, was unprepared for his youngest niece as she catapulted herself into his arms – 'Uckie David!' – almost knocking the whisky glass out of his hand. Laughing, he placed the glass down and proceeded to plant raspberry blows on any visible skin until Betsy demanded it was her turn, whereupon Rose, spotting the Christmas tree, surrendered 'Uckie David'.

'Do break it to me gently,' Bertha said, wishing to know who her younger sister Clara had brought with her this Christmas.

'According to Susan,' David said between blowing raspberries, 'a jazz player.'

'According to Clara's introduction,' Susan corrected.

'A jazz player!' the Taylors echoed – Stephen intrigued, Bertha shocked.

'Mummy, no toys!'

'Silly... Rose,' Betsy gasped between raspberries, 'Father Christmas... comes... on... Christmas... Eve. Enough... Uncle... David!'

'One more for good luck... *There!* Now, why don't you show Rose the bearded man's *favourite* Christmas tree.' Jumping down from David's lap, Betsy took her sister's hand and led her across the cavernous hall towards the drawing room.

'Mind you don't touch any of the adults' boring presents already delivered by the elves,' Stephen cautioned, 'the magical dust will give you away!'

'*I know*, Daddy!'

'A jazz player,' Bertha repeated. 'You don't mean...?'

David, amused by his sister-in-law's discomfort, smiled.

'And what of Uncle's latest wife?'

'His usual type,' a voice answered, its vessel descending the grand staircase.

'Clara!' Bertha embraced her sister.

'Though when I say "usual" I'm obviously not referring to sweet, dearest Catherine – bless her soul, wherever it wanders! – who had only her family's heritage to recommend her.'

'And why is the "usual type" not here to greet us?' Bertha asked.

'Snoozing. You'll have the honour at dinner. David, darling' – Clara gave her cigarette holder two sharp taps – 'I hadn't realised you were here… Where's dearest Ava?'

David removed a lighter from his pocket to light his wife's youngest sister's cigarette, her eyes not leaving his. 'With your uncle.'

'Of course she is.'

'But what of our new aunt?' Bertha broke in, flumping down onto the settee.

'Oh, must we talk of her! Why is it, Bertha,' Clara wondered, while opting for the arm of David's chair, 'Uncle who sees everyone through those critical lenses of his has blurred vision when it comes to the gold-digger?'

'I think we know the answer to that one, eh, David?' Stephen said.

'I think I'll reserve my judgment.'

'Oh, David,' Clara said, her voice huskier than usual, 'you know full well what to expect.'

'Do I?'

'Yes. You. Do.'

'Very well… I'll play along. I expect ripe lips the colour of a virgin's blood, curvaceous child-bearing hips and a bosom that threatens to expel the sweetest of milk, in which case, if I'm right, the old man miraculously continues to enjoy twenty-twenty vision.'

Stephen chuckled.

'A most accurate description – isn't it, darling?' Clara said, directing the tag to her guest as he stepped off the bottom step.

'Of who?' he asked in a smooth southern American accent.

'*Whom*,' David muttered into his drink.

'Really, Chester – wife number three!'

'Her! Yeah. A picture of virility.'

'*Fertility*.'

Susan gave David a warning glance, but she needn't have worried for David's correction rolled off the shoulder of Chester's dinner jacket.

'One child would suffice,' Stephen commented.

'Providing it's male,' Clara added.

'Oh man, I've never seen a bedroom so huge!' Chester remarked.

'It's teeny, darling, half the size of mine…' Clara said.

'Get outta here!'

'… which is half the size of Ava's.'

Chester looked to Bertha. 'No way!'

'No, that's Bertha, not Ava. And "yes way". Ava's room's always been in the east tower apartment – isn't that so, David?'

'Really, Clara, does one speak of such topics?' Bertha lectured as David converted 'Ava's room' to 'our room'.

'Oh, *pooh*, Boots, don't be a snob!' Clara said, addressing Bertha with the nickname she'd given her when the three sisters were still adolescents – when their uncle had upbraided Bertha to re-tie her laces. 'Careful you don't snap them… *Boots!*' Clara had taunted as she watched the strain Bertha was putting her riding bootlaces through. 'You'd take off a boot and let Uncle kick you in the buttocks with it, if he only asked!' There wasn't a progressive bone in Bertha's body, Clara thought. 'Yes, Uncle. No, Uncle.' Once Mr Stephen Taylor came on the scene it was 'Yes, Stephen. No, Stephen.' Just the sort of compliance Stephen was looking for in a wife. He soon had a ring slipped on Bertha's finger and she, only too readily, swapped her dreary boots for a pair of wedding slippers. Stephen had become the patriarch whom Bertha sought to please – Uncle Henry had been relegated.

'Fawcett,' Susan thanked the butler, who, inwardly criticising Miss Clara's gentleman friend for the error of already being attired for dinner, was dotting tea and plates of dainty sandwiches round the coffee table.

'At least you have only to climb one flight of stairs,' Stephen said to David. 'I don't know how the old man still manages all those spiral steps. Accident waiting to happen.'

'How high up is he?' Chester asked, his mouth full.

'Fourth floor. Violet's on the floor below,' Clara replied.

Lighting her own cigarette, Susan said, 'Says it does him the world of good.'

'I say the reason he's at the top of the tower,' David disagreed, 'is so he can lord it over the rest of we mere mortals.'

'You would say that,' Susan said.

'I wonder if it feels lonely all the way up there…?' Stephen thought aloud.

'I'd rather be there,' Bertha said, 'than in the lady of the manor's apartment. Is she aware, Clara, she shares the floor with the attic?'

'Oh, I'm sure she's had a good snoop around the place,' Clara said.

'Daddy,' Betsy called out across the hall, 'I'm taking Rose up to the attic. We're going to hunt the vermin ghost.'

'Stephen, how did she hear of such a thing!' Bertha cried.

'Sounds like someone's little ears have been a-flapping!' David said, tickled.

Stephen, doing a poor job of stifling his laughter, collected a handful of sandwiches and assured the 'old girl' he'd act as their spiritual vanguard.

'Vermin ghost?' Chester asked when father and progeny had left. 'What's that, a poisoned rat back for vengeance!'

'You'll hear all about it later. I've a little surprise planned,' Clara forewarned them.

'Oh, you haven't, Clara!' Susan chided.

'It won't do to rub him up,' Bertha agreed. 'Stephen says Uncle always takes a rubbing the wrong way.'

At that moment, the study door opened and Ava, seeing her youngest sister sitting on the arm of her husband's chair, opted for the east tower.

———

Bertha recognised David's description immediately upon the 'usual type' making her late entrance to dinner. The present Lady de Trouville – wife of the Tenth Baronet of Crowthwaite Castle, Lady of the Manor of Crowthwaite – appeared to be the earthly embodiment of all goddesses of fertility (whose names Bertha could never remember) and Bertha wondered whether she should prepare herself for an announcement from her uncle.

Sir Henry – who'd been watching the door from the head of the dining table – demanded his young wife take notice of his reproaching glare. Violet, though, glided into the dining room in a floor-length evening gown with her chin up and lashes down as though unaware of the facts of Sir Henry de Trouville's marriage record. Except Violet Olsen *was* aware of the baronet's marital history prior to their first meeting, in particular that his previous wife was still in existence, tagging her 'title for life' onto her Christian name.

When Violet did look up from her seat at the opposite end of the table, it was not her husband she took notice of. *How could a woman be expected to see her old and sour-faced husband,* she planned to later tell her maid, *when the man sitting next to him was not only handsome but truly beautiful!* Susan, not alone in witnessing the sexual attraction, was remembering Frances, Lady de Trouville, Violet's predecessor.

'It will not do, Susan,' her cousin had informed her. 'The de Trouvilles have enjoyed an unbroken line of male heirs since the time of my ancestor crossing the channel with the *Duc de Normandie…*' Soon after, he'd petitioned for divorce on the grounds of adultery. *Just like his namesake, Henry the Eighth*, Susan thought, before apologising to 'Catherine Howard' for the family's arrivals having clearly exhausted her.

'Well, I suppose I was tired *but* that's only to be expected. I don't believe many women would be able to carry out the duties of lady of the manor.'

With her acquired skill for expressing sincere platitudes, Susan replied she didn't suppose they would.

'What's this I hear of duty?' Sir Henry said.

'As you requested, Henry, I used my afternoon welcoming your family.'

'Our family, Violet.'

'Not quite the *whole* afternoon.'

'What's that, Clara?'

'Aunt Violet, Uncle, was not present for *everyone's* arrival.'

'Violet?' Sir Henry probed.

'That's not true, Henry! I met Clara, and her man… and…?'

'Susan,' Susan reminded her.

'But what of Ava's arrival?' Sir Henry asked.

'Ava?'

'Ava – my eldest niece!'

'No. I didn't meet Ava.'

'As lady of the manor what possible reason could you have for not meeting our guests?'

'It's not my fault if people were late, Henry; you know it's essential a lady has her afternoon nap!'

'Afternoon naps! Really, Aunt, you sound just like Boots! Other animals eat, toilet and nap…'

'The dinner table, Clara, is no place for crude language!' Sir Henry reproached.

'Being a mother is tiring!' Bertha justified herself to Clara.

'As I was saying, other animals eat, toilet and nap,' Clara repeated, unperturbed, '*humans* dance, we learn to play an instrument, we invent, we look for cures… we love…'

'Niece, I've not the slightest interest in your peculiar lists; what concerns me is my wife's neglect of her duties!' Sir Henry interrupted.

'David and I *were* running late,' Ava told her uncle over Fawcett's soup-ladling arm.

'*We* were hardly late, Stephen!' Bertha broke in.

'You're right, old girl, our train arrived in at Appleby on the dot.'

Dabbing her chin, Clara muttered through her napkin the irony of Uncle's fuss when none of the family had been invited to his wedding – the joke at the time being he couldn't believe himself as innocent as the injured party his solicitor had claimed him to be.

'Speak up, Clara!'

'I was wondering, Uncle, do we raise a glass?'

'Whatever to?'

'Why, the happy couple!'

'That, Clara, was toasted at the wedding breakfast.'

'Oh, well… *CONGRATULATIONS!*' And she raised her glass anyway.

Sir Henry transferred his disapproval from Clara and her insubordination to Ava and her lack of appetite. Bertha, meanwhile, increasingly feared the possibility of a different toast.

'I'm sorry' – Violet was addressing the man seated on her immediate left – 'but who are you?'

'James. James Bowes—'

'I meant, why are you *here*?'

'James is the son of Henry's oldest friend,' Susan explained.

'What's that?' Sir Henry said.

'I was just saying, Henry, James's father and yourself were the best of friends,' Susan replied.

'James? Of course we were – God rest his soul! Who says we weren't?'

'No one is saying you weren't. I was filling in Violet on James's connection with the family.'

'If she had been there to greet him upon his arrival, or even seen fit to grace us with her presence pre-dinner, there wouldn't be the need for such vulgarities at the table.'

'*Again*, I don't understand why I'm to blame for others being late!' Violet pouted.

'Rest assured, Aunt, we can all vouch for James,' Clara said. 'He spent so much of his time growing up alongside us he's almost a de Trouville!'

'As sticky as honey on tissue paper,' James agreed.

'I'm sure I never meant he wasn't welcome,' Violet said defensively.

'How 'bout you, Susan, d'you say you and Sir Henry are distant cousins?' Chester said.

'That we are. Isn't that so, Henry?'

'What?' Sir Henry snapped, his tolerance under stress as he observed another drip fall from Chester's spoon. He'd learned to suffer Clara's 'friends' but that was because they'd understood their lowly station and so made very little noise, unlike this one before him.

'I said we're distant cousins, Henry.'

'So distant I'm not sure why you keep receiving invitations.'

'Because Tom sends them out,' Susan replied and advised Chester take no heed of their host. 'I hear you're in a jazz band?'

'That's right.'

'It might not be my style, but I'm not oblivious to the youth setting the tempo these days. You've an energy my generation would have fainted at! *Anyway*, do tell me about your choice of instrument?'

'I'd have liked to play my vocals but as that was never gonna happen I settled for the trumpet.'

'And did you happen to bring your trumpet with you?'

'He's here as my guest, Susan, not a performer,' Clara made clear.

'I should think not!' Bertha agreed, though her objection was concerned with certain circles learning of the installation of a nightclub at Crowthwaite Castle.

'It's not often you speak sense,' Sir Henry said to Bertha, but before she could capitalise on the positive attention, her uncle was once again engaged with Ava. 'I don't know how I'd manage without Tom. I've no need to tell *you* what a support he is…'

'Then don't *tell* her,' David said.

'That reminds me, David, I'd like a word after dinner.'

'Oh, you would, would—'

'*I hear, Stephen,*' Ava cut in, 'that you lost your bet with Susan?'

'I wouldn't say it was a bet, but, yes, he did,' Susan gloated.

'I say, ladies, be gentle! Uncle, you've cost me my pride!' Stephen said.

'What *are* you droning on about?'

'The renovation.'

'It isn't a renovation; it's not the original with pieces of stone miraculously reattached! The family coat of arms has been replaced with an exact replication – and why would that cost you your pride?'

'Ah, I get what it is you're on 'bout, now!' Chester said. 'Just what is that?'

'A coat of arms,' Sir Henry said drily.

'Yeah, you said. But what *is* it? A bird? A snake? And what's the deal with it eating its own tail? Spooked the hell outta me!'

'It's a bird,' Ava answered for her uncle. '*Corvus monedula* to be precise—'

'You're gonna have to be less specific than that!'

'You'll know it as a crow.'

'The little guys I keep seeing 'round the place? The squawkers?'

'Correct. The bird symbolises wealth and the tail feathers in its beak completes its trefoil knot – that's where you're getting confused with the serpent. The trefoil knot represents eternal life, as does the cypress that wreathes the bird.'

'Wealth and eternal life… And how 'bout the words underneath?'

'*Per familia, divitiae et immortalitas affuo,*' Clara articulated, her husky voice ravishing.

'*Per fam*—'

'NO MORE!' Sir Henry bellowed, making Bertha jump.

'Chester, darling, don't take offence. Uncle is overly precious—'

'It's nothing to do with being precious,' Ava corrected her, beating her uncle to a response. 'Family tradition dictates it's bad luck for anyone other than family – blood *or* marriage – to utter the motto within the castle walls.'

'Ava, everyone. My sister… and Uncle's mouthpiece,' Clara said sarcastically.

David and Susan backed up Sir Henry's 'CLARA!'

'The trouble with your "castle walls",' Clara continued, undeterred, 'are the diktats within.'

'I will remind you…!' Sir Henry warned his youngest niece.

'Your uncle's right, Clara,' Chester said, taking the edge off the baronet's sword. 'Believe me, sir, I wouldn't wanna be the party pooper, the person invited to spend Christmas with one of the oldest families in England only to go and leave a curse behind! That *would* be rough.'

'There, Henry, no harm done,' Susan said. 'Chester couldn't have known.'

After a moment of silence, Violet said, 'I've never even seen this coat and arms.'

'Coat *of* arms. And pray, woman, what do you mean, it was one of the first things I showed you!'

'I can't be expected to remember everything, Henry!' Violet replied, her eyes wandering.

'What are you appealing to David for? He wouldn't know; he wasn't there—! You, Bertha, wake up, niece, you look to be falling asleep!'

Bertha's eyelids, in the process of closing, flew back open. 'It's been a long day, Uncle.'

'Are the seats no longer cushioned in first class?' David said.

'It's all the jolting, throwing me around every which way… backwards and forwards… side to side. Uncle, you know I've never been suited to travel!'

'I remember you on a pony...' Sir Henry began.

'I'm sure it was a horse.'

'A terrible sight – not to mention posture. Unlike Ava. No lady sits a horse like Ava.'

'Of course they don't,' Clara said. Unlike Bertha's bootlaces, Ava's didn't require tightening; everything in her eldest sister's life came easily without any effort on Ava's part, or so Clara complained.

'Betsy must take after her aunt then,' Stephen decided. 'Beautiful rise and fall... Oh, don't look like that, Bertha! Surely you wish your daughter to ride well? Come now, old girl.'

'I told you, Stephen, it was the bay hunter to blame.'

'Ah, the bay hunter!' Clara recalled with a smile.

'*Blame* and *fault*. That's all I've heard at this table. Excuse after excuse for one's inadequacies,' Sir Henry complained before asking James about his dappled grey.

'Is that the one Henry gifted you, James?' Susan asked.

'Yes. Just after father's death – that's right, isn't it, Henry.'

'Never mind the dappled grey,' Chester spoke over Sir Henry's grunt of assent, 'how 'bout the hunter?'

'They're both hunters,' David mumbled.

'I said it shouldn't be ridden,' Ava said.

'I said I didn't want to,' Bertha retorted. 'It was Uncle who made me.'

'I knew something was troubling it,' Ava continued.

'Of course there was,' Clara agreed, 'it sensed Boots's nerves!'

'It would have thrown any one of us,' Ava told Clara.

'So, it threw you!' Chester said to Bertha. 'That's gotta've hurt?'

'It was not *nerves*, Clara,' Bertha riposted, ignoring the American. 'Just because one prefers not to ride doesn't make one nervous of riding.'

'I hate horses,' Violet agreed.

'All I ask, Bertha,' Sir Henry broke in, 'is while you reside within my castle walls you at least attempt to *appear* alive.'

'Raising two girls is demanding, Uncle. Isn't it, Stephen?'

'I say children aren't as demanding as all that and I, having raised three girls, should know. And don't look to your husband for support when he's the one who created the problem. I've told you before, Stephen, if you spoil young girls then you're certain to create unnecessary complexities...'

Clara, sipping her wine, thought that no one could ever accuse her uncle of having any such paternal – or avuncular – qualities.

'Are you looking forward to the carollers?' Susan asked Violet.

'What carollers?'

'From the village. They call every Christmas.'

'Another family tradition,' Clara said, 'though tonight, Aunt, there'll be something extra… in your honour.'

'Really!' Violet's eyes twinkled. 'In *my* honour?'

'What are you whispering about down there? What's this "honour" you talk of?'

'There's no whispering, Uncle. Only talk of the carollers. Tonight, Aunt, after dinner we inferior females shall not be separated from our superior males. Instead, we will all gather as equals in the hall to await the villagers.'

Violet's smile disappeared. 'I'm not sure that sounds at all much of an honour.'

'There'll be no carolling until I've dealt with a little matter,' Sir Henry instructed, glancing at David.

'Sounds ominous!' Stephen jested.

'Can a man not enjoy his meal in peace!' David demanded.

The dining room fell silent, and Fawcett, not faltering in

his refilling of James's glass, detected the skipped beat of the valet's footfall as he entered carrying a tray of the next course.

'Actually, Uncle,' Stephen said, a smile on his face, 'I was wondering whether you could squeeze me in first...?'

———

'What now?' Susan despaired.

Ava looked up to see her uncle's pallor sallower than when he'd entered his study with Stephen at his heels. Violet, also reading that her husband's mood had degenerated, was struggling to restrain her own countenance from displaying the repulsion that was taunting the contents of her stomach.

'David, that word, please.'

'Thanks, *chum*,' David hissed as he crossed paths with Stephen, 'you've surely set the old man up most foully for me.'

'David, brother,' Stephen called after him, 'I can assure you he heard nothing from me!'

Susan looked to Ava but Ava's eyes were downcast.

———

Sir Henry indicated David take a seat. 'I shan't insult your intelligence; I shan't ask if you know why I've asked to see you privately.' David *did* know, and he also knew Sir Henry wished to see the younger man squirm and stutter; so David remained silent, and it wasn't long until his faultless composure rattled the older man: 'Do *you* insult *my* intelligence!'

'What did my wife have to say on the matter?'

'Then you *do* understand why I've asked to see you!'

'*What* did my wife say?'

'Ava told me she could neither confirm *nor* deny.'

David thought quietly about his wife's answer.

'Almighty God, David, did you hear what I just said? She could not *deny*!'

'And neither will my conscience permit me to provide you with the answer you seek.'

'Because your conscience is guilty!'

'*Because* I do not have to justify myself to you.'

'Really, David!'

'If my wife wishes to know then that is a different matter entirely. Ava need only ask me and I make a promise to you, as I appear before you now, my answer will be truthful. *But*,' David added, rising from his chair, 'she is the only person who can make any such demand.'

'David…! David, you will speak with me on this matter!' Had David turned around he would have witnessed Sir Henry's face now heated to an incandescent red. 'Then you leave me with no choice but to be of the presumption that you are guilty of adultery with your wife's sister!'

David, opening the door, shouted over his shoulder that he could damn well think what he liked.

'You have disgraced my niece most egregiously… and I… *I* shan't forget!' Sir Henry's threat followed David out of the study and across the hall to the sideboard. 'Where's Clara?' he then demanded of his guests.

'In her room,' Bertha answered. 'She said she'd be back in time for the carols.'

'I want to see her in my study.'

Bertha looked to Stephen. 'Now?'

'Yes, now. Oh, never mind! Fawcett! Fawcett…?'

'Sir?'

'Has Tom returned from the village?'

'He has, sir. He's eating—'

'I would like to see the both of you. Together. *Immediately*.'

The study door closed and David, changing his mind, picked the whisky decanter back up and, while turning his single shot into a double, reminded Ava to breathe.

Minutes later, many pairs of curious eyes followed Tom and Fawcett into Sir Henry's study.

David threw back his drink – his gaze fixed on his wife.

Ava drew a deep breath.

Two

Carrying on another de Trouville tradition, all members of staff had gathered in the hall for the arrival of the Crowthwaite Carollers – a welcome respite during the busy Christmas period.

It was also a much-anticipated time for the local carollers to gain entry to the castle. Any other year Miss Clara's companion would have been the biggest draw, but this year the attraction was Sir Henry's latest wife, *rather* the lady in her newfound capacity. Recent experience – the Lady of the Manor of Crowthwaite's overt lack of deference during Sunday church services as well as her indifference towards those who she had a care of duty for when being chauffeured through the village – had produced a general consensus she would be found wanting. This public feeling wasn't wrong. From where the carollers stood arranged on the steps that led down from the vestibule, they observed the young woman to be no better than the village whore as her attention flitted between inspecting her tinted nails and fluttering her darkened lashes – always in the direction of Mr David.

The locals, however, witnessed something more was afoot within the de Trouville family home. While their practised choral voices rang out, Susan, from the comfort of her seat, heeded the singers' gazes that were one moment disciplined, the next distracted from their collective spiritual aim as their thoughts were fleetingly scattered to Violet's pursuit of David, David's of Ava, Clara's of David, and Clara's and Sir Henry's of Violet. Ordinarily, Susan would have been reminded of one Crowthwaite summer and the bowls competition that had pitted four of the village's uncultivated players against Sir Henry and his three public-schooled guests; she would have remembered the lord of the manor's elation when his bowl struck the head, scattering the opposition's bowls and placing his closest the jack, and she would have drawn a parallel between *then* when four visions had tracked their scattered bowls and *now* with the locals' flitting eyes documenting the interactions before them, and she would have found the Christmas scene entertaining. But, having just witnessed what had passed between Henry and David, Susan was far from entertained and so she experienced the uplifting rendition of 'The Boar's Head Carol' not to be haunting but punctuated with haunted tones that bowled a shiver from her shoulder down her back.

After a complimentary mulled wine and mince pie apiece, the carollers filed out into the late winter night with a keenness, content that their condemnations and caricatures of Lady de Trouville – along with a copious amount of creative conjecture surrounding the question 'Just what were all that 'bout?' – would keep them sufficiently muffled during their walk home.

'Clara' – Sir Henry called out over Betsy and Rose, who were weaving the animate and inanimate together with a thread of '*O Christmas Tree, O Christmas Tree*' – 'my study.'

From where she was standing talking with the barmaid of The Black Feather, Clara caught David's signal. 'Sorry, Uncle, I've promised your wife a treat. *Everyone*,' she added quickly, 'Pearl's agreed to stay behind… Return to your seats!'

'There's a surprise,' Susan, far from surprised, said to James.

Clara directed Pearl to the smoker's chair beside the Christmas tree and Betsy and Rose wove the final thread of their carol into a knot – each bouncing down into a cross-legged seat on the rug directly in front of Pearl, four little eyes wide and unblinking.

'Oh, Stephen, must the girls be subjected to such horrors?'

'Yes, Daddy' – within a moment Betsy was uncoiled and jumping up and down – 'we must!'

'Absolutely not!' Sir Henry said decidedly to the house-maid stationed by the staircase, who, after scooping up Rose, wrestled one-handedly with Betsy's defiant arms that were now locked firmly round her father's legs.

'Daddy? Please, Daddy…? DADDY!'

'Another Christmas, Daddy's Besty Betsy,' Stephen promised while Chester, taking the seat closest to Pearl, was already proving himself to be the most faithful member of the audience.

'I despair,' David mumbled and, without specifying what was actually to blame for this despair, headed for the side-board, en route pausing to light Clara's cigarette.

To the sounds of the odd chink of glass and flames licking round ash logs in the enormous grate, the shadows within the castle's great hall began to settle down, swamping the dotted candles and oil burners as though desirous to hear the newest custodian of Crowthwaite's story. Pearl singled out a disconcerted Violet, honouring the new lady of the manor by putting the question concerning the gathering of crows to her – to which Violet did not have the answer, nor the inclination to reply to. Informing Violet how fortunate she was to hear the spoken words passed down from generation to generation, Pearl said as long as could be remembered, her family, the Bells, had done the storytelling.

'Without the Bells who would do the tolling?' David teased.

'I always said, Mr Rickard, when yer slam yer empty glass down onto't bar for last time, Black Feather'll be poorer for it.'

Raising his not-so-empty whisky glass, David returned Pearl's smile.

'Mr Rickard's right, though, without us Bells, the story o' Crowthwaite'd be lost, 'long with the forest...'

'But we have a forest, Henry?' Violet said, perplexed.

'*Now*, when the forest began to disappear, the birds all took flight in search of another home, 'cept one... the daw – that'd be "jackdaw" to you,' Pearl said, also addressing Chester while Clara explained the jackdaw was the crow Ava spoke of on the coat of arms. 'The daw might be the smallest o't crows, but that's nowt to do with his backbone and in these parts he's always thrived. When humans and sheep arrived, high up on his perch with his thievin' little eye, the daw watched... and he learned. He learned to line his nest and – if yer can excuse the pun – he learned to fleece sheep! This smart little crow discovered grazed ground, sheep dung and middens to be a platter fit for a king; and he also learned, when it came to nestin', nooks in stone were as good as crannies in trees. It's cos o't daw and his relationship with land and people, that these parts were named "Crowthwaite".'

'Then why ain't it *Daw*-thwaite?' Chester wanted to know.

'Contain your excitement,' David said apathetically, 'we're almost there.'

'It's said, right here in Crowthwaite, few centuries ago,' Pearl continued, 'there were a cawin' of a murder o' crows that were carried on a Helm Wind, and as these caws tumbled down the Pennines into't valley, people heard the name... *DAW... DAW-DAW...* straight from't bird's beak! Eventually, its name travelled the country, over time lengthenin' to jackdaw – 'cept here where we know it, still to this day, as daw. So yer can see, village could've hardly've been called Dawthwaite when "daw" didn't then exist, now, could it, eh?'

'There!' Clara said, her long cigarette holder saving her evening dress from the dislodged ash.

'Now yer know o't daws,' Pearl said to Violet, 'I'm garn to take yer back further, long afore Christian word existed' – Pearl's knack for storytelling was impervious to Sir Henry's 'Blasphemy' – 'when forest I told yer of, covered just 'bout all the bottom o't fells… 'cept where the village lies. *There*, there were a clearin' and where now stands the maypole were a hawthorn tree – just the one, mind you. To us ancestors, haw were sacred for it symbolised *fertility…*' Pearl stressed the last word as Tom, who'd been absent for the carols, settled down onto a carpeted oak tread. 'Fertility were associated with all haws but the haw in't centre o't clearin' had particular importance for us ancestors, on account of it bein' only one – plumb centre, at that! Now, when this haw began to bloom it heralded summer, time when hands would be joined in matrimony… love, betrothal, fertility. May first, when all haws then did bloom – afore man messed 'bout with the calendar, there'd be dancin' round the tree and a maiden chosen who were crowned and clothed in haw blossom to represent the spring flower goddess, Blodeuwedd…'

'*Mark the fair blooming of the Hawthorn Tree,*' James recited, '*Who, finely clothed in a robe of white… Fills full the wanton eye with May's delight.*'

'*Chaucer,*' Ava whispered, resisting the temptation to turn around to see if the poet's name was on Tom's lips.

'Oh, now I do like May Day festivities!' Violet said.

'Well, don't expect to see any dancing round the pole for it doesn't happen in Crowthwaite,' Sir Henry informed her.

'Then I don't see the point in having a maypole!'

'Don't encourage the old man, Aunt,' Stephen said, 'he's been waiting for the excuse to order its removal. I'm sorry, but you married a man with a mind that sees a phallic symbol and fears it will lead to depravity in his forest – a regular old puritan!'

'Even worse, on open moorland,' Clara taunted.

'*And*,' Pearl broke in, measuring the level of blood in Sir Henry's cheeks, 'with the arrival o't solstice came another tradition – an offerin' to the hooded fertility spirits. Every summer and winter solstices, us ancestors would gather in't clearin' round the sacred hawthorn tree and priests, cloaked in black feathers and wearin' beaked masks – dressed in nature's spirit, if yer like – the'd offer up a sacrifice o' daws… a *real* murder o' crows.'

Violet gave a little gasp, her flirtation with the story short-lived, and everyone gathered witnessed her hand clutching the arm not of her husband but David. Extricating himself from the lady's grip, David rose to pour her a sherry.

In all the years her grandfather had been storyteller Pearl had never known such a compliment and it spurred her on. '*A murder o' crows*,' she told Violet. 'Slain… and hangin' from't gnarled and thorny branches o' haw… like baubles' – she paused to tap a fir branch, its glass bauble bobbing up and down – 'on a Christmas tree… Us ancestors knew even harder times o' famine and pestilence than we do and so the' gifted a sacrifice o' daws in exchange for a bountiful harvest and good health. *But* there were another blessin' the' sought: *O mighty Mother of us all, Giver of all fruitfulness, Bring us fruit and grain, flocks and herds, And children to the tribe, That we be mighty!*' Sir Henry bridled at the three sisters joining in – Bertha, who'd been dozing, mechanically muttering the lines. 'And as the' chanted the pagan prayer, the daws' spirits rose – "channelled" were the word Grandad used – *channelled* through the haw.'

'Why did they decide on the crow – the *daw* for the sacrifice?' Chester said.

'Because of their number?' Stephen said.

'That doesn't make sense,' James said, pondering Stephen's suggestion. 'If it's being sacrificed then the animal must have some value. I would have thought the rarer the animal, the more unique it is and *therefore* the greater its value.'

'I struggle to see the value in any crow,' Violet said, indifferent to her adoptive family's coat of arms.

'I still don't get it,' Chester said.

'Grandad said it were something to do with Odin and his two ravens, Huginn and Muninn, meanin' "thought" and "memory", who he used to gather knowledge.'

'That mythology is Norse and only goes back centuries,' David said, 'whereas your pagan story, Pearl, is supposed to stretch back thousands of years.'

'And why can the Norse religion not derive from an older pagan religion?' Ava asked of her husband.

'Not my work of fiction and so not for me to prove. But, Ava, if that's what you believe...!'

'I thought the Norse religion only arrived with the Scandinavians when they invaded this country?' Stephen said, trying to remember his fuddled college days.

'I fear we're straying,' Clara – for the first time, envying Bertha's blissful ignorance – apprised Pearl.

'Yes,' Ava agreed with Stephen, 'but it's thought to have originally derived in Germany.'

'I don't know what you're all talking about!' Violet said with the beginnings of frustration.

'I don't have a clue either,' Chester said, equally confused. 'Man, this ain't my history!'

Susan returned his smile.

'Thinking about what Ava said… she could be right,' Stephen posited. 'The Northmen's religion *must* span further back – it tells of the beginning of the world, after all!'

'A flat world?' David mocked, his memory of college being much soberer. '*I* could invent a story, if you wish, brother, of how the world started, but it wouldn't make my "ism" as old as the world itself!'

'I've long believed,' Ava said, returning to David's challenge, 'the sacrifice of the corvid relates to their intelligence. After all, are not *thought* and *memory* intrinsically linked with intelligence? Could it be our ancestors revered the crow in its elevated position and regarded it as the all-seeing eye?'

Pearl looked across to the staircase. 'That's exactly Tom's thinkin'.'

'Ava and Tom' – David raised his glass – 'Crowthwaite's intelligentsia.'

'That might explain the value of the sacrifice to the gods, but what of the value to the pagans?' James asked, determined to get to the bottom of it. 'In what way did the offering of a daw mean they'd made a significant sacrifice? If it was a cow, I could understand that. A whole cow would have fed a lot of mouths, thus, a great sacrifice.'

'Then that would make even less sense,' Stephen replied. 'To sacrifice your food and chance going hungry in doing so, all with the aim of asking God for more food makes absolutely no sense, whatsoever!'

'Could we return to the story!' Clara cried. 'Chester… no more questions.'

Bertha's eyes flickered. 'Has it finished?'

'PEARL!' Clara ordered.

'Some years, though,' Pearl said, expertly picking up from

where she'd left off, 'sacrifice weren't enough, and in times of extreme famine or pestilence or child deaths, the priests'd offer a higher sacrifice… a human sacrifice… a virgin. A maiden who'd not live to see whether she'd be chosen for next May Queen…'

Violet sipped her sherry.

'Just imagine it, eh… daws with eyes nae longer seein', hangin' limply from thorny branches; a virgin tied to the trunk – her arms strung up by the wrists, lichen chafin' her flesh; her throat slit… her white dress defiled. *Then*, as one o't final acts o't sacrificial rites, a priest would spatter the black "baubles" with virgin's blood afore pluckin' a single tail feather and placin' it on her tongue… the bondin' o' the spirits.'

'The sacrifice of a virgin,' James said, 'now *there* I do see the value!'

'A waste,' Stephen agreed.

Chester chuckled.

' *'Course,*' Pearl continued, 'after the arrival o't Romans, and then conversion to Christianity, the pagan rituals died out, 'long with the old customs… *until…*'

'This is where things really spice up!' Clara said to Chester as Sir Henry shifted in his seat.

'… Sir Henry de Trouville…'

Violet and Chester looked to the current baronet.

'…*Third* baronet, that is – us generous host's fifth great-grandfather, who, in winter o' sixteen ninety-nine, found himself in despair when his newborn son and heir took sick. Local doctor did everything he could – often involvin' leeches – but nowt'd improve the child's health and Sir Henry were told all he could do now were to pray to God. Well, Sir Henry did this, and the lady o't manor did this, and so did Sir Henry's two younger brothers – the third baronet even paid a priest to organise continuous vigil at Saint Cuthbert's Church – but, on't eve o't winter solstice, the little lad's health worsened…'

'It would appear,' David muttered, 'Saint Cuthbert's did not live up to its eponym's record for post-mortem miracles.'

'… and Sir Henry's own strength slipped from him and, sinkin' to his knees – possibly on these very flagstones, he forsook the Christian God. *This* is when he remembered the pagan sacrifice. Now, by this time, so-called "progress" had seen us ancestors' sacred haw replaced with a maypole – though puritans had this removed in sixteen forty-four; then by sixteen sixty-one the maypole were returned to where one has since forever stood. So, as I were sayin', Sir Henry sent one of his brothers to take some branches from't haw that stands alone on't lonnin to this manor – a cuttin' of a cuttin' o' the sacred hawthorn – and he ordered his gamekeeper to muster as many daws as he could trap. As midnight approached' – a light snore emitted from Bertha's direction – 'the three brothers set out into't freezin' night, not much different than tonight, and the' walked down to the village, each carryin' three daws – nine, the gamekeeper said, were the exact number he'd been able to trap! – and when the' reached the maypole the' wove the branches o' haw together round its base afore intertwinin' nine daws. Three brothers, each offerin' three daws to one o't three hooded fertility spirits; brothers believin' their sacrifice would be channelled all the more better for the larch pole reached higher than the haw ever did. Now, holdin' hands and standin' in a circle round the maypole with its hideous wreath o' red-ripened fruits and death, the brothers offered the murder o' crows as a sacrifice to the spirits, chantin', *Oh mighty Mother of us all, Giver of all fruitfulness, Bring us fruit and grain, flocks and herds, And children to the tribe, That we be mighty!* Sir Henry, it were said, repeated the final words with much torment... *And children to the tribe, that we be mighty!'*

'Did it work?' Chester was impatient to know. 'Did it save Sir Henry's son?'

'It did, but there were a condition – o' Sir Henry's own makin'. Sir Henry'd made a promise that if his son's life were spared then every solstice he and his offspring would offer up a sacrifice of a murder o' crows.'

'And did they?' Chester looked to Sir Henry, tenth baronet, but his question was met with a countenance far from the 'generous host' Pearl had described.

'By the time summer solstice arrived,' Pearl answered, 'all three brothers were rigged out in cloaks o' daw feathers, their faces disguised with beaked masks. There were even a haw-handled dagger that'd been fashioned, just for the occasion.'

'They became the priests,' Chester said over Violet's 'ugh'.

'Every solstice, same ritual, and aye, Sir Henry's son continued the tradition, and so did his son... One solstice, there were even believed to be a sacrifice of a virgin—'

'Henry!' Violet rebuked her husband.

'Don't look at me in that way, woman, it's all nonsense! Nothing more than a tale told to keep The Black Feather's coffers full!'

This brought about protestations from Stephen and Clara.

'And is this another family tradition?' Chester – ever the optimist – asked Sir Henry. David cracked a laugh, momentarily diverting Sir Henry's spleen.

'Us host's great-grandfather put an end to de Trouville's hundred-year sacrifices,' Pearl told Chester, 'on account o' there bein' sightin's of a spectre' – Violet gave a gasp – 'the spirit o' the de Trouville sacrificial virgin...'

'The vermin ghost!' Chester exclaimed.

'A blood-stained white apparition, crown of haw on her head askew… walkin' 'tween village green and manor, but for some reason we've never fathomed, once she reaches the haw on't manor lonnin she turns a sharp left to walk a straight line across the fields from Crooklands Salkeld to High Field, then on towards the moor… always seen climbin' up the fell, *never* comin' down. And Sir Roger de Trouville, Sir Henry's great-grandfather, believin' the sightin's to be a sign of a young girl in purgatory, said it were confirmation the one true Christian God'd overpowered the pagan gods, for surely if paganism were mightier, then her spirit would've been channelled instead o' bein' doomed to traipse the same path for eternity.'

Chester looked round the room. 'Who's seen her?'

'If it's proof you seek, you'll find none,' Sir Henry said. 'Not for the majority of my sixty years walking every inch of the manor estate have I had sight of any such fabled phantom!'

'Yer know full well, Sir Henry,' Pearl spoke to her lord with familiarity, 'there's them in't village who'd swear to havin' seen an apparition and that it's as real as you and me, only that it's usually spotted on a solstice and now and then durin' a Helm Wind.'

'What rot! I know of no such thing! I've lived long enough to witness countless Helm Winds – not to mention two solstices each year! – and I've yet to see so much as a downy feather blow past me never mind a spirit!'

Stephen, his brow furrowed, wondered, 'Didn't Fawcett say he once saw—'

'Fawcett has more sense than to suggest anything of the sort!' Sir Henry spat.

'How 'bout you, Pearl,' Chester asked, 'you seen it?'

'*Well*... nae – but as I said, there's them that'll swear to havin' done so.'

'And just what is this... *Helm Wind*?'

'I'd rather not know!' Violet said.

'Nowhere else in country have the' a named wind,' Pearl said with pride. '"Helm Wind" is where east air meets west, sendin' the colder easterly tumblin' down Cross Fell, gatherin' up speed as it goes. Remember I told yer 'bout cawin' o' daws bein' carried on a Helm Wind? Well, we say *all* sounds are carried on it and as it travels the valley's villages it scoops up gossip, be it truth or rumour. I mentioned, just now, not many havin' seen a spectre in a Helm Wind and that's cos when it appears with a Helm Wind it's to foreshadow a tragedy, a tragedy for that very person it's appearin' to – a warnin', if yer like.'

Chester whistled. 'You got it all here... the castle, the moor, your own ghost – and now, even your own wind!'

'Haven't you missed something?' Clara reminded Pearl, and when Pearl looked to Sir Henry, Clara prompted, 'The part about the sacrifices the de Trouville family—?'

'No more!' Sir Henry warned.

Ignoring her uncle, Clara snatched the Bells' mantle from Pearl. 'Because we dabbled with the dark arts, Aunt...'

'I'll hear no more of this!'

'... our family has been forever cursed...'

'YOU HEAR ME, CLARA!'

Bertha's eyes shot open. 'Stephen?'

'A murder of crows, it was—'

'ENOUGH!' Sir Henry had now risen to his feet.

'As you said, Uncle, it's only a story. *A murder of crows*, it was foretold, would be the de Trouville family's downfall. Indeed, as the generations passed by, the heirs and spares

37

began to dwindle, until – well, you don't need me to spell it out, Aunt, after all, that's why you're here… wife number three…!'

'You know… I feel… queer…' Violet said, her red-tinted nails finding refuge once again in David's black sleeve. 'I think it's the fire… and all this talk of bloody virgins…'

'CLARA!' Sir Henry spluttered.

'Aunt should realise, Uncle, that she's your final stab at it!'

'HOW-DARE-YOU!' Sir Henry choked while Ava watched Tom cross the hall in a few strides to take Pearl tenderly by the elbow and escort her from the hall.

'That spectacle was not becoming,' Susan told Clara.

'Oh, do shut up, Susan! When did you become such a stickler?'

'I will not keep quiet while you do your best to break up this family.'

'Of course, one can't have one's own thoughts unless they're in complete accord with Uncle's. You and Ava are so predictable – Pearl, what are the names of Odin's ravens?'

'She's left,' James informed her.

'Huginn and Muninn,' Stephen offered.

'Huginn and Muninn! That's who you both remind me of… Uncle's eyes and ears… No matter how many feathers he plucks you'll both be forever loyal!'

'Clara, you had better think before you say any more,' Ava said, her tone that of the superior sister.

'What did I tell you, Chester? For all the sheep on the estate, the only black one you'll find is right here in this castle!'

'Come now, Clara, no one thinks that of you! Do they, Bertha?' Stephen added.

'Yes, Boots, do agree!'

'Take no notice, Bertha,' Ava said.

'Remind me, dearest Ava, which one are you: Huginn or Muninn?'

It wasn't Ava who answered, but David; speaking Clara's name in an intimate tone that made every person present suddenly feel like an intruder.

Sir Henry watched Ava take a moment before rising. In the dim light it was noticeable that her walk across the hall was unsteady – as was the tremble of the crystal decanter as she poured herself a drink. And when uncle witnessed his niece down a whisky neat in one he – unexpectedly to everyone present, including his truly – launched himself across the divide: 'YOU!'

Chester was quick to his feet as Clara's protector. 'Now look here!'

'Sit down, sir! I've seen some of my niece's hangers-on over the years, but you...! As for you, Clara, you really have seen your very last allowance from me. DO YOU HEAR...? NOT. ONE. FARTHING. MORE.'

Turning to leave, Sir Henry looked to his wife and, seeing her hand still resting on David's sleeve, turned back to Clara before returning to Violet and saying: 'Like two bitches on heat.'

Violet, *now* appearing like she may very well faint, made after her husband, the echo of her heels on stone deafening those remaining.

No one looked upon another; only Clara who, desperate for eye contact from *anyone*, said, 'Well, that bloom didn't last long, did it!'

———

Sir Henry, believing everyone retired for the night, descended the smooth pockmarked stone steps created by his forefathers, the candle flame guttering from the keen draught spiralling upwards – or was it downwards? *Gravity*, he inwardly grunted, *is a fickle friend to the infirm.* It seemed, to him, a capricious force that although presently offering his legs assistance was putting those same limbs at odds with their true potential. Checking his pace, his free hand momentarily tightened its grip of the rope rail, the plumping veins ruffling papery skin.

Touching down onto terra firma with a guttural 'thank you' to God Almighty, Sir Henry still wouldn't entertain his not performing the nightly ritual of checking the contents of his safe – the sleeping draught he concocted the very first night he became Sir Henry de Trouville, Baronet – the same as he could never contemplate relocating to the first floor.

Unlocking and entering his study, he was unaware someone was concealed in a corner – a houseplant and shadow for accomplices. When Sir Henry's feeble eyes and flagging fingers slowed the process of turning the safe's dial, this, along with the candlelight, aided the *other* to memorise the combination.

A little later, when his head was settled into a peaceful snore on a downy pillow, Sir Henry was likewise unmindful of the caw emitted from a jackdaw perched on the east tower battlement above his apartment.

THREE

'MR TURNER, WHEN you've finished gawping, I'd appreciate you carrying out the duties Sir Henry employs you for.'

'Do yer see over yonder, Mr Fawcett, just above Cross Fell's table top, eh?' Sir Henry's valet said, looking through the dining room's west window. 'Sky's clear when yer gets a first gander, but if yer know yer stuff, yer'll see birds flyin' in sooner and that's cos the're flyin' through low cloud that's thin to us eyes, yet thick enough to hide 'emselves in't distance. Mark me words, that cloud'll thicken. By end o't day there'll be snow; smelt it, I did, this morning, when bringin' in logs. It'll be nice for the bairns – snow on Christmas Eve, eh!'

'What I see, Mr Turner,' Fawcett – who'd stood patiently to listen to the weather report – said while heading for the door, 'is a *dining table top* of breakfast dishes awaiting clearing.'

'A man can't deny her maiden attraction,' James said to David as Fawcett entered the hall with a tray in his hands.

'Maiden! Are you telling me you doubt Henry's consummated the marriage?'

'Of course not. It's only, well, one looks upon such a creature and sees a maiden, and a man can't help but take on a little of the old sainted spirit!'

'The lady's in need of rescue from sacrifice, is that it? Then you'll be needing to slay the dragon!'

'I fear even if it were slayed she'd not look upon me as "*the* St George", not with you on the scene, *and you*, dear fellow, having already caught the best of them!'

'I had thought, after your couple of years away, you'd return with a bride on your arm – at the very least an intended,' David commented.

'Alas, no. The only thing I returned with was another fracture in the old muscle pump… which received a further fracture when I arrived at Crowthwaite to discover the old man's beaten me to it – again! *Ahh*… the lady of the manor…!' Stubbing out his cigarette – Fawcett, his face impassive, waiting to substitute the full ashtray with a clean one – James made a lip trill. 'Those *violet blue* eyes…! Actually, they're very much like Mother's.'

'Dear God, James!' David laughed.

'I didn't mean *that*; I was only going to say I can understand what Father saw in her… all those decades ago.'

'Violet's certainly muddied your vision.'

'Not you, too, James.' Clara, entering the hall, despaired, the previous evening already forgotten.

James whistled. 'I can't understand this jealousy of yours, Clara. You're well aware you're just as alluring… she a fair beauty, you a dark.'

'One can always rely on you, James, to say the right thing,' Clara said, hoping for affirmation from David.

'That's just it,' James answered, 'I never do know what to say… not really. Like the time I proposed to Ava…'

'From what I heard it was more of a pact,' David said.

'Exactly my point! I'd rehearsed the proposal all summer and, to my ears, it was magnificent, but when it came to its execution I garbled something about if ever the time came and no one would have her then she ought to know I'd take her off the old man's hands! Ava, being the sweet thing she is, never took offence; and, sadly for me but hardly unsurprising, she never took my proposal seriously. Of course, when Henry got wind of the proposal he blew quite a gale! I suppose I wasn't worthy… *Anyway*, in the end the best man won, dear fellow.'

Despite James's compliment, Clara continued to dwell on the female competition, complaining about 'Ava and Violet' being all anyone could think of.

For refuge, James picked up *The Times*.

'*I suppose*, while we're talking of Ava, I may as well ask of her whereabouts?'

'Stables,' David replied.

'With Uncle? Well, if anyone can sweeten his temper, it's Ava,' Clara said.

'She won't be adding lemon to his tea, if that's what you're worried about.'

Clara didn't say anything to that.

'I hope you'll behave today. Your uncle's fair game—'

'But not your wife?' Bending down, she tapped her cigarette holder, and breathed, 'For you… *anything*.' Then, straightening back up, she took a draw of her cigarette before asking, 'Is *he* with them?'

David pinched a tobacco flake off his tongue before issuing a '*careful*' warning just as Chester came down the stairs.

'Clara, d'you get to see the old guy?'

'Not yet, darling. He's out at the stables with Ava. I told you not to worry; last night's overreaction was exactly that… and quite like Uncle. In fact, I've not the slightest concern regarding my allowance. Simply like him to use the threat when in one of his foul moods.'

'You sure?'

'Don't become a worrier, Chester. Tell you what, let's cheer up this dreary old place!' Clara walked across to the fireplace and pulled the ring bell, returning Fawcett to the hall within moments. 'Fawcett, bring in the gramophone from the drawing room, would you. There's a good man!'

'Sounds good to me,' Stephen said, arriving with Bertha.

'At least wife number three managed to achieve something one and two never did,' Clara remarked as Fawcett and Turner carried in a mahogany cabinet between them.

'And that is?' Stephen asked.

'Dragging Uncle over the line into the twentieth century – even if it is only a foot! Now you're here, Stephen, could you clear that area over there – No, Fawcett, don't force it open, it's not a drawer! Chester, darling, would you take over? *Oh*, I forgot,' Clara added, heading for the stairs, 'we'll be requiring some seventy-eights!' When she returned she had an armful of records.

'What d'you say, Chester, to a—?'

'*Charleston!*' he echoed and, grabbing a record from her, proceeded to wind up the mechanical motor.

Peals of brass, percussion, string and wind instruments travelled the hall; an avant-garde melody rising high with the thick stone walls and channelling through the corridor and up the spiral staircase to meet with Violet who, matching the beat, increased her descent to an undesirable tempo.

'Fawcett,' she accosted the butler at the kitchen door, 'who's playing my algraphone?'

'Miss Clara, my lady.'

'Don't take it to heart,' Susan, approaching from behind, told her. 'Like you, Clara has an ear for music but Henry wouldn't permit the "clap trap" instrument in his manor. You, my dear' – Susan looped a fur-coated arm through Violet's and steered her in the direction of the music – 'have worked quite a trick with your husband; you've achieved something neither Catherine nor Frances ever did!' It appeared Susan had *worked quite the trick* with the lady of the manor herself for, by the time they reached the hall, Violet was smiling.

'Ah, Violet,' Stephen said as Bertha took her usual seat, 'you'll join me, won't you.' Before Violet could respond, she was being foxtrotted round Crowthwaite's makeshift ballroom.

Stephen, it would appear, was not as cultured as his sister-in-law, who was engrossed in a dance Violet had not seen before. Perfectly tuned to the rhythm, Clara and Chester were gently embracing; and with their feet turned in, they tapped the balls of their feet down with a twist as they stepped backwards and forwards in unison. Then, unconventionally, they broke contact to dance improvised solos, again tapping and twisting their feet, heels always off the floor, but now their arms were swinging, their heads waggling and their legs kicking out with more zeal – Clara's short dress a-flapping.

Orbiting their modern dance moves in as fast a tempo as Stephen could manage, Violet was infected, the beat reverberating through her body – her knees feeling the urge to snap her legs into the similar reflexes Violet-the-carefree-child recalled. As the music died down and Stephen abandoned her to claim Clara's next dance – 'You must teach me, sister!' – Violet was left reeling, appealing for another partner. Chester was attending to the gramophone while relating that the music and the dance had been brought across the Atlantic barely a month ago by a buddy of his. David showed no sign of wishing to dance, and when Violet's eyes fell on James over the top of *The Times*, he replied how he only wished he'd the feet for dancing. Violet hung around, hoping she could pencil Chester into her card; instead, after finishing his story, he opted for a drink.

'So, this is where the distant cousins are sent,' he said, addressing Susan.

'At the other side of Henry's great hall by the cold

fireplace?' Susan returned. 'I highly recommend the respite for any distant relative *or guest* of the de Trouville family!'

Chester's laughter rattled his cup on its saucer. 'I can't get used to you Brits and your cups of tea. And how 'bout this – how's a man meant to fit his fingers through this?'

'The idea is you don't. You simply grip it with your thumb and forefinger. But what of its taste, *or* do all Americans prefer coffee?'

'We're *havin'* to get used to our cups of joe,' Chester corrected her.

'Ah, the prohibition!' she said with a sudden realisation. 'Yes, I think you're receiving the lesson that you can remove the monarch but that doesn't mean the gap won't be filled with another tyrant.'

'You could be right… I mean, you *still* have your monarch *and* your alcohol – though we ain't takin' back your tea!'

Their laughter caught Clara's attention, who insisted Chester *must* be her dance partner, Stephen having proved she was no natural teacher. When Chester raised his saucer by way of reply, Clara redirected her plea to David.

'Yes, quite the horse face, haven't I!' Susan said, her peripheral vision alerting her to being the object of Chester's study. 'I believe in some quarters I'm known as "Long Susan". It's fine, I'm well used to being the ugly relative! *Again*, another recommendation – every family should have at least one!' When his amusement had subsided, she asked, 'Why are you here, Chester?'

'Clara asked me.'

'My meaning is why do you permit her such power?'

Chester, thinking over Susan's question, noted Clara had settled again for Stephen, having failed to lure David to the floor.

'I apologise,' Susan began, 'but I'm *not* afraid to tell you your *invite* was twofold. Every Christmas is the same. Last Christmas was a penniless poet who'd gone up to London while, as he himself wrote: *His dad chipped away / At coal destined for a sack, His skin, his eyes, his lungs / Lined with black*. You're all handsome, I'll give her that, but you've all got something else in common – you're from a different class. A class that will never belong at Crowthwaite Manor.'

'I get that she wants to provoke her uncle – how 'bout the other reason?'

'I think you know the answer to that,' Susan replied, watching Clara, who – clearly exasperated with her pupil – was making another attempt to wear David down into submission.

'That's just a bit of flirtin',' Chester disagreed. 'It's the way Clara is.'

'Well, it's not for me to tell you how to live your life. All I wanted to say is you deserve better.'

'Oh, I ain't so bowled over by all this to make me think I have any sort of future with Clara any more than I truly believe I'm accepted as an equal among white men.'

Susan regarded him. 'No, I believe you've more intelligence than that.'

After a few moments of silence between the two, Chester said, 'It ain't my name, you know.'

'Chester?'

He smiled. 'I was Samuel. Samuel Johnson. A worthy biblical name for an obedient boy.'

'*Then the LORD called Samuel. Samuel answered, "Here I am".*'

'That was grandpop, runnin' when called: "Here I am!" He used to say to me, "Samuel, we all have a duty in this world." His *duty* was to his owner, and he never resented it…

not before he got his freedom, not after. I can't understand it and I don't think I ever will.'

No? Susan said to herself when Chester, expectedly, abandoned his tea to accede to Clara's request.

'That looked cosy,' James said, taking Chester's place.

'He's a sweet thing,' Susan replied.

'I see... You're worried Clara's going to chew him up then spit him out?'

'Isn't that her form – introducing young working-class men to a different world before cruelly reminding them they're not worthy?'

'I fear you're a little harsh on her.'

'Possibly you're right... possibly you're not. I *do* recognise she's Henry's own creation; had he given her the attention she craved from a young girl then she might now be a settled young woman...'

'Bertha, old girl,' Stephen said while admiring another exemplary performance of the Charleston, 'Betsy and Rose should be permitted to join us. It is Christmas Eve.'

Without another word from her husband, Bertha rang the bell and when Fawcett appeared she asked, 'Fawcett, need the girls remain in the nursery?'

'Madam?'

'Stephen thinks they needn't.'

'I'll send word to Ivy to bring them down, shall I?'

Bertha looked to her husband.

'Much appreciated, Fawcett,' Stephen said.

'It's not at all what I expected,' Bertha remarked when Fawcett went about his errand.

'What's not?'

'Uncle's marriage. I had expected an announcement at some point during the evening.'

'I told you, old girl,' Stephen said, understanding her meaning, 'it all rests with your uncle… unfortunately.'

'Funny how things turn out. There I was preparing myself for a big announcement and he goes and calls her… well, *I* shan't repeat the words.'

'Strictly speaking, he also applied the same term to your sister.'

'Oh, that's nothing new,' she said, waving the parity aside.

'There may have been "doings" between your uncle and sister in the past but never have they escalated to last night's heights. No, old girl, I fear this is not over by a long shot.'

'Do you really believe that? Oh, Stephen, don't say such things…!'

Susan, who'd watched Bertha ring for Fawcett, said to James, 'Clara does like to tease Bertha, but it's not as though she wasn't onto something when she bestowed her with the nickname.'

'She does fit snuggly into her Mary Janes,' James agreed.

'I fear if the shoe didn't fit comfortably Bertha would still squeeze her foot into it.'

'You really are an old maid! Why is it so hard to believe a wife can enjoy pleasing her husband?'

'I forget you only know a select few women.'

'More's the pity.' And gesturing to the coat draped over her chair, James asked her where she'd disappeared to after breakfast.

'I'd gone out to the stables with Henry and Ava. Henry was talking about the Robins having an Anglo-Arab for sale, a pretty little mare, apparently, which he said he was thinking of buying for Violet as her introduction to thoroughbreds. He was asking Ava's advice and, for what my word's worth, I told him I wouldn't. The mare might be an Arab cross but my experience tells me she'll still be a sprightly thing, and judging by Violet's aversion to horses at dinner last night, it would only intensify her fear.'

'And *did* your word have any worth?'

'Henry, forgetting the girls' and his own and John's childhood ponies, said nothing but hot bloods will ever be housed in his stables so his wife had better learn to overcome her irrational fear.'

'What did Ava have to say?'

'She agreed with me and listed through some beautiful warm bloods, and when the young groom, Joe, told her the Anglo-Arab's a chestnut with a white stripe, she said she'd a mind to send word to Peter Robins to register her own interest.'

'She always did have a fondness for Arabs *and* chestnuts.'

'Agreed, but listen, the interesting part was Henry's answer. He then informed us the point is now moot as he's no longer any intention of buying the mare *because* he's questioning whether she's worth the investment.'

'By "she" he was referring to...?'

'Violet,' Susan mouthed as Betsy and Rose bounded down the stairs with a 'DADDY!' There ensued a cacophony of competition between jazz and Clara and Chester's dance energy and the two girls skipping after one another chanting 'Father-Christmas-comes-on-Christmas-E-ee-ve... Lots-and-lots-and-lots-of-toys-under-the-Christmas-tree-ee-ee...' It was when they were on their fifth loop of the great hall that Rose, finally overtaking Betsy, collided with her great-uncle.

'Upsy-daisy!' Ava smiled, extending her hands down to Rose's little figure.

Rose was hesitating when Sir Henry bellowed, demanding to know why the children were running amok downstairs while the adults danced with depravity to base music.

Chester – half of Sir Henry's adult dancers – lifted the tone arm off the record and the room fell silent. Not receiving a response from either parent, Sir Henry looked down to his great-niece for answer, her body frozen except for a quivering lip.

'Uncle, no!' Ava challenged him – halting Stephen – and as she made to pick Rose up, Betsy took her sister's hand and said, matter-of-factly, 'There, Rose, it's only Uncle Henry full of knot hair. That's right, isn't it, Daddy?'

Sir Henry cast his eye on Stephen as a chortle erupted from David.

'You always did say it was just like a child to come out with tommyrot!' Bertha hastened with a slight nervous quiver.

'I was referring to their making excellent spies,' Sir Henry corrected her. 'Walsingham knew this better than anyone.'

'Are you sure you're not getting confused with servants, Henry?' Susan said, trying to bring her cousin round.

'None in service would be more malleable than a child,' Sir Henry said, not for turning.

'Walsingham…' Stephen considered, 'had children within his web?'

'If not, history has just had a little re-write,' David replied, his amusement subsiding.

Ignoring both men, Sir Henry looked to his wife – who, upon his entrance, had been sat forward, her head waggling and her fingers tapping on her knees in time to her shoes that had been swivelling… heels in… heels out – and gestured to the gramophone. 'Are you responsible for this?'

'Oh, come now, Henry,' Susan said, 'the young things have a right to enjoyment, particularly during the festive season!'

'Here, here,' Stephen agreed.

'*That* was not enjoyment,' Sir Henry countered, 'that was

immoral, not to mention a threat to cover my floor with the breakfast I generously provided.'

'It's the Charleston, sir,' Chester enlightened him.

Sir Henry shut out Chester's 'noise' by asking his wife whether she'd taken part in 'this debauchery'.

'Debauchery!' Susan exclaimed. 'Henry, it was music and dancing! The only strength was in the tea, and that was brewed to perfection!'

'Although, Susan,' Clara chimed in, 'Aunt was swooped off her feet… that's right, isn't it, Stephen?'

'Fawcett!' Sir Henry called out.

'It was only the foxtrot!' Violet appealed.

'Fawcett, see to it that the contraption is returned to its rightful place.'

'Sir.'

'Same goes for the children. I've work to do,' he added, overruling the protests, 'and I shan't be disturbed.'

Sir Henry left to hunker down in his study while Violet shadowed Fawcett and Turner in their carrying of her gramophone back through to the drawing room, and Clara, after whispering something in his ear, led Chester upstairs.

Susan's thinking was proved incorrect when they returned within minutes, Clara muffled head to toe in sable fur, Chester only a short Mackinaw for warmth, its collar buttoned up high. Their figures receding down the corridor, Susan informed James he was more astute than he gave himself credit for. He'd understood, she told him, the Charleston was *Clara*: an expression of freedom for the young woman who'd had to learn to live with the knowledge of her mother dying shortly after her birth, notwithstanding her father's unexpected death three years later; a soupçon of chaos rallying against subsequent years of too-much-order.

Their hands held, Clara and Chester headed towards the gun room, which led to the castle rear. Tom, having just returned from his errand to Appleby, watched, from the estate office, Clara lead Chester across the frosted lawn at a pace signifying a youth he feared to be forsaking him. Joining a track, the young couple was soon devoured by spruce, pine, fir and larch, the latter the only species of the four to always succumb to the season, its needles turned golden as though it was dead and not in a trance.

———

George Turner was correct – even if his timing was out by a half hour, his 'end of day' pushed to 'beginning of next' – for when Sir Henry's party stepped out through the church porch, miniature snowflakes were wandering the graveyard. The night sky was George's cloud which *had* thickened to a grey brilliance awaiting instruction from its superior – a bellyful of blackness suspended above Cross Fell.

'It's snowing, Daddy…' Betsy shrieked, kicking her way down from her father's arms, 'IT'S SNOWING!'

Witnessing his eldest child run out into the open and tilt her head back to let the flakes land on her warm skin, Stephen was repaid with joy for having defied Henry, who'd said the girls were too young to attend midnight Mass; concerning Rose he'd acquiesced but when it came to his 'Besty Betsy' he'd had an additional two years in his favour.

'The magic of Christmas Eve is complete,' Stephen said with a smile that was beaming ear to ear.

Bertha yawned.

'MERRY CHRISTMAS!' he trumpeted, his arms stretched out wide to the world.

The chorus that returned his greeting did not include Bertha, who asked him not to frighten her so at such an hour and Violet who complained about the paths being treacherous enough.

Without offering his wife his arm, Sir Henry called for Ava. Violet, piqued, now hatched a plan to remove the small wrapped box from underneath the drawing room's Christmas tree which contained a brand-new hip flask – had she known anything of her husband, she would have realised he wouldn't have been appreciative, anyway, much preferring his relic with its broken stopper hinge. As she made to follow, her right heel slid out from underneath her. Hearing her cry, all of those in front turned around to see David break her fall; momentarily held in a strong hold, Violet exuded an intoxication which Ava had read many a time on Clara's face.

Shaking his head, Sir Henry turned to lead the congregation, shepherding his family and guests, and tenants and staff, down the church lane where lanterns were hanging from fence posts. A different Christmas, when delivering his sermon, Reverend Tyson had told his flock the arrangement of lanterns signified the Father, showing His children the way.

Tom skirted the walkers all the way from the rear with Pearl by his side, perfecting the temporal dimension to converge with uncle and niece at God's last beacon where he, Thomas Atkinson – his lantern rocking on its crook – was ready to shoulder the burden.

A little behind Sir Henry, Susan and David found themselves confounded when the baronet did something unprecedented: taking Ava's arm, he linked it through his own. It was an affection that was decades overdue and they witnessed the warmth escape his body as he related her father had named her for a 'child of this land'.

54

'I never knew,' Ava said, flabbergasted by both the public avuncular display and the revelation.

'Of course, I dismissed it then – as I still do – as balderdash, but that doesn't mean I don't see the fondness you have for the estate. Your sisters, though' – he gave a brief look back down the line to where Bertha had tagged onto Clara (and, reluctantly, Clara's guest) – 'think nothing of it; except what they can take from it – Ava, listen… After much thought, I wish you to know I will instruct John Atkins to act on your behalf, to petition for a divorce. Now, now,' he interrupted her response, while Susan restrained David with a gloved hand, her look warning him retaliation wouldn't help his cause, 'don't make your decision at this moment. I'm advising you to think on the offer. You're here to see in the New Year and I believe you should use the time to reflect on the state of your marriage. Things *can't* go on as they are! Atkins said, as a result of a law passed this year, a wife is legally permitted to divorce her husband on the charge of adultery alone. I see how rotten a deal this is for you and I won't have it – not for a de Trouville! I only wish for you to know if you do decide to divorce then you will have my full support… including until such a time as we find you a better match – No, Ava, listen to me, there's yet the time for you to begin a family! Until then, I will welcome you back at the manor, back to this land where I know you feel a sense of belonging.'

When her uncle first uttered the word 'divorce', Ava thought she had caught Tom cock his head, ever so slightly; now, witnessing his and Pearl's farewell at the village street, she believed it to have been her imagination.

After stealing into the shadows for a secretive nip, Sir Henry disturbed the couple's moment with a reminder to his secretary that his workday was not finished and he'd be expected, as was usual, to attend the toast; meanwhile David, ignoring Susan's advice, took hold of Ava's arm and ushered her ahead of the party.

'Why Henry couldn't let me go in the motor car, I don't know,' Violet complained to Susan from under her umbrella, the snow rapidly thickening and falling at increased speed. 'The outdoors is going to ruin my chignon!'

Crowthwaite's residents heading off down the village street with a 'Merry Christmas', Susan noted their items of outer clothing would be offering their fragile chests less protection than that currently being afforded Violet's hair by a fur hat *and* an umbrella. However, biting her lip, Susan assured Violet, 'Not a strand out of place, my dear.'

'Just look at that!' Chester exclaimed, stopping to take in the small orbs of light from candles in windows either side of the village green, and here and there an oil burner standing on a garden wall – all aiding the parishioners return to their beds. 'There ain't a spark of electricity in sight!'

'It's nothing like the Big Smoke,' Clara agreed, 'and while ever Uncle lords it over the area, there's no chance of Crowthwaite moving with the times – indeed it skipped gas lighting altogether!'

Bertha garbled something about theatre explosions to which Clara pooh-poohed her sister's scaremongering as a regurgitation of Uncle's prejudices 'which are hilarious considering the fool still insists on using naked flames'.

'Change is coming, Clara,' Chester told her, 'there's no stopping it now. Hundred years from now, even this village's tiny streets are gonna be lit up with electricity…'

Betsy tugged on Chester's hand. 'Dadd-y's kee-ping out the co-o-old!' she sang, gesturing to her father swigging from a silver hip flask. After licking away the spillage from his bottom lip, Stephen was stowing the flask into his coat pocket when he realised his audience. 'I do apologise, my new friend, would you care for a nip?'

'Thanks, but I'll pass,' Chester replied.

'I, on the other hand, will gladly accept,' James said.

There was an exchange between leather-gloved hands and after taking an exceedingly generous nip James whistled.

'The liquid fire packs quite a punch, does it not, old friend!'

Laughing, they chased down the party that was now partly dissolved into the white – no sign of Ava and David, who were way ahead.

Ava had waited until they'd made some headway before shrugging David off. 'I won't apologise for you having to endure Uncle's cruelty.'

'Then what will you do?'

'No, David, that's not fair… you don't get to do that!'

———

'If the reality of that man sleeping directly above us isn't injurious enough, the added insult is his taking pride of place for the Christmas Eve toast,' David said with a scowl in Tom's direction where the private secretary was standing with the lord and lady of the manor.

'Come now,' Susan said, 'he resides on the second floor along with every other member of staff.'

'A secretary – in the east tower apartment!'

'I wouldn't bother,' Ava said, cutting off Susan's retort, 'it's a recurring theme – every visit! As though Uncle has no right to offer the largest room to his aide.'

A little of the whisky sloshed over the rim as David raised his glass to his wife.

'Is it too much for Uncle to expect you to abstain... until the toast?'

'The old man's no dominion over me to make any such demand!'

'No one spoke of demand, David.'

'Demands are for the likes of secretaries,' David continued. 'You know, Susan, I've often wondered whether she lies awake, listening for his clumpy boots... her breath held, praying for a pause at the door.' Before either woman could respond, David stormed across to James; passing by Turner – who was following Fawcett into the hall, each carrying a tray, David exchanged his whisky glass for two champagne-filled flutes.

'He's well aware,' Ava began, a little defensively, 'Thomas's door to the spiral stairs is locked and, like all staff, he's only permitted to use the staff staircase.'

For answer Susan patted Ava's hand, incongruously to Sir Henry tapping metal against crystal.

'Madam,' Fawcett said, handing Ava, then Susan, a flute of champagne.

'Nineteen twenty-three...' Sir Henry paused until he had everyone's attention. '*Nineteen twenty-three* has been an *eventful* year, and a year which has brought our family trials. I'm confident, however, we "de Trouvilles" will triumph, for today, Christmas Day, is a reminder of the strength within each of us, *if only* we submit ourselves to the will of God! As we celebrate the birth of Christ we welcome the knowledge that through our travails we will be delivered. It is then that we shall receive our reward. For though we may be mere mortals, it is through our children, and their children, that we will achieve our immortality.'

'Ironic then,' Clara muttered to Stephen, 'the children aren't here to hear how precious they are.'

Sir Henry raised his glass. '*Per familia, divitiae et immortalitas affuo.*'

All glasses were raised into the air, the family members chorusing the motto – with the exception of Clara, who was acting as translator for Chester: '*Through family, wealth and immortality flow.*' Then everyone drank their champagne, David knocking back the whole flute. Beside him, James cleared his throat before joining David by gulping down the remainder.

His duty done, Sir Henry was replacing his barely touched champagne on Fawcett's tray when a choke resounded round the hall. The flute slipped through Sir Henry's fingers and fell to the floor, scattering crystal and champagne. There followed more choking and someone cried out 'JAMES!' as Sir Henry's guest began to violently retch; and, expelling vomit, James collapsed to the ground.

'CHOLERA!' Violet screamed as Fawcett smartly withdrew.

'Don't be ridiculous,' Susan rebuked Violet while David loosened James's collar.

'I've seen it before!' Violet argued.

'Yes…' Bertha uttered, stepping further back, 'James has only recently returned from India – Dear God, Stephen, he'll infect us all!'

'Now, old girl, don't take on. I don't think it at all likely he has cholera. David… Tom, help me carry him up to his bed… Turner,' he added, 'you'll be needed to attend him.'

'How could you have invited him, knowing he'd just returned from that filthy place!' Violet demanded of her husband, who was standing in a stupor, looking after the four men who were carrying between them a writhing James up the grand staircase.

'You are *truly* absurd,' Clara said to Violet. 'You too, Boots!

James returned months ago; he couldn't possibly be infected with cholera from his trip!'

'Has anyone sent for a doctor?' Chester realised minutes later when Fawcett reappeared.

'Yes, send for Norris,' Sir Henry instructed, trying his best not to look at the pile of vomit.

'Mr Smith has this minute left for the doctor's house,' Fawcett informed his employer.

'Clara's right,' Ava said to no one in particular, 'cholera could not incubate for such a length of time. It only needs hours – days at the most to manifest.' And realising James's champagne flute had landed on the edge of the rug miraculously intact, she reached down.

'AVA… NO!' David called out from the stairs, Stephen and Tom close behind.

Ava's expression was puzzled.

'His drink may have been poisoned,' David explained.

'*Poisoned*,' Sir Henry repeated. Looking round the hall, he regarded each and every individual present and, his senses returned, questioned, 'Who here among you would dare do such a thing?'

———

Crystal, champagne and vomit had been cleaned up and James's champagne flute safely removed using a cloth, courtesy of Fawcett, but Sir Henry and his guests were still in the great hall… waiting.

Since Sir Henry's accusation there had been no talk, except for Susan wishing to know if James was any better, to which David and Stephen had regretfully replied he was worse, 'much worse'.

Upon the chauffeur's return with Doctor Ronald Norris, Fawcett immediately led the doctor up to James's room on the first floor where Turner had remained, attending to the patient along with the help of Nan Clarke, the cook.

All eyes were on the staircase, still waiting, when Doctor Norris descended back down into the hall and it was with great reverence that he spoke: 'It is with deep sadness I regret to inform you that Mr Bowes passed away within minutes of my arrival.'

Four

'Although his symptoms were in accordance with cholera this seems highly unlikely, considering he's the only one to have taken ill,' Doctor Norris said when Sir Henry closed the door to his study.

'Then it *was* poison?'

'That would be my hypothesis. However, until I have the results of the autopsy, I won't say so.'

Nodding, Sir Henry regarded the snow hitting the window, each flake intact, sliding down the freezing pane until lodging against a piece of lead.

'How are *you*, Sir Henry? I would very much like to give you an examination?'

Knocking the doctor's concern aside, Sir Henry asked, 'Could it have been accidental?'

'By accidental you *mean…?*'

'Could James have accidentally poisoned himself – it's not unheard of?'

'No, it's not. There has been human demise as a result of handling poisonous substances. Again, I wouldn't discount anything, but let's wait for the results. Right then, if you're sure I can't give you a quick examination…?'

'Perfectly sure.'

'Then I'll be off.'

Placing his hat firmly down on his head, Ronald Norris said he'd get word to the chief constable to attend the manor at first light. Passing through the hall, the doctor told everyone nothing else could be done at present and his advice would be for them all to get themselves to bed.

Pausing at her bedroom door, Susan looked down the landing to where Clara and Chester were speaking thickly. Clara said something, and Chester – after glancing at the room opposite that was now bereft of James – followed her into her room.

Violet was eager to retire but had hung around for David and Ava to make the first move.

'Would you mind escorting me up to my apartment?' she asked David when the three of them reached the small stone landing outside Ava and David's apartment. 'I've no light.'

'Lock the door until my return,' David instructed Ava.

'Let's not add more drama to the night,' Ava said defiantly, making a point of only closing the door behind her.

'Thank you for being so attentive this evening,' Violet said outside her own apartment. 'One should be able to rely on one's husband for protection.'

'I'm certain you'll be safe,' David said, one foot already on the next step down.

'I wish I could believe that; I'm not so sure! I think... if *someone* were to spend a little time with me...?'

'You could send for your maid.'

'Not the maid... no,' she said, running her fingers over the long strand of pearls hanging over her heaving bust.

'Goodnight, Violet,' David replied.

'Do you really think David's correct in James having been poisoned?' Bertha asked Stephen, feeling much safer within the confines of their own room.

'Yes, I believe he is.'

'Oh, Stephen...!'

'Don't fret, old girl,' he said, tenderly pulling her to him, 'everything will be fine.'

Locking up his study, Sir Henry thought of his Christmas toast and how he was indeed being tested on this holy day. Raising his head to the ceiling he promised he would not be found wanting; he, God's servant, would not rest until he discovered whoever was responsible for James's death.

'Goodnight, Tom,' he said to his secretary, their paths coinciding in the east tower where the corridor split into three.

Returning the farewell, Tom wondered if he'd neglected to take notice of the age creeping up on his employer *or* whether the last couple of hours were to blame, for it appeared Sir Henry had taken James's death very badly.

'*Merry Christmas*, sir,' Tom called after Sir Henry's frail figure that was now beginning its climb. Then, with a shake of his head, Tom opened the door to the staff staircase.

The small log in the fireplace was still fresh, awaiting its final end. Ordinarily a fire would have been lit prior to his retiring to bed but, in the night's events, ordinary duties had been interrupted. Tom hoped, though, someone had got around to lighting a fire in Sir Henry's apartment. He was about to think the same for Ava before reminding himself she had someone to keep her warm.

Throwing himself back on his bed, he closed his eyes and let his mind drift back to another life…

Tom woke, shivering. Barely an hour had passed yet much had flitted through his mind in a distorted dream of death, desire and duty. Another shiver forced him to rise, to cut off the draft from the two mullioned windows.

He drew the last curtain on a jackdaw taking off from the top of the tower, its dark shape only fleetingly dissipating the white.

———

When the sun rose, its rays were weak, barely reaching the white landscape.

The snow was no longer falling and that which had had did not prevent Chief Constable Kenneth Watson's driver from reaching Crowthwaite.

Turning onto the manor drive, the police motor car met with Sir Henry's.

'Thank the Lord!' Frank Smith said, jumping out.

The chief constable opened his door. 'What is it, Mr Smith?'

''Tis Sir Henry, sir – he's dead!'

'*Sir Henry* dead?'

'Aye, sir. George Turner found him when he went in to wake him this morning. It were his throat, sir… cut it were!'

FIVE

IT WAS 1438 when the county last recorded the murder of a notable person – a murder which Sir Henry's direct ancestor was charged with but cleared of being implicated in. Coupled with Kenneth Watson having been a close friend of Sir Henry, the chief constable didn't have the appetite for the investigation and so he'd made a call to Manchester City Police's Criminal Investigation Department, which had immediately despatched an inspector.

Chief Constable Watson had lied to the lady of the manor. Having already warned Turner to stop spreading nonsense about finding his employer 'in his blood-spattered bed with his eyes chillin'ly wide', he'd told the widow she could take comfort in the knowledge her husband had been in peaceful sleep when he'd passed. To Detective Inspector Gilbert Dunderdale, upon his arrival late afternoon on Christmas Day, he'd spoken the truth: Sir Henry had been woken before his throat was cut.

'You'll have to speak with the family regarding the significance of the costume the murderer wore,' Watson said to Dunderdale, 'for though I'm aware of Crowthwaite having a ghost story concerning crows, I do not know of its particulars.'

'You mean you believe Sir Henry was purposely woken so he'd have seen, not his murderer, but a character from a local tale?'

'That's my exact belief, and although I would much prefer to think of Sir Henry's final few moments *not* being filled with terror when suddenly woken and confronted with someone cloaked and masked in black feathers, logic tells me otherwise. God rest his soul.'

'Cloaked and masked in black feathers – that was the character!'

'Apparently, some pagan priest. What I can tell you is the costume is one of three identical costumes kept in the attic. We know, with certainty, it was worn during the act of murder for the blood spatter upon it is consistent with the murderer having been in close proximity to Sir Henry. The costume was then abandoned to the floor beside his four-poster bed.'

'Was the blade also abandoned?' Dunderdale asked.

'No. We're still searching.'

'How was the victim lying in bed?'

'On his back… the left side of the bed.'

'The victim's left side?'

'Yes.'

'Are you able to describe the cut?'

Chief Constable Watson rummaged for the police surgeon's findings. 'Short and deep.'

'Tailing off to…?'

'Sir Henry's left.'

'And was the cut angled?'

'Seward's notes say upwards, to the left – again, Sir Henry's left.'

'Then our murderer was right-handed.'

'That's what Seward concludes. *Ah*, it would have been so easy had they been left-handed!'

'I *would* like to establish who's *not* right-handed – immediately,' Dunderdale requested.

'Collins,' Chief Constable Watson instructed the sergeant who was present.

'I'm hoping,' Dunderdale said as the door closed, 'the left-handers currently residing at the manor over-represent the left-handed population. While we wait, have you any early indication of why Sir Henry was murdered?'

'No. Afraid not.'

'Do you know if anything is missing?'

'You mean has anything been stolen? Not as far as Tom is aware.'

'Tom?'

'Atkinson. Sir Henry's private secretary. That also applies to the study. When unlocking it for me this morning, Tom found nothing to be missing or disturbed. He confirmed the spare key is housed in the estate office while Sir Henry had his with him at all times. *That* key was located in Sir Henry's bedside drawer. The only items Tom could not swear to are those locked in the safe which, he said, he wouldn't be able to identify anything as missing for he didn't have knowledge of what Sir Henry kept locked away – that will be for the solicitor to answer.'

'Meaning robbery could still be the motive, but I'm going to say highly unlikely due to the fact Sir Henry was murdered in his bed, not at his desk – though, I suppose, the reason for his being woken could be interrogation…' Dunderdale began to enact the scene in his head.

'Tell me the code to the safe and you'll keep your life!'

'Hmm. What of fingerprints?'

'None lifted from Sir Henry's apartment other than his own, his valet's, the two housemaids' and his secretary's.'

'Not his wife's?'

'I think we must draw the conclusion that conjugal rights were carried out in the lady's apartment.'

Not wishing to draw any such image, Dunderdale asked,

'And is it normal for the secretary to access his employer's apartment?'

'I'm reliably informed in the case of Sir Henry it was perfectly normal for him to ring for either valet or secretary, depending on the errand.'

'What of Mr James Bowes – assuming he *was* poisoned, and I think we have a strong reason for this assumption, based on the doctor's initial findings and considering the subsequent murder of Sir Henry – is there any early indication of why Mr Bowes was murdered?'

'None whatsoever. Complete mystery.'

'Who was Mr Bowes to Sir Henry?'

'Younger son of a close friend – also now deceased.'

'Who else was present during the toast?'

'Sir Henry's wife, his guests, including Tom. And, of course, Fawcett – the butler who showed you in – along with George Turner, Sir Henry's valet. Both were handing out the drinks. Tom was the last to see Sir Henry alive, the two of them retiring at the same time – a little after three in the morning.'

'What time was Sir Henry discovered dead?'

'Turner discovered his body at seven thirty – exactly, he says. Sir Henry's usual wake-up call is at six but, Turner said, Sir Henry had requested a later call due to their retiring at such a late hour.'

'Meaning Sir Henry's time of death occurred within a four-and-a-half-hour window. Does the police surgeon's initial examination support this?'

'It does.'

'And I suppose you're about to tell me everyone was asleep during this time?'

'The whole house – the whole *castle* reports to have been

asleep, including the staff. As we've already ascertained, the lord and lady of the manor each kept to their own apartment, both in the east tower, Sir Henry on the fourth floor, Lady Violet on the third. Incidentally, my wife was instrumental in their meeting. Last summer, as my better half, she organised a garden party at which Sir Henry was present. Among her other invitees was our nephew, Peter Barnes, son to my youngest sister, who brought along Miss Violet Olsen, as was – a childhood friend, Peter said. I remember her entrance rather well… blonde hair and blue eyes with youth on her side. A breath of fresh air for these parts so no one was surprised when she caught the eye of a local lord. Miss Violet Olsen was Sir Henry's third chance of marriage – third chance of producing an heir, if we're being honest.'

'I *see*. What about the sleeping arrangements of the guests?'

'Sir Henry's eldest niece, Ava, and her husband have the first-floor apartment in the castle's east tower. David—'

'Before you go on, sir, is there a west tower?'

'No only the one tower.'

'Then why not simply call it "the tower"?'

'Never thought about it – until now. *As* I was saying, David – Ava's husband – is the youngest son of the Rickards, a very wealthy family which has the great-grandfather to thank for having made a substantial fortune in India. Like Sir Henry, they're not what you would call *aristocracy*; regrettable for David's father, who's eager on using their still "relatively new money" to buy into the aristocratic lifestyle – this is the reason for setting up not only his heir but all of his sons with prestigious positions within his trading company, placing them in either the London or India offices… Bengal and Calcutta, I believe. Sir Henry told me all four sons' positions came with very lucrative salaries, hence why he was determined on the match for his eldest niece, once he learned of David's interest in her. David's position at the head office in the City supports the eldest brother and he and Ava, like her sisters, reside in London for the majority of the year. A very nice income for a very nice life of leisure – a match for any of the aristocrats. *Not* a clergy's life for him, though I dare say he would have filled the pews.'

'When you speak of the Rickards not being aristocracy same as Sir Henry, what d'you mean – I thought Sir Henry to be a baronet?'

'A baronet, yes, not a baron. Had he been a baron he'd be regarded a peer of the Realm. Baronets are officially considered commoners.'

Dunderdale looked about his immediate surroundings. 'There's nothing common about this.'

Agreeing, the chief constable added that money, however, was not capable of buying one a family. 'Not unlike Sir Henry, eight years of marriage and still the Rickards are childless. As for the other nieces, Bertha made an equally – if not more so – advantageous match by marrying Stephen Taylor, heir to Taylor's Shipping. Since their marriage he's been handed full control of the family business, his father having passed away. The Taylors were quick to establish family roots, though only two girls to date. As for Clara, Sir Henry's youngest niece, she disappointed her uncle in not following in her sisters' footsteps and Sir Henry had to be content with two, not three, war-time marriages.'

'The privileged… well insulated back home, concerned with only marrying for money and prestige while lesser men – the *real* commoners – went off to do their duty.'

'Well, now, we shouldn't judge too harshly those that were called upon to keep the country ticking over,' Watson said as the door opened.

'Whom have you been able to rule out?' Inspector Dunderdale asked the sergeant.

'A couple o' staff, sir. Head groom and cook are both left-handed *but* not one member o't family or guests. Only left-hander were Mr Bowes.'

'Our first victim.'

'The very one, sir.'

'So, unless the groom and cook are both ambidextrous, neither is our murderer. Chief Constable, you were saying…?'

'Miss Clara de Trouville, yes. As I said, still unmarried. Rather a character she is. I expect that's always the case with the youngest, isn't it? Anyway, as usual, Miss Clara brought a different… *companion* with her to the manor, a Mr Chester Johnson. I must warn you not to be alarmed…'

'Why would I be alarmed?'

'Mr Johnson is… he's of a different colour.'

'Why should that alarm me?'

'No? Then I suppose you see more of that sort of thing in Manchester… Oh, I forgot to mention he's also American. Now, where was I? Oh yes, as is usual when Miss Clara visits, Sir Henry stipulated she keep to her room and her male guest to his. The final family member is Miss Susan Markham, a distant cousin of Sir Henry, who, from my experience, is always a welcome guest at the manor. Also unmarried, she joins Lady de Trouville, Miss Clara and Mr Johnson in sleeping alone.'

'And, you said, all members of staff were also asleep at the time of Sir Henry's murder.'

'Each statement taken down reports every single living person in this house was asleep. One of the housemaids is responsible for supervising the children during their stay – Collins, remind me of the girl's name?'

'Ivy Bridges, sir.'

'Ivy, therefore, resided with the children in the nursery on the first floor while the remaining staff all slept on the second floor... One more thing,' Watson added, halting Dunderdale's act of stowing his notebook away, 'upon examination, the police surgeon found a feather on Sir Henry's tongue.'

'A *black* feather?'

'A black feather. Approximately five inches long.'

'Five inches!'

'Laid neatly on his tongue so as not to protrude from his mouth, meaning it lay partly down his throat...'

'Mighty Ruler!'

'The blood on the feather thought to be Sir Henry's, not the bird's,' Watson clarified, unsure of the inspector's choice of words.

'And is the feather a match for the cloak and mask?'

'A likely match, but we don't believe it was taken from any of the cloaks or masks. None of the garments show any visible sign of missing feathers... all arrays still in perfect alignment. It's a mess,' Watson added with a shake of his head, 'I don't mind telling you.'

'Hmm,' Dunderdale agreed. 'In the case of Mr Bowes's death, we'll no doubt discover each family member has a whole room ready to testify to their innocence. With regards to Sir Henry, the only alibi is either the spouse or the sandman!'

'Or tooth fairy,' Collins contributed.

'Did I mention,' Watson said, 'Sergeant Charles Collins will be at your disposal?'

'Collins,' the detective inspector greeted his sergeant, 'I hope you're going to prove yourself more thorough.'

'Sir?'

'The tooth fairy would only be present during the event of a lost tooth, therefore, an unreliable witness,' Dunderdale said with no trace of humour before turning back to his superior. 'You said Mr Bowes suddenly took ill during a toast… has his glass been sent for tests?'

'It has.'

'And he collapsed *immediately after* drinking his toast?'

'Yes. The de Trouville's first Christmas Day toast upon the family's return from church. Fawcett informs me the glasses are raised along with the family repeating Sir Henry's final words.'

'"Merry Christmas"… the irony!'

'No, not "Merry Christmas"; the family motto.'

'Family motto?'

'Collins?' Watson relayed.

Collins flipped through his pocket notebook before handing it to Dunderdale, who tried sounding out the Latin: '*Per fam-i-lia div… div-i-tae… divit-i… di-vi…*'

'English's on next page, sir,' Collins told him.

Dunderdale turned the page. '*Through family, wealth and immortality flow.*'

'Preservation o' money through heirs, so Mr Atkinson says.'

'Yes, thank you, Collins,' Watson said, 'I think the meaning is obvious.'

'From your previous comment about Sir Henry's marriage to Violet Olsen, I'm presuming there's no son to inherit?' Dunderdale said.

'Correct… and that reminds me, John Atkins, Sir Henry's solicitor, is scheduled to arrive tomorrow morning at…?'

'Ten, sir, with readin' set for eleven,' Collins answered.

Dunderdale nodded.

'Then I put the investigation into your... *exceptionally* capable hands, by all accounts.'

'Thank you, sir,' Dunderdale replied though not feeling particularly gratified.

———

The Lady of the Manor of Crowthwaite and her guests were still consuming their lunch so Detective Inspector Dunderdale asked Sergeant Collins to give him a tour of the grounds before the day's light – if you could call it that – completely deserted them. Donning his overcoat and Homburg, Dunderdale followed Collins down the corridor and through the gun room to the castle rear.

'Impressive,' Dunderdale remarked, taking in the white that expanded out to a forest surrounding the castle on three sides.

'I don't envy the gardener,' Collins agreed.

'Officially considered commoners, indeed!' Dunderdale scoffed as they set off walking.

'He were fond o' Sir Henry, were chief.'

'Did he express any thoughts aloud?'

''Bout what, sir?'

'Did he say whether he suspected *why* Sir Henry had been murdered? Did he happen to suggest a suspect?'

'Can't say I heard him. Though, few times he did say he found it hard to believe family'd be involved.'

''Course he did. Wouldn't do for a de Trouville to be implicated in the murky world of murder. No doubt he hopes for a robbery gone wrong... or death by misadventure – though the latter can be ruled out with certainty in the case of Sir Henry's murder.'

'Yer think it still possible for Mr Bowes, though, sir?'

'Not really. Not when Sir Henry was murdered only hours later.'

'Do yer think it could be a woman, sir? Poison *is* a woman's weapon.'

'Not always, Collins – by Artemis, do those crows ever rest!'

'That's exactly what the're doin', sir, comin' home to roost.'

'Is it always this noisy?'

''Fraid so.'

The sergeant had led his superior south-east, towards the stable block that was just visible at the forest edge. Coming to a stop, Dunderdale looked back at Crowthwaite Castle's walls of red sandstone blocks, now in full view. 'I'm assuming that's Sir Henry's apartment?'

Collins followed Dunderdale's line of sight to the top floor of the east tower which jutted out from the rear of the building. ''Tis, sir.'

'It's hard to believe people still live in these mausoleums. Just look at that height!'

'A death trap, Fawcett warned us, sir. To do with the battlement bein' really low, hence why 'tis no longer used.'

'That's a relief, then.'

'The battlement round the main castle were the original one. Used to be a lookout for Scottish raiders. *Little bleeders*, by all accounts.'

'Thank you, Collins.'

At the stables, Collins introduced Dunderdale to Constable Ernest Shaw, who'd just finished his search.

'Any joy?' Dunderdale asked, his question competing with a horse's neigh.

'None,' Shaw replied, closing the door in the tall central arch behind him.

'None, *sir.*'

'None, sir.'

'What's next on the list?'

'The attic – *sir.* Constable Donnelly's already up there, makin' a start.'

'You'd better join him, then.'

'Sir.'

'He's a good lad, really,' Collins said as they watched the young constable cross the lawn. 'Just needs a bit of encouragement, here and there.'

'This your first murder investigation, Sergeant?'

''Tis, sir... as sergeant, that is.'

'Then understand I expect every *i* dotted and every *t* crossed with the steadiest of hands, which sometimes entails giving others decidedly more than a "bit of encouragement".'

'Sir.'

Following Shaw at a distance, Dunderdale and Collins turned the front corner of the building to discover Crowthwaite Castle's command of the valley below. Had Detective Inspector Dunderdale arrived a day or two earlier the sky would have stretched all the way west to the Saddleback mountain range.

———

'TAKE THIS ONE, DADDY!' Betsy shouted, pelting a snowball at Stephen – an easy target as he stood close to his daughters on the snow-covered lawn.

'Why, you...!' Stephen laughed as the snowball hit him square in the face. Betsy squealed and, grabbing hold of Rose's hand, dragged her away like a little puppy soliciting pursuit. The adult dog gave chase and gently landed a snowball on each of their backs before leaving the pups to fight it out between themselves.

Shaking the snow out of his strawberry-blonde hair, Stephen said to the two policemen, 'If it hadn't been for last night's events, the day would be perfect.'

'While I, myself, find winter a nuisance, I can't deny the attraction for the young ones,' Dunderdale replied.

'Apparently, more snow's forecast,' Stephen said, gesturing to the two grooms sprinkling salt along the drive.

'Can't put enough of the stuff down for me.'

'Rumoured to be one of the early enterprises where David's great-grandfather made his money… salt smuggling.'

'The Rickards… smugglers?' Dunderdale queried.

'Not smugglers, no. The great-grandfather was employed at one of the checkpoints along a route through Bengal to not only collect taxes but intercept the smugglers, except it proved not to be a lucrative route – for the smugglers, that is.'

'I *think* I see,' Dunderdale said as a snowball landed at his feet; Collins bent down to scrape up a handful of snow. 'On that note,' Dunderdale added, 'I'll take my leave.'

After a quickfire exchange of snowballs – grown-up versus grown-up, grown-up versus child, child versus child, Stephen pulled his hip flask from his pocket, first proffering the sergeant a nip.

'I won't… thank… you… sir,' Collins said, his breath laboured.

'Then I hope you'll understand… under the present circumstances…' Stephen pulled out the stopper and took a swig.

'You like cold, like me,' Betsy told the sergeant. Pushing a lock of hair away from in front of her eye with a sodden glove, she explained, 'Chester likes cold but Daddy doesn't like it so he has his nips.'

'She's a character,' Collins said with admiration as Betsy's little hands began to rapidly compress more snow. 'My Molly could do with some of her mettle.'

'From one father to another, I'm sensing a problem?'

'Spot o' bullyin' by a local girl – Appleby, that is. Wanted to pay her parents a visit, I did. Were just fastenin't buttons on me coat when our lass put me in me place' – Charles Collins was in full flow, forgetful of Chief Constable Watson's reproaches to speak correct English ('Now you're a sergeant, you set an example to others.') – '"Need to learn to stick up for 'emselves", she warned me. *'Course*, next time I saw the pair of 'em, I gave 'em what for!'

'Bravo, my fellow.'

'Do 'owt for 'em, we would.'

Watching his daughters launching ice projectiles at one another, Stephen nodded. 'Give our lives.'

'What's this?' Susan's voice spoke from behind them. 'Surely it's not talk of more loss of life – not after the appalling deaths of Henry and James!'

'We're speaking hypothetically of fathers,' Stephen explained, 'giving their lives for their children.'

'*Ah*, then a noble cause,' Susan said, her tone lightened.

'Do you know, Sergeant, the third baronet's son's life was saved through the father offering his soul to the pagan gods.'

'Come now, Stephen, we don't really believe his son and heir regained his strength as a result of nine dead crows, a few twigs and some garbled words!' Susan said.

'One can always rely on cousin Susan to spoil a good story,' Stephen said jokingly to Collins. 'But, pray, Suzie, what has induced you to venture into freezing temperatures clad in a dress and heels?'

'I'm to remind you of the present opening – I know, it's

not at all appropriate, but life goes on! Or so I'm told. The drawing room… a quarter of an hour,' she added, already heading back indoors – her duty done.

Back inside, to the man sitting deep in a corner, she said, 'Still hiding in the shadows?'

'I wasn't sure you'd seen me,' Dunderdale replied.

'Oh, I saw you.' Her back to him as she walked away, Dunderdale remembered Watson's description of the family and deduced her to be the distant cousin.

She closed the door to the drawing room behind her and the hall returned to its quiet state. Shivering, Dunderdale contemplated moving across to the roaring fire before deciding he preferred the recess's cold comforts.

Listening to the licking of flames on crackling logs – and the occasional wheeze of air which he found odd considering it had been calm outside, Dunderdale regarded the portrait hanging above the empty fireplace. Its small brass plate immortalised the wizened man as *Sir Henry de Trouville, 10th Baronet of Crowthwaite Castle*. Below his title was the inscription of the year *1923*. Startled, Dunderdale caught Sir Henry's piercing blue eyes and in that moment Detective Inspector Gilbert Dunderdale of the Manchester City Police read a statute subjecting him to remain at the Manor of Crowthwaite until the murderer be discovered. Sucking on his humbug, Gilbert narrowed his eyes… man against memory.

The dining room door opened, disturbing the 'stare down', and Dunderdale was able to identify the couple by the man at the woman's side. Sir Henry's youngest niece's raven-black hair was cropped and styled in the latest fashion and the dress she wore exposed a great deal of leg as she moved across the hall while talking of her plans for when they returned to London – mainly consisting of a club. Before disappearing into the drawing room, Miss Clara de Trouville glanced at her uncle's portrait; Dunderdale knew he should have experienced a sense of shock when her reddened lips curled upwards, but during his career he'd witnessed all facets of human nature.

The door left ajar, Dunderdale heard her call out to her 'aunt' and he thought of the likes of 'Miss de Trouville' he'd seen around Manchester city – amongst the classier establishments, that is – and he, indeed, imagined her to be quite a character for the residents of Crowthwaite.

'Stephen!' a voice cried, giving Dunderdale a start as a woman resembling Miss de Trouville rose from the settee in front of the fire. Dunderdale had thought himself alone when all along Mrs Bertha Taylor had been blissfully camouflaged – her snug figure sunken into lavish upholstery, further proof of this being wisps of prematurely peppered hair escaping from what was rapidly becoming the dated Edwardian style.

Bertha's groggy state meant she did not notice her sister approach from the rear corridor as she herself was drawn to the drawing room – towards 'safety in numbers'. Of this woman being the eldest sister, Dunderdale had no doubt. She bore the same resemblance as the other two women but, whereas the youngest sister's cropped hair was a rebellion against the conservatism that still had Mrs Taylor's hair tied up, Mrs Ava Rickard's hair was worn uncommonly free. A shade lighter than her two sisters' with a hint of warmth, her hair was sculptured in waves that swept down from her widow's peak to tumble over her shoulders. As she drew closer, Gilbert saw this woman was also uncommonly beautiful. He'd met many women he would have described as attractive, but he'd never before laid eyes on one with such natural beauty.

Miss de Trouville's countenance had been one of triumph, Mrs Taylor's of panic, and Dunderdale attempted to decipher what was behind Mrs Rickard focusing on nothing in particular and yet fixing on everything in between. *Surely, she saw me?* Dunderdale questioned as a tall, dark-haired man rounded the corner with an air of sophistication that made his footfall appear to glide.

Reaching the hall, the 'pew-packer' immediately spotted his follower. Not averting his eyes, Dunderdale pictured the mere mortal delivering any old dogma drivel as though it was the new enlightenment.

At that moment, the vestibule door was thrown open and a child's voice cried 'Uckie David!' Rose's little legs carried her across the hall, leaving behind a trail of snow. The steely look of superiority evaporated from David's eyes as he lifted his niece up into his arms, the soles of her shoes slick with a watery brown ice that soaked into his pristinely worn wool sweater.

'Uncle David,' Betsy said, her coated arms tucked behind her back and her neck angled upwards, 'Daddy said we will bring a man to life.'

'That's right, Besty Betsy, if we get more snow there may be just enough to bring to life a' – Dunderdale witnessed genuine human emotion between father and daughter as Stephen scooped her up – 'SNOWMAN! Right now, though, it's time to see if Father Christmas got through to Crowthwaite last night...'

''OOK!' Rose exclaimed from beneath the drawing room doorframe. Her shoes thrashing at David's ribs, Dunderdale pictured another Christmas tree, this one's undergrowth rooted with presents.

'What is it, sir?' Collins asked, appearing at his superior's shoulder.

'I was just considering, Collins, what children the Rickards would have produced.'

——

After giving the family adequate time, Dunderdale asked Fawcett to inform them they'd all be expected to meet him – along with himself and Mr Atkinson – in the hall at the turn of the hour.

The first to emerge was a young woman dressed elegantly with her blonde hair trussed up with intricate weaves. From the chief constable's romantic description, Dunderdale knew this to be the lady of the manor.

'A rotten trick,' she said to Chester, 'to go to the bother of wrapping a perfume bottle – Chanel Number Five, at that! – all for the perverse pleasure of watching me open an empty box! I really do think, Chester, that Clara despises me.'

'Now wait up, Violet, I don't think—'

'But it simply must have been Clara! After all, she really is the sort of person to move in such circles… *Chanel Numéro Cinq…!*' she despaired – the French words foreign on her tongue – as they parted ways.

Fawcett was next. His arms laden with wrapping paper, he relayed the family first wished to freshen up.

As the hour hand approached, Dunderdale joined the Christmas party by the heat of the fire. While waiting for the lady of the manor, David put a double shot into a glass and Stephen reluctantly handed the children over to Ivy. In the end, Dunderdale had to ask Fawcett to send word for Violet.

'This really is inconvenient,' Violet complained a few minutes later. 'Why a lady should be interrupted by her maid at such an hour! After what I've had to endure, is it too much to ask I take an afternoon nap!'

'Oh, do be quiet,' Clara said.

'I shan't be spoken—'

'*If* we could begin,' Dunderdale interrupted. 'I believe you've all been made aware of my being Detective Inspector Dunderdale and that I was sent for by Chief Constable Watson after the regrettable deaths of Sir Henry de Trouville and Mr James Bowes. With the help of Sergeant Collins, I will shortly begin conducting individual interviews within Sir Henry's study. Before I do so, while I have you all together, there are a couple of items I'd like to go over. With regards to Mr Bowes's death, we don't presently have the full facts. We do, however, know with certainty that Sir Henry's death was murder. I will not downplay the severity of your host's murder; I will tell you the termination of his life was a brutal one – his throat having been cut. And if that wasn't horrific enough…'

'*Must* we know the details!' Violet fussed.

'Yes, must we?' Bertha agreed.

'We must endure it,' Ava told them. '*Do* continue, Detective Inspector.'

'If that wasn't horrific enough,' Dunderdale reiterated, 'a black feather was discovered lying on his tongue.'

'A black feather?' a few voices repeated.

'Oh, Stephen!'

Stephen took Bertha's hand in his.

'Why would he have a black feather on his tongue?' Violet wanted to know, clearly not as shocked as she claimed she would be.

'The story!' Clara said, not disguising her annoyance.

'Then you believe, Miss de Trouville, the feather to be linked with the local tale?' Dunderdale asked. 'What if I were to tell you the murderer wore a feathered cloak and concealed his or her face with a matching mask?'

Violet and Bertha emitted gasps.

'Then we'd reply you have your answer, Inspector,' David answered. 'All three items provide you with your link.'

'There is *another* link…' Chester began.

'Go on, Mr Johnson,' Dunderdale encouraged.

'It was right above you when you arrived, sir. The screwy coat of arms – you know, the crow with its tail feathers in its beak?'

'*Screwy?*'

'Screwy… freaky… *spooky.*'

'A trefoil knot, Detective Inspector,' Ava explained.

'But *is* the feather linked with the pagan story,' Stephen asked, 'or is it all a joke?'

'One told in very bad taste, if so,' Susan replied.

'You ought to pay Pearl a visit, Detective,' Clara advised.

'Pearl?'

'Crowthwaite's storyteller.'

'Pearl Bell, barmaid at The Black Feather,' Tom elaborated, his tone low-spirited. 'She lives at "Crowdundle", down in the village.'

'Stephen,' Bertha appealed, 'is he talking of the cloak and mask which belonged to Sir Henry, third baronet?'

'Third baronet?' Dunderdale enquired.

'The cloak and mask date back to seventeen hundred… *exactly,*' Clara told him. 'Three sets were made by the third baronet and his brothers… replicas of the one in the original pagan story.'

'The cloaks and masks usually kept in the attic?'

'The attic, yes – that's right, isn't it, Aunt?'

'How could I be expected to know!' Violet protested.

'I just thought, what with you sharing a floor with the attic…'

It was not clear if Clara was implying Violet had the

opportunity to access the cloak and mask or whether she was taunting her uncle's wife for her apartment's solitary location. Dunderdale drew the conclusion it could be both. 'And is the attic usually locked?' he asked the lady of the manor.

'Why does everyone assume I would know!'

'Never,' Ava answered.

'Meaning anyone within the castle could have access. As for the weapon used to murder Sir Henry, does anyone know of any missing blade?'

'Again, how should I know!' Violet retorted, although Dunderdale wasn't directing the question solely at her.

'Nothing's been brought to my attention,' Tom said.

'Except Sir Henry's dagger – third baronet, that is,' Fawcett prompted Tom.

'You mean the one with the hawthorn handle? It's missing?'

'The very one, Mr Atkinson.'

'Mighty Ruler, why didn't you say so before now!' Dunderdale interjected.

'Nobody asked, sir,' was the butler's reply.

After throwing Collins a sideways glance, Dunderdale asked where the dagger was housed.

'It's usually kept in the gun cabinet, sir. In the gun room.'

'And when did you notice it missing?'

'Shortly after I rose this morning, sir. I was passing through the gun room and noticed smears on the cabinet window, and as I rubbed the glass clean that's when I noticed the dagger missing.'

'You're not telling me you rubbed away fingerprints? By Artemis, this gets even better!'

'Had I had the foresight to know of Sir Henry lying murdered in his bed, along with the necessary investigative skills to realise the missing dagger was the weapon used then, I can assure you, sir, I would not have destroyed potential evidence.'

'Yes, yes, Mr Fawcett, I realise you weren't to know. What's done is— *Just a minute!* Myself and Collins passed through the gun room a little earlier and I only now realise the room was unlocked – door wide open, in fact?'

'Because of it being used as access to the outside for family, sir, it is never locked. And "Fawcett" will suffice, sir.'

'What about the gun cabinet, Fawcett, surely its contents always remain under lock and key?'

'Never, sir.'

Letting out a deep sigh, Dunderdale asked Fawcett to accompany him to the gun room.

David raised his empty glass to Ava and, recalling her exact words when they'd retired to bed, he said, 'Let's not add more drama!'

Six

ON INSPECTION OF the gun cabinet Dunderdale found nothing other than that which Fawcett had already attested to: two nails hammered into the oak backboard, spaced approximately four inches apart, now devoid of their charge.

'Least we've found the blade that were used,' Collins said as Dunderdale seated himself down behind Sir Henry's desk.

'Number one, we may have a missing dagger, but it is yet to be recovered; number two, until it is we cannot conclusively prove it was the weapon used in Sir Henry's murder. By the way, Collins, what did you notice lacking from our little tête-à-tête?'

'*Tetta-tett*, sir?'

'The meeting in the hall between police and public.'

'I'm still not sure…?'

'A denial that any of the family was responsible, Collins, that's what was lacking.'

'Matthew did say, sir, something 'bout yer enemies bein' of yer own house.'

'Sounds like an astute man! Talking of houses, what have you heard on your travels round the castle?'

'Turner still tellin' the tale of how he discovered his employer – and him forecastin' more snow to come…'

'By Demeter, I hope not!'

'Mrs Taylor beggin' her husband for 'em – apologies, sir – *them* to go back to London…'

'What did he say to that?'

'He said he'd have to speak with you but he doubted whether the train tracks'd be clear. Mr Rickard agreed sayin' as soon as the passes were open he'd be takin' his own wife home. There's also something goin' on between him and Mr Atkinson…'

'Mr Rickard and Mr Atkinson?'

'Yes, sir.'

'And that something is?'

'Can't be sure, sir, but there must be something when Mr Rickard's makin' knavish comments 'bout Tom's golden-boy era bein' over.'

'Hmm… Anything else?'

'Miss de Trouville were just as bad – not with Mr Atkinson, with Lady de Trouville. Likes to keep callin' her "aunt" which seems a bit odd considerin' aunt's younger than niece.'

'Yes, I've heard the taunts.'

'Oh, and there were more 'bout perfume.'

'The one stolen from Lady de Trouville?'

'The very one, sir.'

'Surely she's not still harping on about it?'

'It were Miss de Trouville, sir, not Lady. She were tellin' Mr Johnson that Mr Atkinson had sent her a letter, not long after the wedding, from Sir Henry askin' her to buy it. Apparently, so Mr Atkinson wrote to Miss de Trouville, Lady de Trouville had insisted she simply must have the *revolutionary* perfume she'd heard 'bout in her new *elevated* circle. By, that were some impressive words I remembered! Well, accordin' to Miss de Trouville, Sir Henry wanted it for his wife's Christmas present but she couldn't get it, see?'

'I don't see, Collins.'

'Miss de Trouville told Mr Johnson *naturally* she'd heard o't fashion designer's perfume but she wouldn't have been able to buy it for her uncle even if she'd wanted to, on account o't perfume not bein' released until twenty-four.'

'Until twenty-four? You mean nineteen twenty-four – next year?'

'The very year, sir.'

'But that doesn't make sense!'

'I don't know anything 'bout perfume, so I couldn't tell yer. *Then*, Miss de Trouville says when she next met with her sister – Mrs Taylor, that is, the' both had quite a jolly old laugh at their aunt's not yet realisin' the perfume weren't on't market. Even more of a laugh – Miss de Trouville were now laughin' to Mr Johnson – were the fact Sir Henry and his new wife must still be in't honeymoon period for him to have made the request in't first place; accordin' to his niece, he weren't the sentimental type.'

'That could explain Miss de Trouville's triumphant look,' Dunderdale said, more to himself.

'She certainly sounded triumphant. By the way, sir, when I were in't servants' hall, Lady de Trouville's maid were whittlin' on to one o't housemaids that she hoped she wouldn't get the blame for the disappearance of her lady's perfume.'

'What makes her think she'd get the blame?'

'She were the one who put the present under the tree.'

'On whose order? Sir Henry's?'

'She didn't know. It were sent through't post, addressed to her very self. Made her come over all fancy, she told the maid, only to find when she opened it, it weren't for her after all, but her ladyship.'

'Keep going, Collins.'

'Although the package were addressed to the lady's maid, inside she found a present wrapped and tagged for *Lady de Trouville*, with a note tellin' her to put it under the Christmas tree, as soon as it went up; but, she said, the note also instructed her *under no circumstance* to tell anyone 'bout the present, not Lady de Trouville, not anyone, for it were to be a most *wonderful* surprise. Havin' done exactly as instructed, she were now fearin' she might be thought to be in on't joke against her lady.'

'Collins, this has been a very long day – and a Christmas Day at that! By Dionysus, this may be all the other half has to worry about, but I, for one, don't need to hear of perfumes that don't exist being secretly delivered and then disappearing again as though they never were in the first place!'

'Right you are, sir.'

'Then let's to work.'

———

'I'm at a loss as to why you wish to speak with me, Detective,' Violet said as Sergeant Collins ushered her into the study.

'As Lady of the Manor it's only right I speak with you first.'

'I'm sure that's correct, but I still can't see how I can be of any help.'

'Let's see, shall we? I do appreciate this is an upsetting time for you…'

'Well, yes, it is rather.'

'You see, I thought I imagined you to be a sensitive soul – no, not in that way! I would suggest the intuitive type of lady…?'

'When you put it like that, I suppose I am.'

'And if I were to ask you to apply your skills in this domain, what could you tell me that might have a bearing on the investigation?' Foxed but flattered, Violet began imitating intellectual thought, but as this only went as far as making the right noises and expressions, Dunderdale had to give her a nudge: 'What about Mr Bowes?'

'James? I suppose *he* seemed a decent sort – though he gave me quite a scare, making me think he had cholera! As for any goings on between *him* and another, I, for one, never heard of anything.'

'But you did *between…?*'

'Henry and Clara,' Violet blurted out, the association having been poised on her tongue all along. 'He threatened – no, not threatened, he *promised* her that in no uncertain terms for all to hear she'd get not a farthing more from him.'

'Not a farthing more?'

'Henry was generous – too generous, I'd say, each year providing Clara with an allowance not even she could hope to spend.'

'Only Miss Clara?'

'Well, yes; she isn't married.'

'I see. And when was it he said this to her?'

'The day the family arrived… The end of the evening.'

'And *why* did Sir Henry cut his niece off?'

'Since her arrival she's been simply beastly to me.'

'*Because…?*'

'I suppose she's jealous of – well, I don't think it's right a lady, such as myself, spell out a thing that is obvious to a gentleman.'

'I'm afraid *this* gentleman insists on each letter being spelled out.'

'I couldn't possibly… There's such a thing as modesty, you know!'

The detective inspector, thinking he'd struggle to insert a gnat's whisker between the two ladies in terms of age or attractiveness, made another attempt. 'Could there be another reason why Sir Henry withdrew his youngest niece's allowance?'

Violet stroked the smooth tinted polish on the nails of one hand.

'An *entirely* different reason, perhaps?'

'Possibly,' she hinted.

'*Yes…?*'

'She'd seduced David.'

———

Clara informed Sergeant Collins she was quite capable of finding her way around the place. 'There's not so much as a creaky floorboard or a chipped stone I don't know of!'

'Don't suffocate the young lady, Collins. Miss de Trouville, I'm much obliged.'

'I'm sure you're anything but. Nevertheless, go ahead, let's get this over with.'

'As you wish. Do you know of any reason why anyone would wish Mr Bowes dead?'

'James! I can assure you, Detective, the intended victim was Uncle Henry *not* James.'

'And how do you come by that assurance?'

'It's not the I'm-the-murderer-so-I-ought-to-know assurance. Firstly, I can think of no reason *whatsoever* why anyone would feel the need to raise their voice to James let alone murder him, unless Violet was offended by his ogling and irrational obsession – which I really could not understand, and neither could David, for that matter. Pitiable James, how unfortunate for him to have been caught up in Uncle's troubles. The person responsible for his agonising death should be more than strung up.'

'*Secondly?*'

'Uncle was murdered within a few hours of James, and lastly, it was Uncle who'd built up a reputation over the years for upsetting a number of people.'

'What about *this Christmas?*'

'I know the honeymoon period was already passed – the way he criticised her was proof of this. Only a little over three months married and it looked as if Violet's future as the third Lady de Trouville was already shrunk. You see, Detective, I only met Violet two days ago and within this time I've witnessed her endlessly fawning over and swooning into the arms of David. Fortunately for Chester, she's obviously prejudiced otherwise he would also have had to endure the delicate flower that is Violet.'

'You're saying Sir Henry witnessed these… *flirtations?*'

'Of course he did – which is why he referred to her as a bitch on heat.'

'Did he indeed! Those exact words?'

'There are stronger words but none Uncle's tongue would permit. It's a pity, really, that she didn't look upon her own husband with a fraction of the lust she'd bestowed on David; had she done so she might have kindled something deep within him.'

'You said *a number of people—*'

'I also specified *over the years*, which makes me wonder what the hidden question is?'

'Very well, Miss de Trouville, why did your uncle cut off your allowance?'

Clara laughed off the suggestion as ridiculous. 'Violet, I take it? Well, she's wrong! If she knew anything of Uncle, then she'd know this was only *one* of his threats.'

'And what were the others?'

'That I'd not receive a farthing of my third share of the inheritance. Ava and Bertha sometimes heard the same threat, though not so much Ava. I, though, was doubly blessed in having both an allowance and an inheritance to lose… lots of forfeited farthings!'

'And what could have induced him to make his latest threat?'

'I think he might have taken offence at my seeing his wife for what she is.'

'Which is?'

'A daw.'

'A daw?'

'A jackdaw, sir,' Collins translated.

'That's right – a jackdaw. A larcenist with an ostentatious appetite for shiny objects.'

'Ah! No other reason?'

'*Should* there be?'

'I forget you prefer directness. Was it, then, your uncle punishing you for having unnatural relations with your brother-in-law?'

'Which one?'

'That's not a denial.'

'What it *isn't* is an admittance of guilt. I'll tell you, Detective, what else I've discovered about Violet and that is she's rather the jealous type and we all know how jealousy leads to prejudice. Now, if that's all.' But as Clara reached the door, she turned back. 'You'll find my eldest sister, Ava, to be nowhere near as forthcoming as I, so I feel it my duty to tell you, upon her arrival, Uncle whisked her quickly away to this very study… Cooped up for some time, they were.'

———

Sitting across from Ava, Dunderdale found himself in awe. Knowing full well it wasn't an aura framing her head, he failed to recall if the combination of lamplight and shadow had created the same effect for the previous two ladies. 'I hope this hasn't been too distressing for you, Mrs Rickard,' he said.

'I thank you for your consideration, Detective Inspector, but I hardly think I can complain while the bodies of Uncle and James lie cold in a mortuary.'

'Quite right, and it is because of this that I have to ask what it was you and Sir Henry discussed in here on the day of your arrival?'

There was a noticeable pause before Ava replied, respectfully, 'All I feel obliged to say is the meeting was of a personal nature and not at all related to the despicable deaths.'

'Come now, Mrs Rickard, I know you would wish for us to concentrate our efforts on discovering who it was that murdered your uncle! I hope you can see why I'm going to insist you allow me to be the judge of what's relevant and not relevant to the case?'

'I have to ask you to trust my word.'

Dunderdale regarded Sir Henry's eldest niece. 'What about your uncle's recurring threat to disinherit you and your sisters?'

'By that you mean as joint beneficiaries all three of us are suspects.'

'I'd like to concentrate on *your* third of that joint beneficiary.'

'I am aware, Detective Inspector, it makes me a suspect and all I can say is to reassure you I had nothing to do with his murder or James's death.'

'Then have you any information which might help with the investigation?'

'No.'

'And I can't induce you to divulge the details of your private meeting?'

'No.'

'I see what Miss de Trouville means 'bout her bein' secretive,' Collins said to Dunderdale when they were alone.

'It may be her being secretive or it could be the lady's elite education instilled into her, and so I'll reserve my judgment. Now for the remaining sister, Sergeant.'

———

'Please, Mrs Taylor, take a seat.'

Bertha loitered inside the door. 'I would prefer for Stephen to join me.'

'I've no wish to detain you any more than necessary. Please, Mrs Taylor, *do* sit down.'

'I suppose this *has* been the most tiring day.'

Dunderdale waited until she'd settled into the leather chair. 'I was wondering if you know of any reason why anyone would wish your uncle dead?'

'Someone with my social standing wouldn't know anything of murder!'

'Possibly you overheard something without realising… say while taking the weight off your legs?'

'I don't think it at all appropriate to talk of a lady's legs, Detective.'

'What about something you heard which you might later have thought odd?'

'I'm not really sure how one's expected to realise something later if they didn't realise it at the time.'

'In certain quarters,' Dunderdale persevered, 'it's thought

there exist ladies with intuition… females who are adept at picking up on things greater men miss?'

'They don't sound like the kind of quarters any ladies *I* know of would associate themselves with.'

Dunderdale drew a deep breath. 'If I could ask about your younger sister. I believe there was an argument between her and your uncle?'

'Clara…? She may have upset Uncle over something… or nothing, but it was his wife who really didn't help matters. Indeed, because of Violet, Uncle said something rather unbecoming for a gentleman.'

'Oh?' Dunderdale said, feigning ignorance.

'A few filthy words which I won't repeat. Really, Detective, I'm not the person to be answering questions of this nature! Besides, I'm not at all sure how appropriate this is for Christmas Day. Uncle certainly wouldn't approve.'

'Unfortunately for your uncle, he's no longer of this earth, and as for what's proper, what's improper is murdering the host and his guest on any day let alone a holy one. Therefore, I'd like next to talk of your uncle's recurring threat of you losing your joint inheritance.'

'It was not only *my* share of the estate he threatened!'

'Yes, I'm aware of the same threat against your sisters—'

'I'll accept my inheritance as my right as a de Trouville, but I really don't need it. My husband, Detective, is a very wealthy man. Do you know' – Bertha suddenly recalled, the colour in her cheeks fading in a trice – 'Clara's jazz player talked of poison…'

Dunderdale and Collins shared a look. 'When was this?'

'Something about a poisoned rat…'

'And when *was* this?'

'*And* he seemed to take an interest in our coat of arms…

Oh, my Lord, he even mentioned it again when talking of the feather in Uncle's mouth – *AND* when Uncle went for Clara, he threatened him!'

'Mrs Taylor, take a deep—'

'I said Uncle was far too liberal in permitting Clara to bring back waifs and strays to the manor!'

'Mrs Taylor!'

Bertha made to rise. 'Where's Stephen?'

'MRS TAYLOR! Please. Calm. Yourself. I have only a few more questions,' Dunderdale added, employing self-discipline to soften his own tone, 'then you'll be free to return to your husband. *When* did Mr Johnson talk of a poisoned rat?'

'The-The afternoon we arrived.'

'What was it exactly he said?'

'I-I don't remember the exact words. Really, Detective, I don't believe I can help you any further.'

'Just one more question. You said Mr Johnson threatened your uncle?'

'I've told you, I'm not the person to help you with your enquiries.'

———

'Mr Johnson… a friend of Miss de Trouville's, I believe?'

'I think you know we're more than that.'

'The question is, did Sir Henry *know* it?'

Chester met Dunderdale's stare; and, the first to fold, he answered in the negative. 'We've been careful to protect her reputation… which is *why* we agreed to give false statements to the chief…'

'The statements in which neither of you was able to provide Chief Constable Watson with an alibi because you were both sleeping at the time in separate beds… separate rooms? I suppose you're now going to change your story and tell me you shared the same bed, meaning each of you does have an alibi?'

'We ain't changin' our stories, sir; we're admittin' the truth. There's a difference.'

'And Miss de Trouville's happy to state the same – for the record?'

'Before I came in, she told me I should be honest with you. She said to tell you Susan'll vouch for us, all right, as she got an eyeful of Clara's invite. After the doctor left.'

'Then I'll check with Miss Markham, though you must agree this all appears convenient for Miss de Trouville.'

'You can't seriously think Clara to be a murderer!'

'Everyone's a suspect, Mr Johnson… including you.'

'Now just you wait a minute!'

'Sit down, Mr Johnson.'

'I'll sit back down when I'm ready to, *not* when I'm told! If this were the USA, I'd have expected a set-up – *dingle, dangle,* no questions asked! – but I thought this country different… Magna Carta and all that!'

'Sit down, Mr Johnson! Whatever you've experienced before now, I guarantee you my saying you're a suspect is founded entirely on your presence alone, the same as every other person who was also present in this castle at the time of the murder. If, as you say, you have an alibi then you've nothing to lose and everything to gain by cooperating. Do, please, take your seat… Thank you… Now, you say Miss de Trouville was with you from the time of everyone retiring to bed in the early hours *until…?*'

'Until the whole house was woken with the discovery of Sir Henry's murder. Another thing, I'm a light sleeper; there's no way someone woulda been able to leave my bed without me knowin' it.'

'Why did Sir Henry tell Miss de Trouville she'd receive not a farthing more from him?' Dunderdale quickly threw the question at him.

'Easy! He didn't like Pearl's story and Clara was the one who'd asked her to stay behind after the carol singers.'

'What of Mr Bowes's death? Is there anything you could help us with there?'

'Doubt it. Hardly knew the guy.'

Dunderdale then asked about the poisoned rat.

'Yeah, the vermin ghost,' Chester chuckled before the implication hit him. 'You got it all wrong! The little gal wanted to go hunt for a vermin ghost in the attic and all I said was "what's a vermin ghost" – who wouldn't question that!'

'And your threatening of Sir Henry?'

'*I* threaten Sir Henry? Just who is this tryin' to set me up, huh?'

'A witness says you threatened Sir Henry when he went for Miss de Trouville?'

'Is that so? Then I have a room full of witnesses who – unless they're also tryin' to pin the deaths on the outsider – will tell you all I did was to stand and block Clara's uncle… no more than that!'

———

'So you know,' David said before Collins had even closed the door, 'as soon as the weather permits, I'll be taking Ava back home to London.'

Fully aware the hill passes would be temporarily closed to trains and motor cars due to the greater snowfall in these regions, Dunderdale responded that was Mr Rickard's prerogative. 'While we wait for the weather, let me ask you about Mr Bowes's untimely death and whether you know of any quarrel between him and another? Any reason why anyone might wish him harm?'

'Feel free to call him James. *Mr Bowes* sounds… cold.'

'If you could answer the question.'

'My answer to *both* of your questions is "no".'

'Miss de Trouville mentioned Mr Bowes had a – *what* obsession, Collins… with Lady de Trouville?'

'Er…' Sergeant Collins scrambled for his notebook. '… That's it, sir – an *irrational* obsession!'

'Mr Rickard?' Dunderdale prompted.

'I hardly doubt any female would feel offended by a bit of harmless admiration from the sidelines. Surely, if anyone were to find offence it would be the husband and in that case your theory is flawed for the husband now shares a mortuary with James. *Unless* you imagine Henry committed suicide after becoming suddenly overwhelmed with a sense of guilt for having murdered his friend over a little misunderstanding?'

Dunderdale read the sparkle in Mr Rickard's pale blue eyes – which were accentuated by his dark lashes – as arrogance. 'Hypothesis.'

'What's that supposed to mean?' David asked.

'Hypothesis *not* theory.'

The sparkle brightened. 'I distinctly remember you saying there wasn't yet proof of James's death being murder.'

'Just because there exists uncertainty doesn't mean valuable time should be wasted. I prefer the two-birds-and-one-stone approach. Therefore, I'd like to ask the same questions for Sir Henry?'

'Yes.'

Dunderdale was momentarily stunned. '*Yes?*'

'I did. Quarrel with him, that is.'

'That's very honest of you, Mr Rickard.'

'There's no point in denying what I know others will be breaking their necks to tell you.'

'And does your honesty extend to you telling us what the quarrel was about?'

'No, it does not.'

'I must remind you, Mr Rickard, this is a murder investigation.'

'I don't need reminding of that fact, thank you.'

'You see, I'm wondering whether the quarrel concerned yourself and Miss Clara de Trouville?'

'There we have it: the propensity to break one's neck!'

'Again, I am compelled to remind you I'm investigating the murder of a man who you yourself just admitted to quarrelling with only the day previous!'

'And yet *I* do not feel a compulsion to divulge the details of a private meeting, particularly one that has no bearing on your investigation.'

Dunderdale observed his interviewee remove a case from his pocket, take out a cigarette and tap the tip of it against the silver metal. 'What of the other guests? Is there anything else you could tell us that might help us with our enquiries?'

'So you want me to do your job for you, is that it?' David said, the cigarette held between his teeth; he lit it with a big draw before adding, 'Well, I'm sorry, Detective Inspector, I won't play the snitch. Now... if that's all.' And without waiting for an answer, he left.

'Just as secretive as his wife,' Collins remarked.

'Hmm.'

'I notice, sir, yer didn't ask him 'bout Mr Johnson – 'bout the vermin ghost or Mr Johnson's threat. Do I take it he's no longer a suspect?'

'I'm not one for hooking red herrings, Collins… nor will I indulge those with nervous tendencies. If Mrs Taylor's put into your head Mr Johnson's our murderer, I suggest you keep him there… though be sure to make space for every other resident of this castle.'

'Very well, sir. Who next?'

———

'Mr Taylor, I hope I didn't cause Mrs Taylor any distress?'

'I've come to understand my wife to be a delicate woman, Detective, as many of her breeding are. I've explained she has nothing to fear from Chester and that appears to have settled her.'

'In front of the fire?'

Stephen appeared a little puzzled. 'Y-e-s.'

'Good. Well then, I'd like to ask you about Mr Bowes and whether you know why anyone would seek to harm him?'

'Then you *do* believe James was murdered! While I don't doubt your skills as detective, I'm struggling to understand why anyone would wish him dead – he was the best of fellows. No, I'm more inclined to agree with Clara, that James's death was meant for Henry.'

'Would you say Sir Henry was also the best of fellows?'

'I know it's a cliché to say I don't particularly like to speak ill of the dead, but I must admit Henry was a different character altogether – and by that, I'm not suggesting this strengthens the argument for his murder; disagreements are one thing, murder, though, is something entirely different. I had actually predicted to Bertha there was more to come, but *murder…* I didn't see that coming!'

'More to come?'

'Apologies, Detective, I presumed you'd already been made aware of Henry's altercation.'

'A different perspective is always welcome.'

'I fear you may be disappointed. Although I, along with everyone else, witnessed something between Henry and Clara, I couldn't be fully sure what it was concerning. Initially, I resolved to put it down to the usual uncle–niece relations we've been treated to over the years, but then I began to experience an inkling something *more* was occurring.'

'And if I asked whether you could put your finger on this something *more*?'

'I could not… just a feeling.'

'But the altercation, played out for all to witness, surely you're able to tell me what transpired between the two of them?'

'I dare not delve into the matter, Detective, for it involves David's marriage and one doesn't wish to involve oneself with the goings on between another man and his wife. What I do know is, no matter what has happened, David is madly in love with Ava. Has been since the moment he was introduced to her. Nothing has changed there, of that I'm sure… I wonder, though,' Stephen added thoughtfully, 'if one can love another too much?'

'They can. I've seen the aftermath plenty of times in my line of work.'

'I don't envy you. Susan's got the right idea, keep your head down and to yourself.'

'D'you know, Mr Taylor, I've hardly heard mention of Miss Markham?'

'Hardly surprising, Detective. The words "bone" and "pick" have never been used in conjunction with Susan's name. Real sport she is.'

Dunderdale nodded. 'You may go join your wife, Mr Taylor.'

'One thing before I leave, Detective. I know you'll appreciate I'd like to return with my girls to London as soon as possible.'

'Naturally, any father would. While I haven't the legal means to force you to remain, I do hope you will all do so until I've finished my enquiries. For your peace of mind, Chief Constable Watson has organised a roster for a police presence at the manor.'

———

'Ah, the *sport*!'

'Sorry?' Susan said.

'The person who prefers to keep herself to herself,' Dunderdale told her.

Susan smiled. 'Stephen's been singing my praises.'

'He told me you keep your head down and to your own business and I'm hoping that makes you my favourite kind of personality.'

'Favourite personality…? You mean you're hoping that, during my time of keeping my head down and to my own business, I observe?'

'I'm relying on you not disappointing me.'

'I'll do my best – not to, that is!'

'Then *do* begin,' Dunderdale said, gesturing to the chair.

'Thank you, Inspector. I think I'll *begin* with the lord of the manor. Please be assured the following is not I saying I did not like Henry, because I was one of the few who did, but what you must understand about my cousin, Inspector, is he was not the easiest of people to get along with. Henry was perfectly skilled in upsetting any individual and this Christmas, unfortunately, was no different from any other time. His first target was Chester. Henry didn't actually spell out his prejudice against Chester's skin colour and circumstance of birth, *nevertheless* it was there. I suppose Stephen was not forthcoming in telling you of his contributing to Henry's temper?'

'He did not. In fact, no one's mentioned it.'

'I don't have the details but it was clear Stephen had upset Henry with how quickly he was booted from the study. Then there was Henry's confrontation with David, resulting in him telling David he wouldn't forget. You want to know what the raucous was about – what Henry wouldn't forget? Unfortunately, it's public knowledge, even if certain individuals don't wish to admit it. You see, Inspector, Clara has had a fixation on David from the moment she laid eyes on him; she's never disguised her attraction for him which began as teenage infatuation. Well, it looks like some time during the summer the temptation proved too much and he slipped himself between her sheets.'

'That's what Sir Henry confronted Mr Rickard about?'

'It was behind closed doors, but when Henry followed him out of the study saying he'd disgraced his niece most egregiously, *that* confirmed our suspicions.'

'*Our?*'

'An unspoken suspicion shared by anyone who knew the family. A rumour began to surface in late August of David's solitary visits to Clara's apartment. If this alone wasn't enough to anger her uncle then add on Clara's attack against his new wife – not to mention, as I said, the grave error she made in bringing Chester with her. *Then* to top it all off she goes and organises for the local barmaid to tell of the village pagan story which, unfortunately for Henry, did nothing to recommend his family name... nor his own virility! By the way, I overheard Henry on the return from midnight Mass offering to facilitate Ava's divorce.'

'She was thinking of divorcing her husband?'

'*That*, I couldn't tell you. What *I* heard was Henry *advising* her to do so.'

'Do you know whether Mr Rickard heard the same?'

'He most certainly did. We were walking together, immediately behind Henry and Ava so there was no escaping my cousin's uncompassionate words. Now, who does that leave...? Oh, yes, the lady of the manor. Violet, bless her, wasn't to know what she'd let herself in for when she'd agreed to marry into the de Trouville family; to a man who'd already buried one wife and disposed of another. It was only natural that a young woman married to an old man would find herself gravitating towards the company of men closer to her age...'

'Mr Rickard?'

'I see Clara got there before me!'

Dunderdale returned Susan's smile.

'Yes, *David*. There is another point I should mention... again regarding divorce, though it was more of an implicit comment and I can't be fully sure divorce is what was meant...'

'Go on.'

'Morning of Christmas Eve, Ava and I were down at the stables with Henry when he spoke of buying an Anglo-Arab for Violet – that's a horse, Inspector. Well, at the end of the conversation, he said it mattered not for he'd no longer any intention of buying the horse because he was unsure as to whether his wife was worth the investment.'

'And you think he was implying divorcing his wife?'

'That's exactly what I remember thinking when he spoke the words. In the end, I dismissed it as caprice – after all, it's not as if divorce is a simple matter, especially for a man only just re-married. Well, Inspector, I don't mean to sound callous, but is there anything else I can help you with, only I must ready for dinner. I really don't know where I shall put one more morsel, but Fawcett is a creature of habit and he wouldn't permit a late Christmas lunch to spoil his plans.'

'Two more questions, first. Do you know of anything which would explain Mr Bowes's death?'

'There, I'm afraid, I cannot help you. James was a sensitive sort; rather unusual in a man – the ones I've come into contact with, that is! – so if his death *does* turn out to be suspicious then I cannot understand it one little bit.'

'Then, for my final question, I believe you can attest to Miss de Trouville and Mr Johnson spending the night together in the young lady's room?'

'I suppose I could, but only as far as seeing the two of them *enter* her room. As to whether they spent the remainder of the night there together, I could not say.'

———

The study door opened and Collins announced 'Mr Atkinson'.

Dunderdale, putting down his pencil and breathing warm air onto his clenched fingers, regarded this man who was not of the fashionable slim physique, but had rugged looks that belied his position.

Tom's mouth opened as though he was about to say something; changing his mind he closed it again.

'Yes,' Dunderdale agreed, 'it must feel strange, our setting up camp in here.'

'It's just that I've only ever seen Sir Henry sit there,' Tom explained.

Deducing David's 'golden boy' comments were not solely down to the colour of Tom's hair, Dunderdale said, 'I imagine you feel his death keenly.'

Tom returned the statement with a furrowed brow.

'I *understand*, as his private secretary, you would have spent a considerable amount of time with Sir Henry... more time than any other employee?'

'Naturally. As did my father before me, and as he did with Sir Henry, ninth baronet.'

'I also understand Sir Henry was fond of you?'

'How did you come by that understanding?'

'No? Then do correct me.'

'I can't think what correction you require.'

'How was your relationship with your employer, Mr Atkinson?'

'I never gave Sir Henry any reason to regret his decision in agreeing to me filling my father's shoes after his death. Father had provided me with all the training I'd need, but I was still relatively young for the position.'

'Then I congratulate you on your accomplishment! And in your role of working closely with Sir Henry, I'm wondering if there's anything you can tell me that might help us understand his murder?'

Tom hesitated before saying, 'No.'

'*No?*'

'I don't feel it my place to be getting involved with family matters.'

'But...?'

'I'm not saying this has anything to do with his murder…'

'Go on.'

'Sir Henry was extremely angered by something concerning Mr Rickard.'

'If you don't believe it had anything to do with his murder, then what had it to do with?'

'I never said I don't believe, I said *I'm not saying it has…*'

'Then you *do* believe Mr Rickard has some connection with the murder?'

'What I am saying is prior to the family's arrival, Sir Henry and I were working together *here*, in his study, and I sensed something was wrong so I asked him if there was anything I could do and he said, "It won't do, Tom. I'll have it out with him. You see if I don't!" "Who, sir?" says I. "David," said he.'

'No more than that?'

'No.'

'And there's nothing else? Nothing between Sir Henry and another?'

'No.'

'Well, it sounds as if Sir Henry most certainly did have it out with Mr Rickard. *Now*, I understand you were the last person to see Sir Henry alive?'

'No. That would be the murderer.'

'Ah, of course. I'll correct myself by saying you are the last *known* person to see your employer alive.'

'As I was most evenings. It was traditional for Fawcett and I to wait until Sir Henry retired before heading up to our own beds.'

'And when you said your final goodnight, last night, was there anything troubling Sir Henry?'

'No, I wouldn't say he was troubled, as such. He *did*

look more tired than usual, but I put that down to Mr Bowes's death.'

'Did he mention anything about Mr Bowes?'

'No.'

'And there's nothing you know of surrounding *his* death?'

'Mr Bowes? Other than the statement I've already given, no.'

'The statement being your having witnessed his collapse and helping him to his bed. Is there anything else which you may have witnessed... say, between Mr Bowes and another?'

'Nothing. You'd be just as well speaking with Fawcett...'

'The butler hears everything, is that it?'

'I was going to say, as butler, he spends more time around the family and guests than I do.'

'That's what I said,' Dunderdale replied.

———

'Could I ask, sir, how long this will take? There's the dinner to consider. A lot of preparation requiring my attention.'

'I promise not to keep you any more than necessary,' Dunderdale assured the butler. 'Beginning with Mr Bowes's death, I understand it was yourself and Sir Henry's valet who handed out the drinks?'

'It was, sir.'

'We'll get back to that in a minute. First, I'd like to know where and when the glasses were filled?'

'That would be in the kitchen, sir. Immediately before bringing the champagne toast out.'

'Who filled them?'

'I did, sir.'

'*Immediately* before them being brought into the hall?'

'Correct, sir.'

Dunderdale took a few moments to visualise the scene. 'After filling the glasses of one tray, while filling the glasses of the second tray, would you say there was the possibility of another person slipping something into a glass on the first tray without you knowing?'

'I assure you, sir, none of my staff would countenance such a thing.'

'Forgetting, for one moment, whether anyone was capable of such a thing, would anyone *have had* the opportunity?'

'They would not, sir. What few of the staff were not already retired were engaged with their work.'

'Who opened the bottle of champagne?'

'I did, sir.'

'Immediately before pouring?'

'Yes, sir.'

'And when were the glasses cleaned?'

'The champagne flutes, sir, are always stored cleaned then cleaned again prior to being used, if storage has been some time.'

'And were the glasses cleaned again when you took them from their storage?'

'Naturally, I cleaned them again; they'd not been used since Sir Henry and Lady de Trouville's wedding breakfast.'

'Then if we could now move to the handing out of the champagne. Who handed Mr Bowes his?'

'Mr Turner did, sir. Mr Turner's tray contained six flutes, mine five. I served Sir Henry and Lady de Trouville, Mr Atkinson, Mrs Rickard and Miss Markham in that very order.'

'What about previous Christmases, did you always serve Sir Henry his champagne?'

'I did, sir. It is traditional for the butler to tend to the needs of his master.'

'In your capacity of butler, I imagine you're often placed in positions where you may hear of "things" – *say* between Sir Henry and another – or Mr Bowes and another?'

'I'm not sure what you mean, sir.'

'Did you hear anything – witness anything – which might indicate Sir Henry's and Mr Bowes's deaths?'

'I couldn't possibly say, sir.'

———

'Don't be long, Mr Turner,' Fawcett said to Turner as they exchanged places. 'There's the dining room preparations to finish.'

Couldn't or wouldn't say? Dunderdale wondered once more while inviting Sir Henry's valet-cum-footman to take a seat. 'I understand you were present when Mr Bowes collapsed.'

'I divn't mind tellin' yer, Inspector, Sir Henry might've looked a right sight – spattered with blood and his eyes open wide, like the' were cuttin' through to me own soul – but to see a grown man thrashin' round in his last agony… *that* could haunt a man for rest of his livin' days, eh!'

'Terrible business,' Dunderdale sympathised. 'And I understand it was yourself who handed Mr Bowes his champagne.'

'There were nae funny business, if that's what yer wonderin'. All I did were follow Mr Fawcett's instructions; 'twere him who filled 'em up!'

'But it was you who passed Mr Bowes his champagne?'

'Nae. I never said that.'

'Then what do you say?'

'I never said nowt 'bout handin' Mr Bowes a drink. If yer

must know, were Mr Rickard who gave it him. He took two glasses off me tray – one for him, one for Mr Bowes.'

'Mr Rickard…? And would you have noticed if Mr Bowes's glass was tampered with after Mr Rickard took it from your tray?'

'I never noticed nowt o't kind! I'm sure if I did I wouldn't have allowed Mr Bowes to drink it and I resent anyone suggestin' otherwise!'

'That's not what's being suggested…'

'And I never said Mr Rickard were a poisoner… even if he does know o' poisons, eh.'

'What's this?' Dunderdale demanded.

'That's what were told me. At the time, I were upstairs, tendin' Mr Bowes, but Mrs Clarke, cook, told me 'bout it. She were on her way up to help me with Mr Bowes and she said Mr Rickard gave Mrs Rickard a right rollickin', tellin' her to leave Mr Bowes's glass for it could very well have poison in it.'

'I see.'

'Well, I didn't see, but Mrs Clarke's nae liar. Though I'd never've thought of a man usin' poison – not on people, at any rate. Again, that's not me sayin' it were a man. For all I know, could be a woman… in fact, most probably is, eh, though I couldn't say who'd be more likely among 'em. Miss Clara, though… she's a saucy one! One minute me and Mr Fawcett's havin' to lump the gramophone into't hall, next we're lumpin' it back out again… like a couple o' muttonheads!'

'How does that make Miss de Trouville saucy?'

'We saw her, me and Lizzie, from behind the grand staircase. Us two saw her barin' her flesh, dancin' like a banshee! Well, Sir Henry caught her at it and soon put a stop to it; Mr Fawcett came to fetch me, sayin' Sir Henry wanted rid o't gramophone, wanted it put back in't drawing room.'

'And you think this is related to Mr Bowes's death?'

'What? Nae! I'm sayin' it put Sir Henry into another of his moods.'

'Then you believe it could be related to Sir Henry's murder?'

'Now why would yer think I said that, eh?'

'Never mind. If we could continue with Sir Henry, I also understand it was you that discovered him.'

'Yer knows I did. I told yer 'bout him covered in blood and his eyes—'

'I believe there are two doors to Sir Henry's apartment?'

'That's right.'

'Were they ever locked?'

'Never. Yer *could* lock 'em but he never wanted 'em so.'

Dunderdale nodded. 'Tell me, Mr Turner, how did you find Sir Henry to work for?'

'I never did wrong by him, if that's what yer wonderin'! Ivy, now that's who yer need to speak to.'

'What can Ivy tell us?'

'I'm sure she won't tell yer nowt unless yer tell her yer know of her bein' threatened with the sack back in September. While yer on it, yer'd do well to ask May what her ladyship gets up to on her Tuesday trips to Carlisle, eh.'

———

'Mr Turner said there was an incident in September?'

'September…?' Ivy pondered over the month. 'Nae, can't say I remember any incident – there were doin's over the she-holly, but that were winter solstice.'

'*Yes…?*'

'Sorry, sir?'

'What happened at winter solstice?'

'Oh, aye! Well, I were bringin' in't she-holly and, forgettin', I went 'head o' Mr Turner through the back door to the kitchen. Well, Sir Henry were comin' back with Tom – 'pologies, sir! – Sir Henry and *Mr Atkinson* were just comin' back from walkin' round the estate and he – that's Sir Henry – shouts "HO, YOU THERE!" and I never realised me mistake 'til I stepped back outside and saw Sir Henry's eyes gawkin' at me holly. "Sorry, sir," said I, and I told Mr Turner to come back out and then gar afore me this time. "WHAT'S THE POINT, NOW!" Sir Henry then bellowed something chronic.'

'*That's* what you were threatened with dismissal over?' Dunderdale asked with incredulity.

'Divn't know owt 'bout a sackin'. All I remember is the rollickin' I got cos 'tis castle tradition for a manservant to carry the he-holly indoors first.'

'Mr Turner was *quite clear* about an incident in September involving the threat of dismissal?'

'Holly's never brought in, in September! 'Course, now it means Lady de Trouville'll rule house in't comin' year, eh.'

'How so?'

'That's just how the sayin' gars. Prediction is prediction. Can't alter – OH, LORD! Yer divn't think it's *my* fault Sir Henry's dead?'

Dunderdale drew an exceedingly deep breath before saying, 'I think it highly unlikely you changed the course of future events by carrying a smooth-leaved holly into the house before the prickly-leaf one, if that's what you're thinking.'

'*I... su-ppose... not.*' Ivy mulled over Dunderdale's rationale. 'After all, that'd be the devil's work and I'm a god-fearin' sort.'

'There you are, then. And you're *positive* there was no incident in September?'

'September... September...? Oh, aye, forgot 'bout the daws!' Ivy burst out, her cheery disposition returned.

'Daws? You mean *jackdaws*?'

'Aye, *daws*. Well, I forgot 'bout 'em and lit a fire in library chimney. 'Course whole room filled with smoke and suchlike. I'm supposed to check the chimney's been cleared o' daws' twigs first, but I didn't – on account o't new mistress. Downright lucky not to be dismissed on spot, so Sir Henry said.'

'Why would Lady de Trouville stop you checking?'

Ivy appeared confused.

'You said you forgot to check the chimney was clear of twigs on account of the new mistress?'

'On account o't manor bein' in excitement, eh. Can I gar now, Inspector? Mrs Taylor wants me back *as quick as* to take the girls back up to the nursery.'

'This isn't me sayin' that the girl's not got a good heart,' Collins said when Ivy had quickly shuffled out of the study, 'but I'd have to think twice before lettin' her look after my own!'

Taking a – what he hoped would be his final – deep breath, Dunderdale told Collins to bring in Lady de Trouville's maid.

———

'It's May, I believe?'

'I prefer Mrs Carver, Inspector.'

'I'll make a promise to you *here and now*, Mrs Carver, anything you tell me in this room is confidential and its origin will not reach your lady's ears.'

118

May looked unsure.

'I'd like to begin with Lady de Trouville's fidelity in her marriage to Sir Henry.'

'My lady was never unfaithful, if that's what you mean!'

'Would you know?'

'A lady's maid always knows!'

'What about a bit of harmless flirting?'

'Well, maybe there was a bit of that going on. Perhaps my lady did tell me, while I used to dress her hair, that she imagined Mr Tom as a Viking – not those brutish gingers with wiry beards, but with him being strong in muscle and him having white-blonde hair, for that's what she would talk of. *Then* how my lady swooned the other day when she told me of seeing Mr David for the first time. Like one of those movie stars, she said. "What's she got that I haven't!" she then said, while looking herself over in the mirror.'

'By "she" she meant…?'

'Mrs Ava. Well, of course, I never dared say back I knew of no lady ever existed as beautiful as Mrs David Rickard!'

'Back to *your* lady, I hear she's fond of weekly excursions… *Tuesdays* to be precise.'

'Who said that? I bet it was *that* spite George Turner! Well, there's nothing wrong with my lady visiting her old school friend, now is there!'

'Old school friend…? Would that happen to be a *Peter*?'

'Who?'

'You said an old school friend and I happen to know she has a childhood friend who goes by the name of Peter.'

'I can't say I happen to know anything about a *Peter*. All I know is it's a friend from school so must be a *she*.'

'But you've never met this old school friend?'

'*Well…* no. When we reach town, my lady's always kind

enough to give me the afternoon off – *and* money for the tearoom. Anyway, it stands to reason it must be another lady. As lady of the manor, my lady would hardly be seen to be visiting a gentleman, now would she!'

'So when Sir Henry referred to his wife as a "bitch on heat" he wasn't referring to her weekly visits to Carlisle?'

'I'm sure I don't know anything about him saying any such words about my lady. From what I heard as they came up their stairs, as I was readying my lady's apartment, he was in bad spirits but I never heard any such name calling.'

'Bad spirits?'

'I heard the sound of his voice that told me he was in bad spirits again and so I made myself scarce by slipping out the other door – as is right for a lady's maid.'

'There was nothing you heard, say *unintentionally?*'

'Naturally, I never wanted to hear any such words between a baronet and his lady, but as I was expected to attend my lady I had no choice but to wait on the other side of the door until Sir Henry had gone up to his own apartment. I assure you, Inspector, I never wanted to hear any words of my lady having only three years!'

'Lady de Trouville only had three years – three years of what?'

'Of marriage. He threatened my lady she'd go the same way as her predecessor if she didn't conceive and deliver of him a healthy son… within three years.'

'He spoke those exact words?'

'Those very. "You, being a woman," he told my lady, "are dispensable the moment your womb withers, whereas I am capable of siring an heir right up until my last breath!" Such words a lady's maid shouldn't have to suffer – I especially didn't want to hear anything more.'

'*More?*'

'It gives me no pleasure to repeat what I next heard *but* I suppose I must speak the truth to you, Inspector.'

'Go on?'

'While Sir Henry ranted on some more, my lady moved across the room so as she was standing right on the other side of the door from me – of course, I hadn't realised until then that I'd left a gap and I couldn't hardly go and close it now, could I!'

'*Y-e-s...?*'

'So, naturally, I heard clearly my lady say, with her back to Sir Henry, "But you, my dearest husband, will be dead long before then!"'

SEVEN

JOHN ATKINS OF Atkins, Bagnall and Jones removed a document from the safe and laid it down on the desk. From where he was sitting, Dunderdale could only read the title:

Last Will and Testament of Sir Henry de Trouville

'I received *this* from Sir Henry,' the solicitor said, while removing an unaddressed envelope from his briefcase, 'care of his secretary, during the evening of twenty-third of December...'

'*Evening?*'

'Yes. Ten o'clock.'

'At such a late hour?'

'Sir Henry was a privileged client.'

'Hmm. Before you tell me about its contents, could you say whether you would know if any item was missing from the safe?'

'I could and there isn't.'

'Then do tell me about the envelope.'

'Prior to Tom Atkinson delivering me this,' Atkins explained, extracting a single sheet of paper from the envelope, 'he and Sir Henry's butler, Robert Fawcett, were called to the study to act as witnesses. You see, Sir Henry wished to add a codicil to his will.'

'I think I *do* see. So, what's in *this* codicil?'

'It was Sir Henry's wish in the event of *not* producing a

legitimate heir *and* it being conclusively *disproved* James Bowes to be his biological son—'

'What's this! James Bowes was the bastard child of Sir Henry?'

'Jane Bowes was adamant Sir Henry was James's biological father. Of course, as Jane was married to Sir Henry's friend at the time of conception, there was still the possibility James was the legitimate offspring of Mr and Mrs Bowes.'

'And so, Sir Henry would not risk a bastard inheriting, is that it?'

'On the contrary, Sir Henry, in his desire to pass the family estate down to a direct heir-of-blood, was quite prepared to take the risk *if* all other options had been exhausted. Sir Henry, therefore, turned to science.'

'He looked to science for disproof in the hope he wouldn't find any then he could go to his grave content with the knowledge of a greater probability than he ever had during his life – is that it?'

'Very good, Inspector, you're *almost* there,' Atkins congratulated him. 'To begin with, Sir Henry and I looked to the genetics of eye colour. Had James's eyes been brown then this would have conclusively disproved James to be Sir Henry's biological son. No such disproof was found: Sir Henry, Jane and James all had blue eyes.'

'The Davenports?'

The solicitor smiled. 'We then looked to the genetics of blood. Through the latest science, by taking a sample of Sir Henry's blood and comparing it with that of James and Jane, one could establish with certainty Sir Henry *not to be* James's biological father *if* James's blood group turned out *not to be* one of the possibilities that would arise from the blood groups of both Sir Henry and Jane – I fear I'm telling you nothing you don't already know!'

'When looking at the inheritance of blood types there are rules. A male of a certain blood type and a female of a certain blood type will parent a child of one or more possible blood types. Meaning, the difficulty would have been in proving James Bowes *was* Sir Henry's biological son. Hence the clause being worded so as to rule out Mr Bowes's claim to any inheritance *if* it was *disproved* he was Sir Henry's son as opposed to it having to be proved that he was. Blood-type testing could never conclusively prove the latter for there are other adult males with the same blood type as Sir Henry.'

'Excellent, Inspector… though I wonder at Sergeant Collins's muddled expression.'

'I think I can just about follow the gist,' Collins replied unconvincingly.

'*That* would have been as far as we could have gone and, as I said, Sir Henry was willing to take the risk. Where you fell short, Detective Inspector, was no such science was to be called upon during Sir Henry's lifetime for he would not countenance making it public knowledge he'd had "relations" with a married woman – even if he was risking the possibility of Jane departing this world before he.' Atkins flicked the document he still held in his hand. 'Back to business! *As* I was saying, in the event of Sir Henry *not* producing a legitimate heir *and* it being conclusively *disproved*, through blood tests, James Bowes *is* Sir Henry's biological son – thus removing any possibility of issue – then Sir Henry wished for the estate to be passed in its entirety to the eldest daughter of his late brother.'

'Mrs Rickard?'

'Mrs Ava Rickard… yes,' Atkins confirmed, handing the document across the desk.

Dunderdale read through the codicil and, nodding his head, returned it to Atkins, saying, 'Before we proceed with Mrs Rickard's good fortune, I've a question. In the event of Sir Henry not siring a legitimate heir *and* it turning out James Bowes not to be his bastard after all, prior to the codicil being written then who would have inherited the estate?'

'Sir Henry would have died intestate.'

'Then the family would have gone to court. Sister against sister. Aunt against niece.'

'Human nature being what it is, I imagine so. Although Sir Henry was careful to stipulate only an heir-of-blood could inherit, I'm prepared for the eventuality that even with the codicil, as his surviving wife, Lady de Trouville may very well pursue a legal challenge. If she does, then I, as Sir Henry's executor, will do my best to ensure the estate is disposed of in accordance with my client's wishes. Miss Violet Olsen brought nothing to the marriage and the marriage only endured three months before Sir Henry's demise, therefore, if she does bring a challenge then I'll be arguing for her to be awarded the personal chattels gifted her by Sir Henry and nothing more.'

'And the codicil is legal, is it? Watertight?'

'Sir Henry correctly documented all that's required, and I would swear to the signature being his. The codicil was also correctly witnessed. Robert Fawcett and Tom Atkinson sub-scribed their names as witnesses and, by signing the codicil, each agreed – as Tom confirmed to me in person – they had observed the signing of the same codicil by the testator, Sir Henry. Therefore, in answer to your question: the codicil shan't fail in a court of law. It was an impromptu request, but *hardly* a surprise.'

'Go on…?'

'Knowing Sir Henry personally, I'd seen for myself his

fondness for Ava, even if he didn't always show it. I did, if I'm honest, think it a bit mean she was never included within his will. *Equally*, I thought it strange Tom being chosen as one of his witnesses.'

'Now you *do* have my full attention.'

'The year before Ava met David she had wanted to marry Tom – each declaring their love for the other. Although Sir Henry was impressed with Tom, this admiration solely concerned Tom's aptitude as a member of staff, *not* as a match for his eldest niece.'

'That explains Mr Rickard's knavish comments!' Collins reminded Dunderdale.

'Sir Henry withheld his permission for them to marry?' Dunderdale asked Atkins, confident of the answer.

'Not quite. Although Sir Henry refused to give his blessing, he left the decision firmly in the hands of Ava; along with the threat that if she did choose to marry Tom then she would not receive her third of the inheritance.'

'But you said Sir Henry would have died intestate had it not been for the codicil?'

'And I stand by those words. The truth that none of the nieces were included in the will did not deter Sir Henry from using the promise of a shared inheritance as influence over each of them.'

'Liked to dangle the inheritance in front of them, did he?'

'More like whip them with it.'

'I've known the type. And Mrs Rickard didn't like the idea of losing out on a fortune, so poor Mr Atkinson was thrust aside, is that it?'

'Quite the opposite. Ava still wanted to marry Tom. It was Tom's decision in the end and he decided he would not allow her to make such an error. By this time Tom was in no doubt of Sir Henry's feelings about his station; he had thought Sir Henry's attentions towards him meant he would not be averse to such a match. Alack, it was not to be. As I said, *considering these circumstances*, I was surprised Tom was chosen to be one of Sir Henry's witnesses.'

'After all, what would stop him running straight to Mrs Rickard to inform her of the possibility of an enormous fortune! You do realise this revelation incriminates them both... Mr Tom Atkinson and Mrs Ava Rickard?'

'That's what's worrying me. A little over twenty-four hours after the writing of this codicil' – the solicitor jabbed his finger at the document housed once again in its envelope – 'James Bowes mysteriously dies, leaving Ava Rickard as the sole beneficiary. And then before the sun is given time to rise, Sir Henry is discovered brutally murdered in his bed.'

'Hmm. And what of Mr Atkinson's employment now Sir Henry has passed?'

'That will be for the new beneficiary to decide.'

'Mrs Rickard.'

'Yes. As well as private secretary to Sir Henry, Tom assisted with the estate management and so I will advise he be retained in his position. A man who not only possesses the intellect for the job but who's a local lad with knowledge of each and every tenant and worker is someone not easily replaceable.'

'All providing he's not implicated in murder, that is.'

'Truly remarkable, sir,' Sergeant Collins commented.

'What is?' Dunderdale asked.

'Investigation only just begun and we've already got our prime suspects. Not much longer now and I wonder if we won't wheedle out a confession – or two!'

'Mighty Zeus, Collins, it is because of the fact the investigation is barely underway that we cannot – and will not – make any such assumptions! I'll agree Mrs Rickard and Mr Atkinson are suspects, but so is every other person who has been present during this Christmas holiday. Let me ask you, Sergeant, whether another thought has occurred to you?' Collins's brow beginning to crease, Dunderdale offered his assistance: 'Let us entertain the idea it is the *inheritance* that is the motivation for the deaths of both James Bowes and Sir Henry and that both Thomas Atkinson and Ava Rickard are not implicated in any way, what d'you think might be the next move for our murderer?'

'Mrs Rickard must next be removed!' the sergeant exclaimed.

'Mrs Rickard's life would indeed be in danger! *If* Mrs Rickard is our murderer then we'll get to the bottom of it. Until that time, I'll not risk the lady's life.'

'Potential murderer *and* potential victim, eh!'

'Thank you, Collins. Mr Atkins, I suggest you carry out the will reading as planned. Before you begin though, I'd like to know whether you believe Sir Henry will have spelt out, in actual words, the contents of his will in the presence of Mr Atkinson and Fawcett?'

'No, Detective Inspector, I'm confident he will not have done so. Furthermore, as you read for yourself, the codicil has been carefully worded to say: "In the event of the clauses in my last will and testament not being met…"'

'But Sir Henry *did* spell out to both witnesses Mrs Rickard would become the sole beneficiary if the clauses were not met?'

'When Tom handed me the codicil, I read it through privately before asking him to confirm all of its contents as what had been made known to himself and Fawcett, and he was able to recall Sir Henry's wishes verbatim.'

'Then both he and Fawcett were in possession of the

facts of Mrs Rickard being named as the sole beneficiary but neither knew of the contents of the will. Who, then, *did* know the contents of his will?'

'Myself in the capacity of both solicitor and executor, and Sir Henry of course, and the two witnesses, my associates, Arthur Bagnall and Andrew Jones. I did advise Tom to ask Sir Henry to reconsider and do the same for the codicil but Tom replied that Sir Henry told him I would say that and he was to reply his employer was insistent on it being added to his will, *there and then.*'

'Therefore, other than yourself, Sir Henry, Mr Jones and Mr…'

'Bagnall.'

'… and Mr Bagnall, no one else knew of the contents of Sir Henry's will?'

'Correct.'

'*Then*, it couldn't have been Mr Atkinson and Mrs Rickard,' Sergeant Collins volunteered, 'because the murderer would've had to know 'bout Mr Bowes, and you, Mr Atkins, just said Sir Henry didn't tell Mr Atkinson or Fawcett what were in't will.'

'When you look at it from that angle, what you say is true. But then – working with your reflex angle, Sergeant – the only suspects are myself, Mr Jones and Mr Bagnall.'

'So, we're back to square one.'

'Everyone's a suspect,' Dunderdale agreed. 'And what about the combination for the safe, Mr Atkins – was this known only by Sir Henry and yourself?'

'Correct.'

'Then if Sir Henry's inheritance *is* the motive, how in Athena's name did the murderer discover James Bowes to be the sole beneficiary?'

'*That* I'll leave for you to discover.'

'Mighty Ruler, I can feel this case is going to leave me questioning my sanity! One more question before we move into the hall.'

'Concerning?'

'Miss Clara de Trouville…'

———

Sir Henry's sitting for his portrait had coincided with his meeting the young Violet Olsen and so one would have expected him to endow his 'perpetuity' with a benevolent guise. Ava though – blocking out the chatter – recognised her uncle to have concealed nothing of his soul and it was because of this that she was viewing his image with pity.

Does she already know that which Atkins will shortly announce? Dunderdale asked himself while they waited for the solicitor.

'If it wasn't so early,' Stephen said to David, 'I'd raise a glass to the old man.'

'And I'd have joined you… My thanks for damn good scotch!'

The clock chimed the eleventh hour and John Atkins made his appearance. As he seated himself in the smoker's chair, the room fell quiet.

'According to Sir Henry's wishes,' the solicitor began, 'and in his exact words dictated to me as witnessed by Arthur Bagnall and Andrew Jones on the first of September nineteen thirteen, his last will and testament is as follows: "I, Henry John de Trouville, Sir Henry de Trouville, Tenth Baronet of Crowthwaite Castle and Lord of Crowthwaite Manor, hereby revoke all former testamentary dispositions made by me and declare this to be my last will and testament. I appoint John Atkins of Atkins, Bagnall and Jones as the sole executor of this will."' Atkins cleared his throat and, adding an edge to his voice, said, '"I, Sir Henry de Trouville, direct my executor to distribute my estate, *in its entirety*, to only an heir-of-blood. Upon my death, my executor will therefore distribute my estate, *in its entirety*, to my eldest legitimate male issue. Failing male issue, my estate, *in its entirety*, is to be distributed to my eldest legitimate female issue. Failing legitimate issue, my estate, *in its entirety*, is to be distributed to James Bowes *unless*—"'

The glint in Violet's eye metamorphosed from expectation to perplexity. '*What?*'

'Stephen?' Bertha said. Stephen, though, appeared as shocked as his wife and could offer her no explanation.

Chester looked to Clara who, stubbing out her cigarette, appealed to David, but David was busily employed in trying to work out what it meant. Ava's eyes were still downcast, as were Tom's; and Fawcett, standing by Tom's side, was Fawcett: his mouth set rigidly in the butlers' code of discretion. Susan simply observed and Dunderdale had the impression she was enjoying herself a little.

'"*Unless*,"' Atkins continued, '"it is conclusively *disproved*, through blood tests, James Bowes is my biological son. If—"'

David burst out laughing. 'The hypocrite!'

Ava flinched.

'Did you know of this?' Clara accused Susan.

'Sorry, dear, I knew not one jot of it! Though, it does explain the dappled grey!'

Bertha looked to her husband. '*James... Uncle's son?*'

'From what Atkins is saying, I don't think it's been proved, but yes, old girl, it looks that way.'

'I'm confused,' Violet said, still looking very much so, 'does it mean it has to be proved James was Henry's son or not?'

'It could never be proved but it could be *disproved*,' Atkins explained.

'Still doesn't make sense…?' Bertha seconded Violet.

'Spin it,' David told the two women. '*Unless it's proved James was not the old man's son.*'

'Then why didn't he just say that!' Violet replied.

'Because the emphasis was to be on the disproving!' David was emphatic. 'You've just heard Atkins say it could only ever *conclusively* be disproved!'

'"*IF*"' – the solicitor's voice cut through – '"*If* I have omitted to leave property in this will to one or more members of my family, the failure to do so is intentional."'

'THE DECREPIT BASTARD!' Clara drowned out Bertha's 'How could he!' and Violet's 'But I'm his wife!'

'James is dead,' Chester assured Clara, 'so it's gotta be as he always promised.'

'*HOWEVER*,' Atkins called out and the conjunction was instantly welcomed as everyone waited for the clause, 'on the evening of the twenty-third of December, Sir Henry added a codicil to his last will and testament, stating in the event of the clauses of his last will and testament not being met, thus removing any possibility of issue, *then* he wished for the estate to be passed, *in its entirety*, to his heir-of-blood' – Atkins gave a dramatic pause, a moment to browse his audience; the majority of which had failed to hear his three stressed words and so were waiting with baited breath – 'the eldest daughter of his late brother… Mrs Ava Rickard.'

Dunderdale witnessed Ava turn her head, ever so slightly, in the direction of the staircase where Fawcett and Tom were standing; in Tom's cheeks, two little dimples.

'What does it all mean?' Bertha wanted to know.

'It means James was murdered for an inheritance the poor man never set his sights on!' David answered her ungraciously.

'The inheritance is *one* possible motive,' Dunderdale conceded.

'Of course the inheritance was the motivation!'

'I think, David,' Stephen said, 'the detective is saying it's still early days and nothing can, as of yet, be ruled out.'

'Then he'd better get a move on, for in the meantime – what of my *wife*!'

'I see,' Ava whispered.

Tom's dimples disappeared.

'The detective's promised a round-the-clock police presence within the castle – that's correct, isn't it, Detective?' Stephen said.

'It is, Mr Taylor… for everyone's safety.'

'Ought I be the one who should be worried?' Violet wondered.

'My dear, you've just heard the will reading,' Susan told her. '*I'm* Henry's widow!'

'But was it essential for James to die for you to gain your widowhood?' Clara deplored, baring more teeth than usual.

'James was nothing to me.'

'James was *something* to us,' Stephen informed Violet.

'You're all being beastly… twisting what I mean!'

'But what of my inheritance… What does it all mean?' Bertha repeated.

'It means, old girl, you have no inheritance.'

'We're to receive nothing?'

'I don't think Atkins would joke about—'

'AVA!' Bertha bellowed, forgetting her education. 'Ava, it's only right I receive my share – Uncle promised!'

'Not now,' Susan despaired.

'There, old girl, don't take on. We still have our own wealth.'

'Stephen, I was Bertha de Trouville – it's my birthright!'

'Yes, don't take on, Boots, we shouldn't be surprised,' Clara added, and looking across to her other sister, she demanded, 'Is this why you were locked up with Uncle... disinheriting your sister because you couldn't satisfy your husband?'

David was as quick as the echoes of 'CLARA!' that bounced off the stone walls and, pulling Clara to her feet, he proceeded to shake her. 'GOD HELP ME, CLARA, NO MORE... NO MORE!'

'David, darling...!' Clara appealed to her lover, while Dunderdale – he and Collins already restraining Chester – commanded Mr Rickard to let go of the lady.

His chest rising and falling, David looked down upon Clara and, with a heavy breath, he gave her a final caution with a 'No more'.

In the silence that followed, Violet looked across to Atkins, who was in the process of packing up. 'Surely, there's been some mistake?'

'There's no mistake, my lady.'

'Then I really get *nothing*?'

'Nothing.'

The lady of the manor rose to her feet and, as she turned to leave, completed an ovation-worthy swoon.

It was Tom, standing to her rear, who caught her.

———

'You can leave the motorcycle here for a moment while you take a walk with us,' Dunderdale instructed Shaw as the constable met with his two superiors on their walk down to the village, to "Crowdundle". As Chief Constable Watson had commandeered Smith to chauffeur the detective inspector and sergeant between Appleby and Crowthwaite, Collins had lent Shaw the use of his police motorcycle, saying it had to be quicker for Shaw's travelling back and forth, and surely safer than his push iron.

'Go ahead, then, Constable,' Dunderdale said as Shaw kicked the motorcycle's stand into place, 'what have you got for me?'

'Few things, sir. Feather on Sir Henry's tongue's been identified as the tail feather of a jackdaw.'

'As we thought. The next thing?'

'Clothes Mr Bowes were wearin' when he'd taken bad, inside his trouser pocket were a matchin' feather.'

'By Demeter, another one!'

''Fraid so, sir.'

'You know what this means?'

'Sir?' both sergeant and constable queried.

'It means he was murdered.'

'That were goin' to be me next piece o' news, sir,' Shaw replied quickly with the air of one in the know. 'Autopsy confirmed he were poisoned.'

'With?'

'Arsenic... arsenic *something-or-other*, sir.'

'I would hope, Shaw, to discover your forgotten word in your notepad, *and* I would imagine that word to be "trioxide".'

It was clear by the look on the constable's face his notepad contained no such scribbling, but he did confirm it sounded like the very word the chief constable told him of.

'Odourless and tasteless... makes sense,' Dunderdale said, ignoring the urge to lecture. 'I imagine it was a substantial dose?'

'Enough to make it lethal in a very short amount o' time, sir, so the chief constable said.'

Over on the lawn, Stephen was in the midst of another snowball battle; no further snow had fallen, but Turner was still insistent more, *much* more, was most certain to come.

Betsy and Rose moved in on the attack, pelting their foe, who, before dropping to his knees in defeat, waved across to the policemen.

Doffing his hat, Dunderdale said, 'Do either of you happen to know how long Mr Bowes wore the trousers for on Christmas Eve?'

Collins looked to Shaw and Shaw to Collins.

'Never mind! Were the clothes his formal dinner attire?'

'The' weren't, sir,' Collins answered.

'Then we know he changed clothes sometime after dinner but before leaving for midnight Mass.'

'Meanin' there were time for the murderer to slip the feather in his pocket,' Collins advanced.

'Correct, Collins… By Hermes' – thinking better of the humbug he'd just pulled from its packet, Dunderdale stuffed it back inside – 'did it have to be arsenic trioxide!'

'Easy for the murderer to get hold o',' Collins told him. 'Sir, could I ask, just what are these names yer keep spielin' off?'

'Hermes?'

'That's one o' them.'

'They're Greek gods and goddesses, Collins.'

'Ah… right,' Collins replied, none the wiser.

Unsatisfied, but not yet skilled in the art of the open-ended question, Shaw asked, 'You a bit partial to *these* Greek gods and goddesses, sir?'

'Let's just say I find them more tolerable. Now, if we can return to the poison…'

'I bet,' Collins began, 'Mrs Clarke'll have some arsenic… in her larder, for killin' rats.'

'Similarly, as would surgeons for preserving dead bodies, but I hope – whatever the reason for its purchase – the poison's not being stored in anyone's larder! *Yes*, Collins, while I've no doubt Mrs Clarke will have a stockpile, any individual could walk into any pharmacy in any town and buy the vicious substance. *No*, Collins, we'll be chasing our own tails if we go up that road! Any other "things", Shaw?'

'One last one, sir. Champagne glass has no trace o' poison.'

'That's *not* what I wanted to hear.'

'Nor, sir, does it have any trace o' champagne.'

'Someone had washed it?'

'That's right, sir. Spotless it were.'

'So now there's no way of knowing whether Mr Bowes's champagne was or was not laced with the arsenic trioxide!'

'I think it stands to reason it were, sir, otherwise why bother washin' it!' Collins told him.

'Hmm. Go on then, Shaw, get yourself to the castle and ask Mrs Clarke if she's something to warm your insides. Then, you'd better relieve Donnelly.'

'Oh!' Shaw halted. 'Did Donnelly tell yer what he saw last night?'

'No…?'

'Personal thing, it were, sir. Donnelly were doin' his rounds o't first floor and, headin' back to the staff staircase for the next floor, he saw Mrs Rickard sat on edge of her bed with Mr Rickard – as drunk as an ass on fermented apples, Donnelly said! Knelt on floor he were, apparently, sayin' all sorts o' soppy things such as from time he'd laid eyes on her how he'd prayed to a deaf God – Donnelly's blasphemous words, sir, not mine! – that he'd prayed to God for her to love him. And Mrs

Rickard sayin' back to him, didn't he think she'd tried! Well, Donnelly said, Mr Rickard next said he were sorry for what he'd done to her but didn't she realise what she'd made him become… that "she'd created a monster". That were when Mrs Rickard, seein' Donnelly through the gap, went and closed the door… apparently she weren't best pleased he'd heard that.'

———

Pearl swung the black iron arm out over the stone hearth and, clutching the kettle's handle with a rag, dismissed an offer of assistance. 'Yer a guest, Mr Dunderdale. Besides, I've been liftin' this kettle since afore ma and gran passed. Now then, what can I do yer for?'

'You'll have heard about the incidents up at the manor?'

'The murders, yer mean? We all have.'

'Yes, there's always a lot bandied round a public house and though much is absorbed along with the alcohol, I imagine, Miss Bell, a barmaid always keeps a sober ear?'

'I've known plenty o' butterin' up in me time to recognise it when I hear it,' Pearl teased, 'so, if what yer hopin' to hear is a whisper of a murderer then I'll give yer two names – though the're obvious ones on account o' bein' offcomers.'

'Offcomers?'

'New to these parts.'

'Ah, now I understand! And *yes*, I am expecting you to give me the names of Lady de Trouville and Mr Chester Johnson?'

'That's 'em, and I'm wonderin' if yer already knew this then what's the real reason for yer visit?'

'I've heard of a local story that may have a bearing on the investigation and Miss Clara de Trouville said you're the one who does the telling.'

The door to the rear yard opened and the young man who came in was too slow to conceal a brace of pheasants behind his back.

'Don't worry about us,' Dunderdale reassured him. 'We're only interested in murder of the human kind.'

'Me brother, Mr Dunderdale. William, not in here! To the outhouse with yer.'

'Just one moment, William,' Dunderdale said, forestalling a quick exit. 'I suppose you would know who's responsible for keeping the carrion birds on the estate in check?'

'That'd be 'Arry James…' William replied hesitantly, '… gamekeeper…'

'And what does Harry James do with his kills – hang them as a warning to other birds?'

'Aye, he does that!' William replied, reducing in height as he relaxed. 'Grandad once said there used to be daws all round the estate, hangin' everywhere, but Sir Henry divn't like to see his family's symbol all limp and dead – mind, he divn't particularly like to see 'em all alive and worryin' chicks either! Anyway, 'Arry James hangs 'em from branches in't forest, where Sir Henry divn't venture much. Though I divn't suppose he'll be doin' any venturin' now and mebby new lord won't mind where daws is seen hangin'. That all, sir?'

'It is. Thank you, William, you've been of help.'

Tipping his flat cap with pride, the door closed and Pearl pushed two cups of tea across the table. 'So, Mr Dunderdale, yer wantin' to hear 'bout a murder o' crows, eh…?'

'Naturally, it's all nonsense,' Dunderdale said as they walked back up the village green that had no greenery in sight.

''Tis that, sir, so we'll waste no more time.'

'On the contrary, Collins, we will give the tale our full attention.'

'Sir?'

'Because our murderer has provided us with a link between *it* and the two deaths – Sir Henry's in particular.'

'Sir.'

'Good. Now, let's see if we can track down that gamekeeper.'

Harry James was in the estate office with Tom and as he was going out to check on the birds anyway he said he'd show them where he hung the daws.

Much to Charles Collins's disappointment, his superior had chided him on there not being the time to stop and eat – many thanks had been bestowed by the two policemen upon Mrs Clarke for the Boxing Day lunch leftovers – and so, knocking the crumbs from the double breast of his greatcoat onto the narrow forest track, he experienced a sinister *Hansel and Gretel* moment. *No bloody wonder*, he remarked to himself as he craned his neck back to take in the dense coniferous canopy high above their heads.

''Tisn't right,' he said; his breath, he thought, issuing from his mouth like steam from the iron horse's funnel, 'an animal needs light!'

'Yer'll not get light in here,' Harry James replied from up front. 'Yer can see not even snow got through much.'

'How do yer not get lost?' Collins said, projecting his voice.

'Been workin' this forest for decades and for 'em that know it like I do, there's always ways o' findin' a path out – *Whisht!*' Harry James ordered, coming to an abrupt stop – they were in *his* territory. 'Hear that?'

'Pheasant?' Gilbert Dunderdale guessed.

'It's their alarm call. Must've picked up on vibrations from sergeant's big police boots! I'll get down to 'em soon enough... scatter some seed, I will, and that'll soothe 'em.

Now, if yer were to keep followin' main path yer'd come 'cross me birds, but as yer want to see daws, this is where we leave.'

Collins followed Dunderdale, and Dunderdale, Harry James – a snake weaving in and out of pale trunks – and soon enough, the wise head of the snake halted its body's progress.

'Here's a fresh 'un,' Harry James said – his walking stick the snake's tongue, pointing out the black object hanging silently from a branch. 'Bert must've been out this morning.'

'Bert?' Dunderdale enquired.

'Young laddo from village.' Then, leading them into the darker depths where all the lower trunks were bare except for dead branches protruding like the remains of spears embedded long ago and where the only other sounds were echoes – mainly the cawing of jackdaws – Harry James told them they'd see more from thereon in. 'I like to hang 'em in a circle, a perimeter, if yer like. Reminds daws what's in store for 'em if the' come anywhere near.'

'Does it work?' the snake's tail asked.

Harry James shrugged his shoulders. 'Whilst the' keep breedin', I'll have Bert keep shootin' 'em. Terrific shot, he is, so I use him to do most o't killin'. Divn't make that noise, Sergeant, I've me job to do, same as you have. If yer really that squeamish, now's time to take a gander elsewhere, 'cos here's more o't little blighters – see?'

Collins did see, and it recalled to him the image Pearl had already inserted into his mind. Dunderdale, on the other hand, was thinking they looked like a trophy display. Regarding one in particular, its body crudely staked onto a splintered branch, he said, 'I don't suppose Butcher Shrike was to blame for this one?'

'Ah, well, Bert gets carried away now and then. Nae harm done when daw's already dead, now is there! Now then...

what's happened here?' Harry James wondered while picking up an expired jackdaw from the forest floor. 'Not only has it been pulled down, but every single tail feather's been plucked!'

'*Tail feathers?*' Dunderdale repeated.

Harry James gave an affirmative grunt.

'Bert?'

'Nae. Bert wouldn't play a trick as to pull it down. He always keeps 'em hangin'… least 'til the' start decayin' bad.'

'What about feather plucking, is Bert partial to a bit of that?'

'Never as I've witnessed. Ah, well,' Harry James resolved and proceeded to hang the jackdaw back up by the twine tied crudely to its feet.

Bending down to where the bird had been lying on a bed cushion of needles, Dunderdale collected a pile of tail feathers and proceeded to count them from one glove to the other. 'Tell me, Mr James, does—'

''Arry James.'

'Tell me, Harry James,' Dunderdale corrected, 'does each bird species have a specific number of feathers?'

'Course. There's patterns all round, if yer care to take a gander.'

'Then how many tail feathers does a daw have?'

'Twelve.'

'How many have yer, sir?' Collins asked.

Dunderdale displayed them between two gloved palms. 'Ten.'

———

'What does this tell us, Collins?' Having departed company with Harry James at the forest path, the inspector and sergeant were free to discuss the investigation.

'Murderer always planned on killin' two people.'

'In which case he or she knew of the contents of Sir Henry's will. Equally…?'

'Equally?'

'Equally, Collins, it could be that Sir Henry was always the only intended victim resulting in our murderer, after making a grievous error, having a busy night.'

'Trudgin' through *that* place in't dark' – through the low light, Collins looked back across the grounds towards the forest – 'to get another feather before comin' back, climbin' up to the top o't tower and murderin' Sir Henry!'

'Yes, I agree, it seems far-fetched. Plausible, nevertheless – providing our murderer knows the forest as well as Harry James,' Dunderdale added, opening the door to the gun room and finding Tom waiting for them.

'Detective Inspector, could I have a word?'

Dunderdale and Collins followed Tom next door, into the estate office. After closing the door, Tom said, 'I'm wondering what your interest is in culled daws?'

'Why d'you ask?'

'It's only that after you left with Harry James I was reminded of something… from Christmas Eve.'

'Go on.'

'Late in the afternoon, I was standing here, by the window, and I saw Miss Clara lead Mr Johnson into the forest; and since you've been gone I got to wondering your interest in dead daws when I remembered Pearl's story of the sacrifice of a murder of crows and their feathers, and then there's the feather that was found with Sir Henry with no feathers missing from the cloak or mask and so – well, I put two and two together, though now I'm wondering whether my arithmetic might be out!'

143

Gilbert Dunderdale put his hand into his coat pocket and when he pulled it back out it was clutching a bunch of jackdaw tail feathers. 'One bird, twelve tail feathers plucked, ten remaining.'

'Only ten?' Tom said with surprise.

'A tail feather has also been found in the pocket of Mr Bowes's trousers.'

'Then...?'

'*Then*, Mr Atkinson, I'd say there's nothing wrong with your sums!'

EIGHT

FAWCETT TOLD DUNDERDALE that Mr Turner could be found in his room on the second floor. 'At the top of the *staff* staircase, turn right. His door is the second on the left.'

It took a couple of knocks before George Turner answered the door.

'Ah, Mr Turner, sorry to bother you on your break,' Dunderdale said and, taking the valet unaware, forced his entry into the room with Collins in tow. 'We shan't take up much of your time.'

George quickly ran around to his bed and, picking up a magazine – Dunderdale had seen more of these round Manchester than he had the likes of Miss de Trouville – stuffed it into his bedside drawer. 'I haven't long, Inspector.'

'As I said, this won't take long. I remember you saying it was yourself and the cook who tended Mr Bowes when he took ill.'

'That's right.'

'Just the two of you in his room the whole time, was it?'

'I helped Mr Rickard, Mr Taylor and Mr Atkinson carry Mr Bowes upstairs, then they went back down and Mr Atkinson said he'd send for Mrs Clarke to help me look after him. It weren't long, at all, 'til she came up. If that's all—'

'We're not done yet, Mr Turner. Who undressed Mr Bowes?'

'Me and Mrs Clarke, 'tween us. Mrs Clarke said he should be in bed in his undergarments not lyin' atop of it still dressed for church.'

'What if I told you a feather's been found in Mr Bowes's trouser pocket?'

'I divn't know nowt 'bout any feather!'

'Do you believe in coincidences, Mr Turner?'

'I'm not sure…?'

'A feather discovered on Sir Henry's tongue and you were the one who found him dead—'

'That were nowt to do with me!'

'A feather found in Mr Bowes's trouser pocket and you being the only one left alone with him.'

'Not for long, I weren't, and yer've already been told that! Any one of 'em downstairs could've put it there! But I see that won't do… better it be a lowly servant' – George gestured his bleak surroundings – 'than one o' their own!'

'That's not what I'm saying, Mr Turner, but you must admit you had opportunity.'

'I won't admit nowt o't sort!'

'Then did you happen to notice anyone else meddling round Mr Bowes's trouser pockets?'

'I only God damn wish I had!'

———

'I'd much prefer to say I've heard a rumour,' Dunderdale began, sensing the humiliation sticking keenly to the lady opposite, 'but I won't pretend I didn't hear Miss Clara's words, so instead I'll say I am in possession of *a certain knowledge* between your husband and your youngest sister.'

'Then, Detective Inspector, you now know of the reason why Uncle wished to see me upon our arrival,' Ava replied.

'And also the reason for Sir Henry wishing to speak in private with your husband?'

Ava nodded.

'Prior to this morning, had you any knowledge of your uncle's will?'

'No. If I had I would have told Uncle to dispose of the estate as he thought right.'

'What about the codicil?'

'*Codicil?*' Ava pondered over the word.

'Drawn up at the eleventh hour,' Dunderdale added.

'Yes… I think I see what you mean. It does look suspicious – I now being the sole beneficiary. Coming from me, I suppose the refutation will be meaningless.'

'You're saying neither the will, nor the codicil, was discussed between yourselves?'

'That's exactly what I'm saying,' she said, her tone now assertive.

'Even though the meeting has been reported as considerable in length of time?'

'I'm not sure what you wish me to say.'

'What if I tell you it has been confirmed Mr Bowes was poisoned, is there anything you have to say about that?'

'There's no mistake?'

'None whatsoever.'

'Then I'd say I'm heartily sorry to hear of this.' Ava regarded the detective inspector before adding: 'I fear this doesn't help my situation.'

'If you're not in any way implicated in either murder, *then*, Mrs Rickard, there's nothing to fear. I would, however, like to ask you about this morning when Mr Atkins read the contents of the codicil and your instinct to look to Mr Atkinson?'

'Again, I'm unsure what you expect me to say.'

'I expect you to speak facts and truths.'

'Then, the truth is I don't remember doing so,' Ava replied, the worn leather giving a comforting creak as she shifted in her seat.

'I understand you were considering a divorce?' When Ava's beautifully sculptured lips remained clamped – the silence punctuated by another creak, Dunderdale advised her to answer the question.

'Uncle offered his assistance, *should* I wish to divorce David.'

'Which provides your husband with a motive.'

'David… Uncle's murderer…? No, Detective Inspector, I can't believe that… David's no murderer.'

'No?' Dunderdale said. 'Well, Mrs Rickard, rest assured that until the investigation is closed, there'll be a continued police presence at the manor.'

'Then, like David, you believe my life to be in danger?'

Wondering if her refusal to link the possibility of the vast fortune with the two deaths to be genuine, Dunderdale told her it was a precaution and Mrs Ava Rickard exited the room as she had entered, like a woman burdened and not one whose shoulders should be free of weight.

'She pretendin', sir?' Collins asked.

'I'm not sure,' Dunderdale replied truthfully. 'Did you hear her reaction to her husband having a motive?'

'That's natural, sir. No wife'd like to think her husband a murderer.'

'That's just it, Collins, her first reaction was not to refute her husband's guilt but to question his innocence.'

'*So* Mr Rickard's our prime suspect, sir?'

'What I'm saying is Mrs Rickard's reaction told me she doesn't know her own husband. An affair will do that to the injured party, Collins. It shatters their previous understanding of that person.'

———

'I don't see there's anything I could possibly say today that wasn't said yesterday,' Violet complained to Collins.

'It's purely routine, my lady,' Dunderdale tried to explain.

'It's cruelty, is what it is, for someone still suffering with a fit of the vapours!' Violet said while appearing as fresh as a daisy.

'The sooner we begin, the sooner you can return to your bed. Yes…? Then if we could start with the night of the story-telling and Sir Henry referring to you in a derogatory term concerning the female dog – and, yes, I'm well aware the same was said of Miss de Trouville.'

'I already told you, it was Clara who'd upset Henry. Though, I must say, he's upset me a great deal: to go and make enemies and get himself killed is bad enough but to leave me with nothing – *nothing*! Well, I shan't be pushed aside like Frances!'

'Is that what he was doing?'

'What?'

'Trying to push you aside?'

'I'm sure I don't know what you mean.'

'How did it make you feel when your husband threatened you with divorce should you fail to deliver him a son?'

'How did you hear about that?' Violet snapped.

'If you could answer the question.'

'How do you think I felt? And why was it to be my fault, that's what I'd like to know!'

'I can only imagine you experienced strong feelings?'

'I've just said so, haven't I!'

'Strong enough to commit murder?'

'What is it you're trying to say?'

'Did you feel desperate enough to kill your husband?'

'Why would I be desperate? I'd still three years – plenty of time!'

'Then why the need for threatening your husband's life?'

'What makes you say that?'

'Did you or did you not, Lady de Trouville, say your husband would soon be dead?'

'I don't remember saying any such thing! *Anyway*, it couldn't have been me if I'm not the one to inherit, now could it!'

'I'll only arrive at the truth, my lady, by disproving all possible motives.'

'Does that include the spectre?'

'Sorry?'

'Could the bloody virgin have had something to do with Henry's death? He *did* die like her... what with him getting his throat slit and then there's the black feather!'

Dunderdale breathed out. 'I'd say we can rule out anything not of this earthly world. But while we're on the subject of beings no longer of this world, I would have thought, as lady of the manor, you'd have enquired whether there's an update on the death of your guest.'

'Is there?'

'There is. Mr Bowes was poisoned.'

'Oh, that's a relief!'

'I beg your pardon?'

'I had feared it to be cholera.'

'You find poisoning to be preferable?'

'Of course I do! Cholera would have spread through the manor like wildfire; a foolish man drinking something he shouldn't have will hardly affect anyone else.'

'My lady, Mr James Bowes was murdered!'

'You never said anything about him being murdered!'

'Then let me state, for the record: your guest, Mr James Bowes, was murdered with arsenic trioxide poisoning.'

'You should be clearer, Detective, I ought to know of all murders taking place in my own home!'

'Then there's nothing you can help me with regarding Mr Bowes's death?'

'Why would there be?'

'And you also deny threatening the life of your husband?'

'You've no proof of any such thing.'

'But Sir Henry *did* threaten you with divorce?'

'I told you, Clara had put him in a beastly mood! She's frightfully horrid, Detective. You saw her this morning, her anger – I really did fear for my life! And then the way she and Bertha went at Ava over the inheritance! I wouldn't at all be surprised if they're in on it together. Really, though, it shan't do them any favours – squabbling over the money! – for it'll all come my way. I'll make sure of it.'

'To return to the threat your husband made against you, are you sure it had nothing to do with your Tuesday trips into Carlisle? You see, I'm wondering,' Dunderdale continued, capitalising on the drop of Violet's lower jaw, 'since your marriage, whether you've remained in contact with your old school friend... Mr Peter Barnes?'

'There's nothing wrong with two friends meeting up!'

'Not at all, my lady. And what of Sir Henry? Did he agree with this sentiment?'

'He never forbade my visits, if that's what you mean.'

'Ah, but did he know *whom* you were visiting?'

Violet's silence provided Dunderdale with his answer and he told her she could return to her apartment.

'What did the chief have to say 'bout his nephew's meetings?' Collins asked Dunderdale.

'He said until there was evidence it was his nephew Lady de Trouville had been meeting with he'd do nothing. If it could be proved the two childhood friends were still in contact with one another then, naturally, he'd establish his nephew's whereabouts for this Christmas; though he imagined, as with every other year, it was with his parents back home in Carlisle, where he still resides. He *did* admit his nephew was as poor in character as he was in money, but stressed he wasn't the murdering type – as though there is the *one* type! More of a bit of a scoundrel, he said.'

'Well, sir, he now has his evidence.'

'Yes, Collins… he does.'

———

Clara swanned into the study, grabbing a small bowl as she passed by the bookcase. Sitting down on the warmed leather, she crossed one leg over the other. 'Aunt's just provided us with a nauseating melodrama of James's poisoning… I hope you'll remember I was right, Detective Dunderdale.'

'And what is it *exactly* you were right about?'

'I said James's death was linked with Uncle's.'

'*You said* your uncle was the intended target due to his having upset a number of people over the years.'

'Regardless of how their murders are linked, they're linked, are they not?'

'Additional evidence has turned up, substantiating this – but we'll return to that. First, I'm interested in your reaction when you discovered you were to receive none of the inheritance, as I am equally interested in how you spoke to your uncle's widow – it does appear you've quite the temper!'

'Have I not a right to human emotion, like any other? I

told you yesterday, Uncle had promised all three of us were to inherit. *Regardless*, I've every confidence Ava will do the right thing…'

'I'm sure she will,' Dunderdale said, knowing full well they had different ideas of what that 'right thing' was.

'As for Violet, is there a different way to react when one learns of the reason for a dearly loved friend's heartless murder? The woman's clearly deluded herself she's to inherit, which suggests she does have the kind of temperament necessary for a cold-blooded murder – wouldn't you agree?'

'Hmm…'

'What is "hmm" supposed to mean?'

'It's supposed to mean "hmm". Now, Miss de Trouville, if I could ask you about the afternoon of Christmas Eve…'

After a long draw of her cigarette, Clara exhaled through red-puckered lips and, her head still tilted, said, 'Oh?'

'When you were witnessed leading Mr Johnson into the forest behind the castle?'

'Oh dear, did we shock whomever it was!'

'I'd like to know if your excursion had anything to do with feathers – daw tail feathers?'

'I don't know what the gossip has been, nor do I know what you and Mrs Dunderdale get up to – providing there is a Mrs Gilbert Dunderdale? Whatever's been said, I can assure you no feathers were involved in our activities. If you must know, Detective, our excursion was linked with the story…'

'Yes, I've heard the local tale of "A Murder of Crows".'

'Then you did pay Pearl a visit! Well, Chester, having also heard it, was intrigued – no, not intrigued, I think the word I'm looking for, if my memory serves me correctly, is "aroused". Oh, dear me, I fear I've shocked your sergeant!'

'Did you and Mr Johnson venture out to the culled jackdaws?' Dunderdale demanded.

'Why, what a peculiar question – now you've aroused *my* curiosity! The answer, I'm afraid to disappoint, is no, we did not. So, go ahead, tell me the significance of the daws.'

'It's the additional evidence I spoke of. A daw tail feather was found in Mr Bowes's trouser pocket.'

'*Now* I understand – just like the one discovered on Uncle! *My* turn!' Removing her cigarette from its holder, she stubbed it out into the crystal bowl and, sitting forward, said, 'Do you really believe I'm the only member of this family who knows the location of where Harry James displays his kills? Do you know how tedious it was, Detective, growing up in a place like this? Three young girls had to find ways of entertaining themselves and, sadly, much of the entertainment consisted of shadowing the staff. Therefore, I recommend you ask my sisters about dead daws… I imagine they'd show more interest. Anything else?'

'Yes. I find it convenient you neglected to tell me you were also referred to as a—'

'*Like two bitches on heat,*' Clara spoke the words for him. 'No, Detective, it was perfectly obvious the slight was directed at Violet. The only convenience was my being Violet's cover. I assure you I took no offence. *Besides* you've heard Chester's testimony, you know I have an alibi for the time of Uncle's death.'

'Ah yes, the alibi which, initially, you were not so forthcoming with. By the way, Miss Markham *did* witness Mr Johnson accompanying you into your room. What she could not swear to was whether you remained together for the remainder of the night.'

Clara's eyes narrowed, then, smiling, she said, 'It's fortunate, wouldn't you agree, that Violet's been spared the misfortune of having to insert her Christian name before her title… spared the humiliation of divorce, that is.'

'You seem certain of their divorce?'

'Of course he'd have divorced her! You don't believe that rubbish about Violet being the one to sire his heir, do you? Dear Detective, you should not believe that any more than you should believe James to have been his son. We all knew Uncle was at fault.'

'A regular Henry the Eighth?'

'Is that so hard to conceive?' she said, pleased with her choice of word.

'While I do have thoughts of my own, I'm more concerned with those of others… particularly those who are economical with the truth. I especially enjoyed your answer to my asking whether you'd been carrying on with your sister's husband: "What it isn't is an admittance of guilt."'

'Then you did understand my meaning! I must admit, Detective, I left the interview quite underwhelmed.'

'I think we've established your uncle was not best pleased with the carryings on between you and Mr Rickard and that was why he cut off your allowance. I believe, Miss de Trouville, this time he really did mean it.'

'You see, Detective, that's where we differ. I still say he did not, and *I* am the expert in these matters. After all, I heard the threat repeated during each of my visits so I should know if I was hearing the same empty threat. Furthermore, I still haven't confirmed the rumour.'

'I apologise, Miss de Trouville, I forgot to mention I no longer seek confirmation of the affair. I'm reliably informed on the morning of Christmas Eve your uncle sent Mr Atkinson on an errand to his solicitor in Appleby, to instruct him to remove your yearly allowance with immediate effect. So, you see, what I choose to believe is immaterial; it is what your uncle believed that has significance and the fact that this time he *did* cut off your allowance is enough confirmation for me. What, no rejoinder, Miss de Trouville? Then let me suggest to you that come the first of January you literally will have not a far-thing to your name, and I believe this fact provides you with a strong motive for murder – a very strong motive indeed!'

'Has she or has she not been carryin' on with her brother-in-law?' Collins wanted to know as the study door slammed shut. 'I thought her outburst at will readin' this morning were her admittin' it!'

'And that she was.'

'But the riddle?'

'Implicitly, Collins, she was admitting to the affair. The explicit admittance she talked of referred to her not experiencing any guilt over the matter.'

'The—!'

'Quite, Collins. I think we'll see Mr Johnson next.'

Chester Johnson had nothing to add or subtract from Clara's statement on their forest outing; the only thing Dunderdale learned being when Chester was not on the defensive his cheekbone structure was the perfect ingredient for a most wonderful smile.

————

'Look at that!' Stephen exclaimed.

Dunderdale turned to the study window to see the snow George Turner had been threatening had begun to fall – thickly.

'Betsy and Rose will be overjoyed!'

'I'm glad someone will be,' Dunderdale replied sullenly.

'I've been doing my best to keep them preoccupied,

shielded from all of this,' Stephen explained. 'Terribly bad business for all of us, *but* I'm hopeful you'll soon discover the culprit. Right, Detective, I take it we're looking at two murders, one murderer. Naturally, this is what I deduce after learning of James being the old man's son *and* he having been set to inherit everything – not to mention the talk out there' – he gestured towards the door – 'of it being confirmed he *was* poisoned?'

'Your deduction appears to be correct, Mr Taylor. A feather matching the one discovered lying on Sir Henry's tongue has been found in the trouser pocket of Mr Bowes.'

'Then it's conclusive.'

'Yes, I would say so.'

'Poor dearest James...! I've been thinking – wondering if he died knowing the truth of his existence, whether it was a secret shared between father and son?'

'It's thought to have been a secret shared only between Sir Henry and Mrs Bowes – and Atkins, Bagnall and Jones, of course.'

'Then it's a shame, is what it is. For a man who wished for so long to have sired a son not to have acknowledged his own all because of two rituals and their corresponding slips of paper which declared the child to be a bastard.'

'*If* Mr Bowes was his son.'

'*If*,' Stephen acknowledged. 'I realise I'm in danger of going on about "shame", but I feel strongly that society's shame, which the old man feared and would have had to endure, would have been nothing to the years of pleasure he would have derived from his recognition; as a knowing father, *I* would have taken my chances. *I* would have damned all the proofs and possibilities and consequences and cold shoulders!'

'Then you're made of sterner stuff than most men! I

157

understand it was yourself and Mr Rickard, along with Mr Atkinson and Mr Turner, who carried Mr Bowes up to his room?'

'That's right. Pitiful sight, he was.'

'You see, Mr Taylor, I've been wondering *when* it was that the murderer secreted the feather inside Mr Bowes's pocket?'

'I can't help you there, Detective, for not only am I *not* your murderer, with all that was going on I couldn't say I noticed any other person tampering with James's clothes. Is it *definite* the feather was placed in his pocket at that time?'

'That's what I'm trying to ascertain.'

'Then I'm sorry I can't be of any help.'

'There is something you could help with and it concerns your private meeting with Sir Henry on the evening of your arrival.'

'Nothing unusual there, Detective,' Stephen replied. 'As men of business, we would often have an informal chat in his study. From one chief to another, we'd discuss the City and current investment opportunities. As it happens, I asked Uncle if he was interested in joining me in an investment but the old man turned me down.'

'Were there many investments that required Sir Henry's financing?'

'*I* wouldn't say I needed Uncle's money for investments.'

'Then what would you say?'

'I'd say if there was a lucrative investment then I'd give him a heads up.'

'And will you still be investing?'

'I've the rest of Christmas to mull it over, though I don't suppose such things are worthy of consideration at a time like this. Sort of puts things into perspective. *Family*, that's what's important.'

'I heard Sir Henry was not best pleased with your asking him?' Dunderdale posited.

'It was a joint investment offer, Detective, not a loan request,' Stephen clarified. 'When I come to think of it I suppose he was more antagonistic than usual, but I suppose that had to do with him learning of the affair.'

'Ah! The rumour concerning Mr Rickard and Miss de Trouville, though I do remember your reluctance to comment upon others' marital affairs.'

'Had it been down to me, you'd still be none the wiser. I expect it was only a matter of time before it all came out. I apologise for whining on, but it's been a shocking time: two murders as well as learning one's own brother-in-law – who one regards with the highest esteem! – has been... *well*, carrying on with one's sister-in-law!'

'I'd be interested in your thoughts on your brother-in-law?'

'I know David comes across as the arrogant sort, and I suppose he is, but he's harmless enough. The trouble is, Detective, as the youngest son, he was indulged. Couple his spoiling with his magnificent looks and, well, I don't think I'd be too far off the mark if I say he's often permitted the freedom only usually afforded a demigod – though, in Clara's eyes, I suppose that's exactly what he is.'

'Your description of Mr Rickard's upbringing goes some way to explaining Miss Clara.'

'On the contrary, Detective, Henry wouldn't have known how to spoil any person, least of all his youngest niece, who arrived at Crowthwaite Manor at the age of three. No, Clara, I'm afraid, cannot lay the blame of her character on a lavished and indulgent love. Even knowing my sister-in-law *all too well* it was still a surprise to discover there was substance in the rumour after all. Of course, we all knew Clara was besotted with David, the story being she has been since she was eighteen. When Ava brought David to Crowthwaite Manor for approval, she never realised she'd receive it from two quarters. Poor, sweet Ava. When one looks upon her, Detective, one really can't blame the old man for threatening to cut off Clara's allowance.'

'No, I suppose one can't. *Well*, thank you, Mr Taylor, that will be all.'

'Did you ask him?' Bertha – standing outside the study – demanded of Stephen as soon as the door opened.

'Ask me what, Mrs Taylor?' Dunderdale called out.

Bertha turned around to scan the hall behind her before hurrying into the study. Collins closed the door again.

'Please, Mrs Taylor, do take a seat. Collins, another chair for Mr Taylor. Now, Mrs Taylor, what is it you'd like to know?'

'Now you have proof James was poisoned, I'd like to know why you haven't arrested him?'

'Arrested whom?'

'Why Mr Johnson, of course!'

'Ah, his having spoken of poison! I understand he was simply responding to your daughter's talk of hunting a vermin ghost.'

Unconvinced, Bertha turned to her husband. 'Stephen, his bedroom adjoins ours – I simply can't tolerate knowing a murderer is on the other side of the wall while I sleep!'

'I'm sure, old girl, the detective's right and we have nothing to fear from Chester – besides, I'm confident he's been sharing Clara's room all along.'

Bertha's eyes widened with disgust. 'This is Violet's fault – it would never have happened in Catherine's day!' Then, grasping Stephen's hand, she appealed, 'Have you told him?'

'Told me what?'

'That we insist on returning to London!'

'We won't get through, old girl. Look out there,' Stephen added, waving a hand towards the windows where the snow perching on the stone sill was beginning to mount the glass pane.

'Oh, Stephen!'

'We'll be fine,' he said, gently massaging her hand. 'You've seen the police round the old place. No one would be stupid enough to try anything now!'

'Rest assured, Mrs Taylor, between them, Constables Shaw and Donnelly have the castle under police protection,' Dunderdale said soothingly. 'Now, if there's nothing else?'

In answer, Bertha rose, telling Stephen as she did so that she'd asked her.

'I wish you hadn't,' Stephen replied.

'Asked whom what?' Dunderdale enquired.

'Ava – about my inheritance, but she won't be moved to partake in civil discussion! Clara may have her faults,' Bertha said to Stephen as he guided her towards the door, 'but I fear she's right... Ava's bitterness is preventing her from instructing Atkins to give me my share!'

Collins opened the door for the couple and Mrs Taylor's mouth clamped shut.

———

'Thank you for coming to see me again, Miss Markham.'

'Did I have a choice?' Susan said with that devilish twinkle in her eye which Dunderdale admired.

'One *always* has a choice. With regards to this morning's revelations...'

'You mean Atkins announcing James as Henry's son? *First,*

Inspector, I understand you have some news concerning James's death? News I'd much rather not hear, but go ahead, confirm the rumour filling the hall.'

'I commend you for your consideration, Miss Markham. The rumour you've heard of Mr Bowes having been poisoned *is* correct.'

'Has the poison been identified?'

'It has. Arsenic – arsenic trioxide to be precise.'

'Ah, isn't it always! How unfortunate for James, for his untimely death to be inextricably tied up with Henry's! *Apologies*, Inspector… ask away.'

'Regarding the revelation of the possibility of James Bowes being the illegitimate son of Sir Henry, I recall you saying you knew nothing of this?'

'That's correct.'

'No suspicion?'

'Not the slightest – for which I'm greatly disappointed in myself! Though I had joked to myself some time back that Henry had gone Roman – you know, adopting a full-grown spare from his closest friend. How close to the truth I now realise I was!'

'Extremely close! My observations told me everyone else present was surprised by the revelation – would you disagree with this?'

'No. I would agree.'

'I was hoping you'd seen something I'd missed – alas, another disappointment!' Dunderdale bantered before asking: 'When we spoke yesterday you told me a great deal *yet* you left out the detail of Mrs Rickard and Mr Atkinson.'

'Because, Inspector, it's history… consigned to the past.'

'You really believe that?'

'No. I believe there are regrets on both sides and I believe

162

their love endures. What I *don't* know and what I *struggle* to countenance is anything more between them.'

'You mean you don't know of any interaction since the lady's marriage to Mr Rickard?'

'Exactly.'

'Do you think Mr Atkinson knew of Sir Henry's offer of facilitation?'

'I'm not sure whether or not it's something Henry would have discussed with his secretary, but I wouldn't be surprised if Tom overheard him when we were returning from midnight Mass; he was immediately in front of Henry and Ava.'

'Ah! And would you discount an alliance between Mrs Rickard and Mr Atkinson?'

Susan reflected on the insinuation. 'I wouldn't *think* it possible.'

'But looks and deceit and all that?'

'I hope we're right,' Susan said with sobriety and, reaching across for the crystal bowl-cum-ashtray, knocked off her cigarette ash just in time. 'They'd make a beautiful couple though, wouldn't you say?'

'More beautiful than the Rickards?'

Susan smiled.

———

'I hope you'll permit me to comment that to have been a spot of good fortune!' Dunderdale said to David.

'I won't if you imagine it to be a fortune we expected – or needed, for that matter. Though, I did always say Henry would never allow the estate to be divided.'

'Unexpected? Even knowing of Sir Henry's fondness for his eldest niece?'

'Fondness! I wouldn't have said so! *Yes*, unexpected, and unsolicited. I'd have sooner Ava not inherited at all.'

'Hmm. Could you tell me, Mr Rickard, whether you'd heard of any rumours, up in London, concerning your brother-in-law?'

'Stephen? Which kind of rumours?'

'If there are different rumours then all of them, but, for starters, I'm particularly interested in those concerning his financial affairs.'

'*That* rumour. Yes, there is one, but I'm afraid as far as my own knowledge goes, that's all it is… a rumour. A few unfaithful friends whispering beneath Turf's cigar smoke; a story circulating of Taylor's Shipping.'

'Can you be more specific?'

'No, I can't. All that's reached my ears is the company's currently experiencing financial difficulty. Nothing I've not heard before so I'm not sure one can set much store by it – he certainly doesn't live like a man with money troubles. Either way, it'll not trouble my night's sleep.'

'You're not overly fond of your brother-in-law, are you, Mr Rickard?'

'There it is – that word again! *Fondness* has nothing to do with it. A man's business is his and his alone, though I understand that won't stop *you* digging. And yes, I'm aware that's the essence of your job, Detective Inspector; mine, however, is to protect my own interests, and that includes my wife and so I demand to know how much longer this investigation of yours is going to take?'

'You're still planning on returning to London?'

'Why not, it's our home, after all!'

'Ah, now I understand!'

'Understand what?'

'Your preferring your wife to not have inherited. It's perfectly fine, Mr Rickard, no response required. Now then, we spoke of *other* rumours?'

'*You* spoke of other rumours.'

'So there are no further rumours concerning Mr Taylor?'

'As I said, I keep to my own business.'

'And that's noble of you, Mr Rickard, but—'

'But this is a murder investigation.'

'A *double* murder investigation,' Dunderdale updated him.

'Then I'm more than doubly sorry for James's early demise, and if I believed any knowledge I possessed would help you catch his killer, you would know.'

'On the contrary, Mr Rickard, you do have a knowledge that I'm interested in: only you alone suspected Mr Bowes of having been poisoned *when* you told your wife not to touch the champagne glass?'

'The rationale was James was the only one who took ill immediately after drinking his champagne – and I never believed for one moment he had cholera. Of course, I see you are of the opinion the first person to talk about the method of murder is the most likely suspect; a tactic to throw everyone off the scent for surely the murderer would never be stupid enough to utter such words!'

'And yet it also transpires you were the one to hand Mr Bowes his champagne glass?'

'Flute. Champagne flute. And, yes, I took one for each of us, but that's all.'

'Very well. How would you rationalise a feather, matching the one discovered on Sir Henry's tongue, being found in Mr Bowes's trouser pocket?'

'Had a feather not been deposited on Henry's tongue, I'd have rationalised James could easily have pocketed the feather

165

for some study *or* for no particular reason at all. However, as you say, knowing of two feathers, I can't rationalise other than to say they're a cruel calling card.'

'A murderer with a twisted sense of humour, wouldn't you agree, Mr Rickard?'

David met Dunderdale's stare. 'Yes, I did have the opportunity to slip a feather into James's pocket when I helped him to his room. As you're also aware, so did my brother-in-law, Henry's valet... *and* the secretary.'

'*And* the cook.'

'And the cook.'

'I understand you were in possession of the knowledge of Sir Henry's offer to facilitate your wife's divorce against you?'

'Tread carefully, Inspector, you cross a delicate boundary into an area that has nothing to do with your investigation – or you, for that matter.'

'I'm wondering whether you've yet the compulsion to divulge the details of your quarrel with Sir Henry? No? Not to worry, your wife has been forthcoming in confirming the rumour surrounding yourself and her sister to be accurate.'

Dunderdale watched the colour in David's cheeks rise as a frost clouded his blue eyes. 'Damn your condescension, damn your suspicions and damn your questions! I've told you I had nothing to do with the murders and I won't stay here and subject myself to any more of your prying!'

'Let him go,' Dunderdale told Collins.

————

Dunderdale asked Fawcett why Mr Bowes's glass had not been placed in a secure location.

'I was instructed only to move the champagne flute out of harm's way, sir, and not to wash it.'

'Forensics have confirmed it's been washed clean, *meaning* we have no way of proving whether it contained poison let alone champagne!'

'That's unfortunate, sir. However, I would swear an oath to it having contained champagne.'

'On account of you filling it... yes, you told me that yesterday; what you didn't tell me is you were called in to witness Sir Henry's writing of his codicil?'

'I was never asked, sir.'

'Then if I could ask you now: whilst acting as witnesses, was the conversation between testator and witnesses one-sided?'

'Sir?'

'In other words, did Sir Henry ask either of you for your advice in the writing of his codicil?'

'He did not, sir, and no unnatural thought would ever occur to a master.'

'There was no coercion from Mr Atkinson?'

'There was not, sir.'

'And, finally, do either yourself or Mrs Clarke know of any meddling with or an unexplained depletion of your stock of pest control substances – arsenic trioxide to be precise?'

'I do not and Mrs Clarke would take exception to any such suggestion.'

———

'Ah, Mr Atkinson!'

Tom still looked uncomfortable at taking the seat opposite anyone other than Sir Henry.

'I noticed you were the first to offer your congratulations to Mrs Rickard? A smile can speak volumes,' Dunderdale added, quickly cutting off Tom's denial.

'I believe Ava to be the rightful *and* deserving heir,' Tom admitted.

'Is that what you told Sir Henry?'

'I knew nothing of Sir Henry's plans until he invited me into his study along with Fawcett. Fawcett can vouch for my being merely a witness to the codicil, just like him.'

'I'd like to ask if you know the combination to the safe?'

'Why should I?'

'I never asked whether you *should*, I asked if you *do*. But, to answer your question, Sir Henry could have entrusted you with the safe's combination in the event of… *say* any forgetfulness – not unheard of for a man of his age?'

'If Sir Henry did consider the likelihood of forgetting the combination then I couldn't tell you whether his Plan B was to have it written down somewhere *or* if he'd entrusted another with it. I would say the sensible course of action would be to give the combination to his solicitor.'

'That's exactly what he did do.'

'There you go then, there was no reason for a third person to know the combination!'

'But you did know of the contents of the codicil.'

'We've already established that fact.'

'You knew, Mr Atkinson, that upon Sir Henry's death Mrs Ava Rickard would become a wealthy woman… a very wealthy woman, indeed.'

'No, I didn't. Not until Mr Atkins read the will did I know this. What I *did* know was that upon certain conditions not being met *then* Ava would become the sole beneficiary. What I *did not* know was what those conditions were.'

'Very well. Whose idea was it for the secretary to attend the family toast?'

'Sir Henry's, naturally.'

'You never planted the seed?'

'If by that you mean did I wheedle my way in with the intent of murdering Mr Bowes, then it must have been a plan years in the making.'

'You and Mrs Rickard were childhood sweethearts, that's right, isn't it?'

'It's public knowledge that I loved Ava and she me.'

'Loved?'

'Very well, then, if you must know, I'm still in love with her!'

'And she you?'

Tom paused at that before saying, 'I honestly couldn't tell you.'

'Over time a man might turn bitter and resentful against the person who prevented him marrying the woman he loved.'

'If you know of our history then you'll know it was my choice in the end. Ava was ready to give up her promised inheritance and I admire – *love her* all the more for it.'

'Then it's not that, minus her inheritance, she wasn't such a good prospect after all?'

'I've already told you, I didn't know the conditions of Sir Henry's will.'

'So you did. If we can talk of your carrying Mr Bowes to his room…'

'Along with Mr Rickard, Mr Taylor and Turner.'

'Along with Mr Rickard, Mr Taylor and Mr Turner. Remember my telling you earlier this afternoon of the feather found in the pocket of Mr Bowes's trousers?'

'Yes.'

'I'm trying to work out when the murderer concealed it there and I'm wondering if the best opportunity would have been when he was taken to his room?'

'No, Detective Inspector, in answer to your question, I was not the one who slipped a feather into Mr Bowes's trousers. What I can tell you is I now understand that which enshrouded Sir Henry when he last retired for bed to have been "loss".'

'Like a father mourning a son?'

'Yes, I think that's exactly what it was. I apologise, Detective Inspector, but I've still work waiting for me.'

'Yes, you may go.'

'There's the possibility Mr Atkinson's actin' alone,' Collins said. 'Gettin' rid o't obstacle to him and Mrs Rickard bein' together, at same time givin' her riches beyond his wildest dreams!'

'Except it appears he knew Sir Henry was actively encouraging his niece to divorce her husband, so surely all Mr Atkinson needed to do was sit back and wait.'

'Yes, sir, but I'd put my weekly wage on Sir Henry *still* not lettin' his niece marry the secretary.'

'Hmm,' Dunderdale agreed.

———

Contrary to Fawcett's claim, Dunderdale found Mrs Clarke – as he'd suspected – to be most affable. Wiping her floured hands on her apron, she took no exception to being asked about her storage of arsenic trioxide. Regrettably for the investigation, she had no meddling or depletion of stock to report.

'When Mr Bowes took ill, I understand yourself and Mr Turner undressed him and put him to bed?'

'That's right.'

'I would ask you to keep in mind my questions are purely for the purpose of fact gathering…'

'I've nae problem with that.'

'Then, did you check Mr Bowes's trouser pockets?'

'I only wish I'd time to rummage through young men's britches, eh!' Mrs Clarke answered with not one ounce of offence taken, 'but the answer's nae, I didn't.'

'Did you happen to notice if anyone else took an interest in Mr Bowes's clothes… his trousers, in particular?'

'Mr Turner yer mean? Nae, I never saw owt o't sort.'

'Then Mrs Clarke, I thank you for your much-valued time.'

'Afore yer go, Inspector, would yer be wantin' more sustenance?'

'No, thank you, Mrs Clarke, we're to return to Appleby,' Dunderdale said, and Collins's mouth closed again.

———

Dunderdale and Collins had sat quietly while Smith carefully negotiated the country roads – the inspector reflecting on the day's revelations while the constable dreamed of the mutton Mrs Collins would be stewing.

Mesmerised by the snow hitting the windscreen – every flake that was wiped from existence soon being replaced with another, Dunderdale finally voiced the question that had been puzzling him as Smith pulled the motor car up outside the offices of Atkins, Bagnall and Jones: 'Why poison? Why arsenic trioxide?'

The mutton stew evaporated from Collins's mind. 'Yer said yerself, sir, yer can't taste or smell it.'

'Yes. But why *arsenic trioxide*…?'

'I'm not sure I understand, sir?'

'Never mind, Collins. Thank you, Smith.'

The two policemen stepped down from the car, their black shoes immediately soiled by a mush of snow, soil and manure.

'Quick as you can, Collins – Chief Constable Watson should contact Scotland Yard before the day's end. Tell him to pull on whatever strings he has in his web... I'd like to know if Mr Taylor has need of a begging bowl.'

Putting his faith in salt, Dunderdale pooh-poohed the idea of taking hold of the iron railing and mounted the stone steps unaided.

'Detective Inspector Dunderdale?'

'Mr Atkins, a moment of your time if you wouldn't mind offering a little respite.'

'Not at all! Please, take a seat.'

'Thank you... I wanted to ask whether Sir Henry ever entered into any business dealings with Mr Taylor? Any investments between the two businessmen?'

'Never. Now if you were to ask whether Sir Henry asked me to draw up a contract of loan for Mr Taylor then I can confirm he did – on a few occasions. The repayment of his last loan, I'm afraid to say, still being outstanding.'

'And does this outstanding money amount to a substantial sum?'

John Atkins wrote a figure down on a piece of paper and handed it across to Dunderdale.

'That's a no, then,' Dunderdale answered himself.

'Not a substantial sum for the likes of Sir Henry or Mr Taylor, at any rate!'

'Though I've known a lesser amount put a man in his grave, I don't believe it to be the kind of sum Mr Taylor would find worth murdering for. I must say,' Dunderdale said while undoing the buttons on his overcoat, the blazing fire in the solicitor's office a cold reminder of what awaited the policeman back in the study at Crowthwaite Castle, 'the characterisation I'm building up of the baronet makes me wonder at him agreeing to the loans in the first place.'

'Sir Henry may have loaned Mr Taylor out of a sense of duty to his niece but he was always careful to dictate strong terms. He wasn't the type to risk his money. Of course, he himself made investments during his lifetime as lord of the manor – and he enjoyed some remarkable returns which, when added to the family's accrued wealth and his own scrupulous spending habits, explains the vast estate he leaves behind.'

'I don't suppose...?' Dunderdale solicited, proffering the paper between two fingers.

Atkins, obliging, took back the sheet and, after scribbling down another figure – with more columns – he handed it back.

Dunderdale whistled. 'And only a commoner, at that! *Do you know*, Mr Atkins, the thought never occurred to me before now, but if a male heir was so important to Sir Henry then why didn't he pass the estate and title on to a distant cousin?'

'Ah, that! There *are* some male distant cousins – much more distant than Miss Markham – but Sir Henry said they were so far removed their blood would be positively anaemic of the de Trouville line.'

'It sounds a pity I never got to meet the man in life!'

'Yes, he was quite a character,' Atkins agreed.

'One more thing before I depart: Lady de Trouville is quite insistent on fighting for what she believes she's entitled to – by which she made clear to mean the inheritance in its entirety. I wanted, once again, to ask your professional opinion on the matter?'

'Unless she were to prove herself to be with child at the time of Sir Henry's death – *is this* what she's claiming?'

'No.'

'Then it's as I explained this morning – Ava still stands as the sole beneficiary.'

NINE

THE NIGHT'S SNOWFALL was piled to each side of the manor's track by the time Dunderdale and Collins returned early afternoon the next day. As the motor car's tyres crunched closer to the castle the sergeant exclaimed at the impressive snowman on patrol: a real northerner with a flat cap on its bulbous head, a pipe protruding from a slit for a mouth and a good foot of walking stick buried in snow. The policemen tracked its creator down to the attic, wondering, as they climbed the last few steps to the third floor, at his recital – '*Once, and but once found in thy company, All thy suppos'd escapes are laid on mee; And as a thiefe at barre, is question'd there / By all the men, that have been rob'd that yeare…*' – and it didn't become apparent until they rounded the corner that it was Stephen's unique way of counting up during a game of hide-and-seek.

'*… So am I, (by this traiterous meanes surpriz'd) / By thy Hydroptique father catechiz'd…* COMING, READY OR NOT!'

Dunderdale and Collins waited until father had located both daughters. 'YOU PEEKED,' Betsy squawked, 'you peeked, Daddy!'

'I most certainly did not, it was Miss Schoe-Schoe's swishing frills which gave you away!'

'Miss Schoe-Schoe,' Betsy addressed the newborn doll suspended between two plump hands in front of her face, 'you are a most silly girl not to keep still when told!'

Rose giggled and Betsy went on to demand it was her turn to be seeker.

'Sergeant,' Dunderdale said, 'take father's place, would you.'

Stephen, leaning into the sergeant's ear, instructed him to hide in the wardrobe in the far corner. 'It'll be her first choice!' he whispered.

Betsy, after sitting Miss Schoe-Schoe down on a low stool, planted plump hands over her own eyes and began to count.

Charles Collins headed for the far corner, Rose running back to her usual hiding place – her teddy bear swinging wildly by one paw – and Dunderdale gestured Stephen to follow him out to the landing. 'When you, Mr Taylor,' he said in a low voice, 'spoke of investments, what I heard of was "begging bowls".'

'Begging bowls? Someone's being inventive!'

'Then I look forward to your simplified explanation,' Dunderdale said as numbers began to bounce off objects deep within the attic.

'I might have asked Uncle for the odd loan – a little something to tide me over, that is. Being in business some-times demands the juggling of funds. Heading a successful company is not for the faint-hearted, Detective!'

'Then why not tell this when asked?'

'I see where this is leading, but you're wrong. It's a tem-porary hiccup, nothing more. Certainly nothing that can't be fixed with another stab at the sales ledger – if you can forgive my poor choice of noun…! I've been here before, you know…'

'Yes, I do know, hence my use of the plural.'

'WELL DONE!' father congratulated triumphant daughter who'd outwitted another grown man. 'Apologies, Detective, but I do not agree with your semantics. It all comes down to the company's generous terms – once we're paid what we're owed then we settle our own accounts; now and then a creditor digs its boots in, hence the ha'p'orth of a loan. *This* is why I decided it wasn't worth the mention. At the time, I believed it would only provide ammunition for a non-existent gun. Of course, I now see I should have told you – would have saved you a lot of trouble! In fact, I thank you, Detective, for broaching the topic for it has reminded me, I've still a loan outstanding… though, I suppose it's now owed to Ava…'

'Stephen?' Bertha called.

'You mark my words, Detective, the old family business won't die on my watch.'

'Stephen!'

'There, don't take on, old girl, you've found us.'

Dunderdale saw Bertha's shoulders squeeze together, as though she were a tiny plasticine figure being manipulated by a child's hand, and decided the explanation to be a combination of a drop in the temperature and the reality of dust.

'Stephen, what are you doing all the way up here?'

'We've been having a game of hide-and-seek, old girl.'

Betsy appeared, one arm wrapped possessively around Miss Schoe-Schoe's waist. 'I told you, Mummy.'

Still carrying the scars of one Halloween spent in the attic and Clara's suggestion of connecting with the spirit world through the Ouija parlour game – and Bertha's continuing fearful insistence the three young sisters had released something unnatural into the living world – Bertha said she wished Stephen wouldn't play with the girls, not 'up here'.

'We're done now – that's correct, isn't it, Detective?'

Dunderdale agreeing, Stephen bent down for Rose and 'Mr Ted'. 'Come along… besty seeker in the whole wide kingdom.'

Dunderdale, still disregarding Fawcett's repeated requests for all members of the law to use the staff staircase, tailed the family and was rewarded with Bertha's voice, which wound its way upwards, round the spiral steps: 'I know you told me not to worry…'

'And I meant it, old girl.'

'… but I really don't like how David treats you as his inferior.'

'Only a bit of brotherly banter!'

'Is there any need for his incessant facetiousness! I mean, this morning and his jibe when he said he'd not hear the kettle call the pot black!'

'He's got a lot going on at the moment.'

'But what did he mean? I asked Susan, but she said she didn't know.'

'Who does know, old girl, who does?'

'Stephen will join us, won't you, Stephen?' Clara said as the Taylors entered the hall.

'Always game for anything…'

'A moorland winter walk,' an unenthusiastic Susan informed him.

'You shan't douse Stephen's fire, Susan. He's never missed the traditional Christmas walk… although, we are a day late,' Clara added with an accusatory glance in Dunderdale's direction.

'I'm up for it, Clara, honey,' Chester said.

'How about it, Detective?' Stephen asked. 'I know Betsy has been chomping at the bit.'

'YES, DADDY, YES!'

'Oh, I'm not sure, Stephen…' Bertha began.

'I am,' Violet chimed in, 'and I shan't be going anywhere!'

'Detective?' Stephen urged.

'Providing you acknowledge Constable Shaw will be accompanying you,' Dunderdale acquiesced.

'Don't trust the murderer among us not to bolt?' David suggested.

'David!' Bertha reproached him.

'You're quite right, Mr Rickard, though there is still another possibility—'

'The murderer's an outsider?'

'Nothing can yet be ruled out.'

'Then it's decided… I shan't go, after all,' Bertha said.

'Well, I for one shan't be frightened to live within my own skin!' Stephen declared. 'What about you, eh, David?'

'I'm not about to let Ava go alone, if that's what you think.'

Violet gave Ava a look of resentment.

'Stephen, must you go…?'

'Yes. We. Must. Mummy,' Betsy told her.

'Surely, you're not taking the girls!'

'Yes. He. Is. Mummy!'

'No, just Betsy. Now, now, she'll be fine, Bertha! You heard the inspector: not only have they their father and uncle for protection but a policeman!'

'Oh, do join us, Boots. I'm sure there's a spare pair of Wellingtons that will fit you perfectly!' Clara said.

'I tell you what, Bertha,' Susan said, 'we'll have a quiet and cosy afternoon together in the drawing room. What d'you say, Violet?'

'I suppose,' Violet answered ungraciously.

———

Dunderdale watched the walking party set off north of the castle, their path taking them through the forest's outer perimeter, each member muffled up and their footfall sure. Thinking of The Black Feather's greeting for Crowthwaite's 'offcomers', Dunderdale suggested Collins introduce him to the local tap – 'my treat!'

His Homburg planted firmly on his head and the lapels of his overcoat up high, Dunderdale looked up to the sky. 'Thank Demeter it stopped! I *was* worried we might not get through today.'

'Up here, sir, we learn to live with all weathers. No choice, really, but to.'

'You ever thought about a transfer, Collins?'

Collins reflected. 'No, can't say I have.'

'You ever been up there?' Dunderdale asked, a gloved hand pointing to their right where a thick white bar of cloud was hanging above Cross Fell, parallel with the Pennine hill's flat peak.

'Not me, sir. Farmer's only one with need to venture up those parts. Dreary, by all accounts, but that doesn't stop these so-called fell walkers comin' for the privilege. Can't make out some folk.'

'On that, I think we can agree.'

A gust of wind blew a flurry of snow off the branch of a hawthorn tree onto Collins's arm. Knocking the bitter misdemeanour off his three chevron stripes, he asked, 'What do yer think 'bout Mr Taylor, sir?'

'Until we hear back from Scotland Yard all we've learned is that the borrowing of monies is part and parcel of being in business. At best it's circumstantial. By the way, Collins, Barnes is a blank. Chief Constable Watson said he was sorry to hear a married woman of Lady de Trouville's standing had been meeting in secret with another man; he also said his nephew may be a bit untrustworthy but not his sister, who swears her son has been, remains and intends to remain with the family in Carlisle the whole Christmas.'

'That's that then, sir.'

'Looks that way.'

'Though, doesn't mean it weren't Lady de Trouville that did it.'

'No, Sergeant, it doesn't.'

At The Black Feather, Pearl 'kicked' a local out of 'Grandad's' seat. 'Yer know me rules,' she threatened with the gravitas of the court jester.

'Aye, I know 'em, alreet,' he replied, always up for a friendly exchange of words with Pearl Bell, 'offcomers get best seats in't house, eh!'

'Be gone with yer, Drew, I'm no offcomer!' Collins laughed.

'Nae, Charlie-Boy, there's always a hoo-doo for you here!'

'Enough, yer doilem!' Pearl said while shepherding Drew towards the bar.

A little of Dunderdale's ale sloshed over the rim of his tankard as he sunk deeper than expected into the chair Pearl had evicted Drew from. After blotting the creamy froth from his trousers, Dunderdale sipped at the local drink and stared into the guttering fire. When Collins began to speak, Dunderdale showed him his palm to indicate all that was required was silence, to focus on the public house chatter.

Disappointingly, none of the discussions surrounding the 'goings on' up at the manor told Dunderdale anything new and so he relaxed deeper into the chair and waited for the activity of electrical signals to communicate within his grey matter – the process of consolidation of his recently acquired knowledge.

More disappointingly, while sitting in 'Grandad's' seat – Pearl remarking to herself how she'd never seen anyone sit so still for such a length of time and astonished at having never known a man take so long to down his ale – Dunderdale was no closer to understanding how the murderer had succeeded in poisoning James, nor to which one of the suspects had turned murderer.

During this time, the comings and goings of locals, the exchange of money for drink and the guzzling and chattering had all been dismissed as ordinary. Not even when each 'coming' arrived with small talk of the weather had anything occurred to the detective inspector – after all, that was the British way. It was only when a local gasped 'Sweet God!' as he was blown across the threshold, that something piqued Dunderdale's interest, interrupting his thought process.

'Helm's gettin' up!' the local exclaimed to his fellow patrons. 'If it keeps up there's a good chance it'll blow horns off a tup!'

'A tup?' Dunderdale asked Collins.

'Ram, sir.'

'Afore day's up,' the local said to Pearl as she pushed his drink across the bar, 'there'll be 'nother whisper makin' the rounds – yer can mark me words…!'

Extricating himself as quickly from his seat as the worn seat padding would allow, Dunderdale, grabbing his hat and coat, told Collins to finish his drink 'double quick!'

Fighting a headwind, Collins caught up with Dunderdale a little up the village. 'SIR…! Sir, what is it…? What's the rush?'

'You shouldn't need me to spell it out, Collins…' Dunderdale shouted with breaths that threatened to drown him, 'WE'RE IN A HELM WIND!'

———

Close to exhaustion, Dunderdale pushed open the heavy oak door to the vestibule to find the walking party already returned and surrounding one of the settees, along with Violet, Bertha and Susan. 'God, no!' he cried.

Constable Donnelly tapped Constable Shaw on the shoulder of his cape. Turning around, Shaw was clearly relieved his two superiors were back.

As fast as Dunderdale's jellied legs would carry him, he headed to the epicentre of the commotion, praying his fear would prove incorrect.

Seeing Ava lying inert, a profanity was about to spew from his mouth when her eyes flickered. 'Thank you,' he breathed, lifting his head to the not-so-almighty from whom he neither sought, nor expected, forgiveness.

'Doctor's been sent for,' Shaw told him.

Susan took the cup and saucer from Fawcett and handed it to Ava. 'Just little sips.'

Dunderdale looked down on Ava and although the marks round her neck answered his question, he asked, 'What happened?'

'What happened is some bastard tried to murder my wife, that's what happened!' David fumed over Stephen's 'Most terrible, Detective!'

Pulling David to one side, Dunderdale appealed to his better nature: 'While we await the doctor, with your permission, Mr Rickard, I'd like to begin my enquiries whilst everyone is gathered; it prevents the chance of collaboration – you understand?'

David agreed.

'I suggest we all take a seat,' Dunderdale said while stripping off his outer garments. 'Come on, people, give Mrs Rickard air! Fawcett, afternoon tea all round might do the trick to settle nerves.' Fawcett headed off to the kitchen and Dunderdale signalled Shaw to begin.

Unclasping and removing his cape, the young constable went straight on the defensive, saying naturally he'd kept his distance. 'I weren't too far back, sir, just enough to be respectful. 'Course, I'd heard o' Helm Winds but as the' always blow 'emselves out afore reachin' Appleby, I'd never really known one afore now! By the time I realised I were in one, it were too late for it'd brought thick fog with it as well! Well, I tried me best to get the group back together but as the'd already split up it were difficult, 'specially as…'

'Especially as…?'

'I'd lost sight of 'em, sir.'

'What, all of them?'

'It wasn't the bobby's fault, Detective,' Stephen said. 'We'd all lost sight of one another.'

'Damn fog!' David said, vexed.

'You say you lost sight, Constable…'

'That's right, sir.'

'What about sound? Could you *hear* any of the group?'

'Now I think on it, I could hear Mr Rickard and little lasso laikin' somewhere up-front o' me…'

'Playin', sir,' Collins translated for Shaw.

'… and I could hear voices comin' from't old building – faint the' were…'

'Old building?'

'It's a derelict and dilapidated farmhouse,' Clara told him. 'The voices the constable could hear were myself and Chester. I was showing him round the old place.'

'What then, Shaw?'

'As I said, I heard Mr Rickard and little lasso and I shouted out to 'em to stay exactly where the' were and not to go any further. I then made me way into't old building.'

'And whereabouts was the building in relation to Mr Rickard and Miss Betsy? You said uncle and niece were ahead of you?'

'That's right, and farmhouse were to the right, much closer to me than Mr Rickard were... I think.'

'Be sure, Constable.'

Shaw, concentrating on the plates of sliced buttered breads which Fawcett was dotting round the tables, thought on it before saying, 'Yes, sir, farmhouse were closest.'

'Mr Rickard? Did you hear Constable Shaw call out to you?'

'No. I didn't.'

'That seems odd, sir, wouldn't you say? If the constable could hear you, how was it you couldn't hear him?'

'Nothing odd about it, at all. He was downwind of us. Surely you know the law of sound! Now, where the hell is that doctor?'

'Mr Smith left immediately for him, sir,' Fawcett answered, now setting down a tiered stand of scones, rock buns, and slices of plum and caraway seed cakes – the hall looking more like a tea party than an inquisition.

Dunderdale turned back to Shaw. 'What next?'

'I realise now I should've waited 'til I'd had a response from Mr Rickard – to make sure he'd heard me. Not thinkin', I went off to the old building in search of who were in there, to tell 'em to wait 'til I found the others, but when I got inside I could hear no more. I searched through every room. It were clearer in there; somehow the fog hadn't found its way in... strange that, when yer think of it not havin' any doors or windows... just openings...'

'Concentrate, Shaw.'

'Right you are, sir. I didn't want to risk gettin' lost and, thinkin' the group would surely try to head back to the manor on account o't fog, I waited at the front door – opening, I mean.'

'Miss de Trouville, why was it the constable couldn't locate yourself and Mr Johnson? You, yourself, said you were both in there.'

'And we were. The only possible reason must be that I'd already shown Chester round. I'm assuming by the time the constable arrived inside, Chester and I were at the rear of the building.'

'And what were you doing at the rear of the building?'

'Nothing that concerns you, Detective.'

'You could say that, but then I'd have to remind you your sister has just been strangled within an inch of—'

'Just answer the damn question!' David commanded.

'Go steady,' Chester warned David. Bertha, a full plate in one hand, inched closer to her husband.

'If you insist on knowing,' Clara said, directing her answer to David, 'we were taking action to keep warm.'

Violet scoffed and Bertha coughed: 'Fawcett, now Uncle's no longer with us, must you continue to ration the butter? Todd *lavishes* our afternoon tea with it!'

No sign of offence taken for the comparison, Fawcett handed Bertha a cup of tea.

'And when you were… sufficiently warmed?' Dunderdale asked Clara and Chester.

'We were at the back the whole time – that was 'til we heard the disturbance,' Chester told him. 'We got round to the front just as David was carryin' Ava into the building.'

'Thank you, Mr Johnson. Shaw, you're standing in the opening that's the front door, you've not been able to locate members of the party who you thought were inside the building, talk me through what happened next.'

'As I said, I waited, knowin', quite rightly, the group'd pass that way—'

'Why quite rightly?'

'Because o't footprints, in't snow, sir. Stood to reason anyone with half a brain would think to retrace their footsteps once the' could no longer see which way were up or down. So, I waited and while I waited I called out their names… Mr Rickard… Mrs Rickard… Mr—'

'And then…?'

'I'm not sure how much time had passed afore I heard Mr Rickard callin' out for help. I shouted back and I'm thinkin' it must've guided him for he appeared through the fog carryin' Mrs Rickard with little lasso by his side. Then, as Mr Johnson said, him and Miss de Trouville appeared.'

'From?'

'Side o't building.'

'What about Mr Taylor?'

'He appeared at the same time. Now yer come to mention it, I heard his voice afore I saw him… callin' for Betsy.'

'That's right, Detective,' Stephen said. 'I'd got split from the group and when I realised we were trapped in the fog, I got myself into quite a panic… Images flitting through my mind of possible tragedies that could befall Betsy… a slip on some ice… a trip over a snow-covered boulder… all alone, walking round and round in circles…'

'Oh, Stephen, don't say such horrid things,' Bertha said, another slice of bread in hand, 'you know I'll come over all ill!'

'I imagine it's every parent's nightmare.'

'It is,' Stephen agreed with Dunderdale, 'and I never want to experience anything like it for as long as I live.'

187

'Could I ask, Mr Taylor, how it was you managed to get yourself split from the remaining group?'

'It was a stag, Detective. A lowland red to be precise, and what a specimen he was! Didn't know he was there until we rounded the old farmhouse. Though he knew we were there, by Jove he did! *He* had no respect for any of David's laws; upwind but did that stop our scent reaching him? No, it didn't! A streak of rust-red cutting through snow at lightning speed – cleared the wall, no bother! By the time I reached the boundary he was already at the other side of the moor that borders the forest. Fortunately for me, he hung around its edge.'

'I saw him, Daddy!' Betsy's little voice said, her face peering out between two spindles. 'You pretended your arm was Winnie and you shot him with your finger!'

'Betsy, no!' Bertha started. 'Where's Ivy?'

'It's fine, Mummy. I was only going to tell Dunderhead about Daddy's stag. We saw it, didn't we, Uncle David?' At that moment Ivy arrived, her chubby face swollen pink with apology.

'Get yourself back to the nursery, Besty Betsy!' And, cocking an invisible rifle, Stephen got his eldest child in his sights and... *POOF!*

'DADDY!' she screamed, making Violet jump.

'Just one moment,' Dunderdale told Ivy. 'Miss Betsy, is there anything else you'd like to tell me?'

'After we found Aunty Ava, I heard Daddy shouting my name and I said, "I'm fine, Daddy, I'm with Uncle David and Aunty Ava" – but you kept on shouting... silly Daddy!'

'Thank you, Miss Betsy. Off you go with your nanny.'

'She's not my nanny. She's just a housemaid.'

'*Dunderhead?*' the inspector said to Stephen when they'd gone.

'Yes, sorry about that!'

'Hmm. Then it was a stag that was to blame.'

'Personally, I don't understand the obsession. We see them all the time,' David said.

'The sheer beauty, David!'

'Then why stalk the poor creatures?'

'The beauty, as you well know, brother, lies not only in the animal but within the art of the hunt.'

'I'm sure it does,' Dunderdale interrupted. 'If you excuse my saying so, Mr Taylor, you've demonstrated yourself to be a loving father, which makes me wonder how it was you lost sight of Miss Betsy?'

'Don't, Detective…! If I *must* think about it, I'd say I knew she was quite safe with David. Betsy adores her uncle, and he her.' David's steely expression did nothing to support his brother-in-law's character reference. 'I'm sorry, old girl… she really was in the best of hands. Larking around they were, having quite a jolly. In fact, I remember, David, brother, you caught me with quite a whopper of a ball on my lower back!' At that, a gratifying glint formed in David's eye, just as the doctor arrived along with an eddy of wind and snow.

'About time!' David said, the glint short-lived.

Doctor Norris requested the patient be moved to the drawing room for examination. Refusing offers of assistance, and ignoring Ava's own objection, David picked his wife up from the settee with relative ease.

'You can continue, Constable,' Dunderdale instructed.

'Where were I? That's it, everyone were back at farmhouse! I told Mr Rickard to bring his wife into't building where there were a little shelter. After givin' her the once over, I found she were conscious but confused. It were then when Mr Rickard, seein' her neck, looked to me, and I told him it looked very

189

likely someone had strangled her. Well, sir, his face turned all angry and he demanded to know who'd done it…!'

'Did he, indeed! And what was the response?'

Shaw cast his eye quickly over the group and said, 'I'm 'fraid, sir, I never gave 'em time for much other than instant denials for I told 'em we must get Mrs Rickard back to castle.'

'What time was this?'

'I remember lookin' at me watch as we set off downhill and it said two forty-five which means it couldn't have been much earlier than two forty.'

Just as Dunderdale recorded the times in his notebook there were urgent footsteps and then Tom was standing in the hall, still dressed for the outdoors and his face flushed. 'Where is she?'

'Now, Mr Atkinson—'

'WHERE'S AVA?'

'Mr Atkinson, lower your voice!'

'She's with the doctor,' Clara answered, her eyes directing him to the 'where'.

'HOW DARE YOU!' David's voice carried through to the hall as Dunderdale was telling Shaw and Donnelly to 'stay put' and Collins 'with me'.

'This is not the time,' Doctor Norris told Tom.

'I couldn't agree more,' Dunderdale said.

'Who did this, Ava?' Tom asked.

David getting to his feet, Ava managed a hoarse, 'David… no!'

'Enough, both of you,' Norris commanded, 'you are adding to Mrs Rickard's distress!'

'I'd sooner scoop out my own heart with a blunt spoon than grey one hair on Ava's head! *Ava*, tell me what happened.'

'*Mrs Rickard* to you,' David reminded him. 'You're staff,

Atkinson… though not for much longer.'

'That will be for *Ava* to decide – for it was *she* who inherited the estate—'

'Who are you to speak to me of *my* wife!'

'We all knew the danger she was in and I'd believed, as her husband, you'd at least know how to protect her – what a fool I've been!' His meaning was ambiguous as to whether he was referring to not self-knighting himself as Ava's protector *or* for not marrying her all those years ago.

'A GREAT LUMBERING FOOL…!' David acknowledged and then one doctor and two policemen couldn't prevent two men, both in their prime: David threw the first punch but Tom managed to counter before each man was clumsily restrained.

It was the object of their desire's 'STOP IT!' that put an end to their struggles.

His appearance dishevelled, Tom looked once more upon his teenage sweetheart then left.

Doctor Norris told Ava his examination was complete and she was free to return to the hall. Shaking off David's help, Ava left the room unaided while Dunderdale quietly instructed Collins to go after Tom to ask his whereabouts for the afternoon.

'Obviously you'll receive my report later, Detective Inspector,' Norris said when they were alone, 'but I can tell you the swelling and marking to Mrs Rickard's neck is consistent with strangulation that will have resulted in her losing momentary consciousness.'

'Suggesting there was the need for her attacker to flee the scene before one could say knife?'

'Looks that way! Bruising will follow and I've advised liquid food only and plenty of fluids – Fawcett should keep those warm honeyed-teas coming!'

'What of evidence? Were there any thumbprints which could be lifted?'

'None, I'm afraid. Looks like her attacker wore gloves.' Regardless of the castle's thick walls, Norris lowered his voice: 'I don't know what's going on here, Detective Inspector Dunderdale… the lord of the manor murdered in his own bed, his *son's* champagne poisoned *and now* Miss Ava strangled while out walking, but I don't like it – not one little bit!'

'Neither do I. It also doesn't look good for the county, *apparently*, which is why the chief constable wants the murderer delivering into his hands *pronto*. So, based on your examination, would you say we're looking for a man?'

'If I was called upon to make an educated guess…'

'Which you are.'

'Then I'd say yes, her attacker was male *but* as I couldn't say with certainty, I wouldn't swear to it.'

'Before you leave, do you advise against my speaking with your patient?'

'*That*' – picking up his leather bag – 'I leave for Mrs Rickard to answer.'

'Absolutely not!' David said when Dunderdale put the same question to Ava.

'We must know who it is, David, and for that Detective Inspector Dunderdale needs delivering of all the facts.'

'Then, Fawcett, another dose of honeyed-tea, please,' Dunderdale instructed as Collins returned. 'Mrs Rickard, ready when you are.'

'You'll want to know why I was stupid enough to be walking alone and the honest answer is I sought solitude.' David's jaw twitched. 'I knew we were headed for a Helm Wind – I saw it when we set off, lying over the Pennines.

For those of us who've spent a significant amount of time at Crowthwaite, those of us who've enjoyed exploring its moorland in all weathers, we've learned the lie of the land and the tricks of the weather, so when the wind increased and the fog descended I was not perturbed. Of course, I didn't know what was to befall me – not even when I saw the figure.' A morbid curiosity instantaneously gripped the group – Violet's and Bertha's postures rigid with fright. 'I'm not for one moment suggesting it was Crowthwaite's spectre *though* its movements were ghost-like, like a cloud of blanket weed in a disturbed pond. Naturally, I dismissed it as a trick of light and fog… *and yet* I remember the scene that played out in my mind of a young woman in white, walking ahead of me on the left… the same uphill direction – and then it was gone, consumed by the fog. I do realise, you know, it to have been the figment of an overactive imagination, probably brought about through the amalgamation of a pagan story and the horrific murders of Uncle Henry and poor James.'

'No, Ava, don't you see,' Stephen said with an animation that would become Betsy, 'it was a warning – the apparition was foreshadowing danger!'

'Don't be ridiculous, man!' David said.

'Good Lord,' Stephen, not to be discouraged, told Ava, 'if only you'd been thinking straight and returned to us!'

'You truly believe it was the spectre?' Bertha addressed her husband. 'To think I could have been there!'

'Well, I for one shan't venture out into that ghastly place ever again,' Violet said, determined.

'Did anyone else see this figure?' Dunderdale asked, to which no one replied they did and Ava reiterated there was no such thing as a spectre and that she certainly never experienced any fear as she trudged on. 'As I climbed the slight incline all that was audible was a bracing, driving wind.' Gripping her teacup, she looked into the flames. 'There's something majestic about Crowthwaite's surroundings, something transcendent and yet humbling at the same time… cathartic. I remember my hair' – instinctively, she reached up to tuck a lock of dark hair around her right ear – 'whipping against my face be-before…'

'Have another sip,' Dunderdale advised.

'I say she's had enough,' David asserted.

Ava, understanding his meaning, picked up from where she'd left off: 'That was when I was grabbed… from behind… hands that went straight for my throat. There was no scent…' She shook her head and soon regretted it. 'No perfume. No sound, nor words to identify my attacker. It was as if they were no longer human… only the wild animal consumed with the business of murder…'

Violet put the back of her hand to her deep red bow lips. Bertha returned the caraway seed cake to its plate.

'Take a deep breath, Mrs Rickard,' Dunderdale bade with the voice of a hospital matron.

'Stephen was right,' David said, his cooled temper beginning to simmer, 'you shouldn't have gone ahead on your own!'

'I did try to fight back,' Ava assured Dunderdale, 'I scrabbled to fight, but it was in vain… gloved hand against gloved hand… My breath failing me, the very last thing I remember was a distant voice… calling my name.' After a brief glance at David, Ava revealed, 'I'm thankful James was spared further pain by being ignorant of the fact his impending death was murder… Uncle, God bless him, wasn't so fortunate. To know another can so easily wish you dead…'

'I give thanks I had the foresight not to go – I wish you hadn't, Stephen… and Betsy,' Bertha tagged on as if an afterthought. 'Uncle has put you in quite a predicament, Ava.

Had he shared the inheritance between the three of us – as he always promised – then all three of us couldn't have been attacked, it would leave the murderer exposed… sitting alone.' Bertha spoke the last words while shifting her line of sight from Chester to Violet.

'I wasn't even there! You truly are a most wicked family! When Henry asked for my hand, he never explained there'd be horrid murders and ghost stories and family feuds over what's mine!'

Susan, steadily exhaling cigarette smoke into the air, thought of the malign presence that had hung over the family during the carolling.

'No, old girl,' Stephen reminded his wife, 'it won't do to bring up matters of the materialistic at such a time as this.'

'Ava isn't insisting on a fuss,' Clara said, unsympathetically, 'so I don't know why others are. No real harm's been done.'

'I ain't so sure,' Chester replied quietly, 'and I'm beginnin' to feel glad you're not up for the bills.'

'Shut up the lot of you!' David snapped and, reaching for Ava's hand, he said, 'I thought I'd lost you.'

Dunderdale and Susan both read the envy in Clara's expression. Ava noted it too, and taking back her hand she asked to be excused. 'I think a lie down might do me some good, Detective Inspector.'

'Of course, Mrs Rickard. Donnelly, from this point forward, I want you shadowing Mrs Rickard,' Dunderdale instructed.

'That won't be necessary—'

'I'll be perfectly safe with the constable outside the apartment door, David.'

'I *would* like your own account, Mr Rickard,' Dunderdale agreed.

'You've already heard what happened.'

195

'I've heard other accounts; now I'd like *your* account. From the beginning.'

Resuming his seat, David quickly rolled off: 'Betsy took my hand as soon as we set out and part of the way I lifted her onto my shoulders. When we arrived at the moor, Betsy immediately set to, launching snowball after snowball at me; she sent one in her father's direction but the deer proved itself to be more of interest—'

'I say, David, that's a bit harsh!'

'As he said, I sent him on his way with a magnificent bowl – though it was meant for his head. At this time, I could still see my wife ahead of us; Clara and friend, I couldn't say. As for the constable and his "respectable distance", I'm now beginning to wonder at he having been chosen for the job.'

'Let me be the judge of that, Mr Rickard. *Then?*'

'*Then* I asked Betsy what she thought about angels and she rode my shoulders until we found a decent sort of patch of snow where we could lie down, side by side. I'm damned if I don't know how I failed to recognise the beginnings of a Helm Wind! There we were with our eyes to the hidden heavens, thrashing and flapping our arms and legs like two crazed birds when it suddenly dawned on me we were being eaten by fog! Not daring to let Betsy out of my grasp' – 'Oh, Stephen!' – 'I began searching for Ava, but as I received no response to my calls, I didn't know if she could hear me. You remember my wife telling you of the family's knowledge of the area, Inspector? Well, I knew mine and Betsy's exact location and I knew Ava's direction of travel – the last I saw of her before we began making those damn angels! What I *couldn't see* was any trace of Ava on the ground, telling me Betsy and I had strayed to the right – east, that is.' Breaking off, David cleared his throat. 'I told Betsy we'd do a bit of the old detecting ourselves, to see if we could find Aunt Ava's footprints in the snow and thus, carrying my niece, I walked a straight line west until we came upon Ava's path where I tracked her uphill, all the while calling her name…'

Susan passed him a shot of whisky.

'It was when I saw the other set of footprints that I knew she was in real danger.'

'Other footprints?' Dunderdale asked.

'Coming down from the north-east.'

'Roughly, how much distance was it between you discovering *these* footprints and your wife?'

'I don't like guesswork, Detective Inspector, for its foundation is built on assumptions and conjectures – a "Plan B" to aid one's arrival at a position which can't be found through facts and truths.'

'I entirely agree with you there, Mr Rickard, but sometimes a rough calculation is all we have to work with.'

'Thirty yards, then, but I shan't be held accountable for one bungled foot which might make all the difference between a guilty man walking and an innocent one swinging.'

'Thirty yards,' Dunderdale contemplated, 'of a set of footprints made by an unknown person following Mrs Rickard's.'

'That's just it… *these* footprints didn't follow Ava's; they disappeared.'

'The spectre?' Bertha asked Stephen.

'If phantoms do exist, old girl, then they either do or don't leave their imprints behind – they can't have it both ways.'

'There was no spectre!' David responded.

'Then what do some footprints disappearing in the snow matter!' Violet said.

'Surely you know what it means?' Chester addressed Violet and Bertha.

Bertha eyed him with suspicion – that which had momentarily been transferred to Violet returned.

Clara told Chester his attempt was futile.

'What Mr Johnson is trying to say,' Dunderdale said, 'is it means Mrs Rickard's footprints were stepped into from that point onwards – that's right, isn't it, Mr Rickard?'

'Correct.' David reached for his glass; finding it empty he knocked it away again and instead removed his lighter and cigarette case from his pocket. 'I've never covered a distance so quickly in all my life! Betsy in my arms and wind and fog and incline all working against me. It felt an age... and then there she was... lying in the snow...'

'I would say you're to thank for your wife's life, Mr Rickard, for I believe your quick gut reaction was what interrupted her attacker. Had you arrived any later... well, we'd be looking at another murder.' While Dunderdale had spoken, Clara had substituted her seat for the absent one beside David, who, though fully aware of the two taps Clara gave her cigarette holder, after lighting his own cigarette, had stowed the lighter back into its pocket; Clara spoke a couple of words that sounded like 'ridiculous, darling' and Chester and Shaw competed for the privilege – Chester getting there first.

'Well done, brother,' Stephen lauded him, Chester seconding, but David preferred Susan's praise that came in the form of a refill.

'I apologise for keeping you at the scene of the crime, Mr Rickard, but do you happen to remember seeing the attacker's footprints fleeing?'

'Yes. They headed away in the same direction as that from which they'd joined Ava's footprints: north-east.'

'That would be ahead of Mrs Rickard's direction of travel, but to the right?'

'Correct. She was travelling due north.'

'Do you happen to know what time it was when you discovered your wife?'

'As it never occurred to me to check the time at such a critical moment, no, I don't.'

'What about the amount of time it took for you to reach the farmhouse after discovering Mrs Rickard?'

'Damned if I know!'

'Why not take another guess, Mr Rickard?'

'You already know my thoughts on guesswork, Inspector, but very well, ten minutes is what you've got to work with.'

'Ten minutes... That would make the time of the attack roughly fourteen hundred hours thirty. And how much time does it take to travel from the manor to the moorland?'

'I'd say it took us about an hour to reach the derelict farmhouse,' Stephen answered.

'Making it approximately fourteen hundred hours when you arrived at the moor. To summarise, everyone's account tonight confirms none of the group was further ahead of Mrs Rickard, meaning everyone else was further back, south or south-east. Did any of you see anyone else while out walking? From the moment you set off to the time you got back to the manor...? Not a single other person?'

'Not unless you count Ava's spectre.'

'What about any other footprints?' Dunderdale asked, ignoring Clara's flippancy.

'Having been up front on our walk up there, I think I can speak for everyone when I say none whatsoever,' Stephen said. 'The snow was unblemished.'

'Anyone disagree with Mr Taylor...? Then we can discount our culprit having travelled the same way and lying in wait for there would have been evidence of their footprints—'

'Unless the' went some time before and waited it out?' Collins suggested.

'In winter? I hardly think it likely! And, considering the snow had stopped, this would also rely on sufficient time for them to cover their tracks. Talking of tracks, are there any other tracks or paths that lead to the same section of moor?'

'We accessed the moorland from the track west of the manor,' Stephen said, 'but yes, there's another track east of the manor. Bit of a longer slog, Detective, but doable.'

'How much is a "bit"?'

'Actually, it's more like double the time.'

'This is all quite elaborate,' said Clara.

'Go on, Miss de Trouville?'

'To suggest, Detective, my sister's attacker was someone outside our immediate family is dependent on your murderer having known about the event in advance.'

'I am aware of that—'

'Oh, I forget,' Clara added, 'the staff will have known… as did Bertha, Susan and Violet. Violet, Aunt, I heard from Tom that Uncle took you on a tour of the estate back in autumn?'

'You are simply beastly!'

'Take no heed,' Susan told Violet.

'I was here the whole time!' Bertha appealed to Stephen.

'Don't worry about Clara, old girl, you know how she likes to tease.'

'Oh, is that what I'm doing, Stephen? Firstly, Boots, may I point out that Stephen is hardly in a position to be called upon as your alibi for at the time in question he was out on the moor chasing a *red-head*, and secondly, I will remind you all that each time another tragedy occurs the suspect looks all the more likely to be one of us!'

Looking directly at Clara, David said, 'When I discover

who it was that dared to put their hands around my wife's neck – as God is my witness, *I* will choke the life out of *them*!'

'From this point forward, the only choking that will be carried out will be done at His Majesty's pleasure after *I* have conducted *my* investigation,' Dunderdale reminded him. 'Now, I'd like to leave the moorland and return to the manor. Lady de Trouville, Mrs Taylor and Miss Markham, if you could tell me, one at a time, your movements from the time myself and Sergeant Collins left for the village – that would be just after the walking party set out until the time of their return to the manor? I remember you organising a sit-together in the drawing room?'

'Yes, that was the plan, wasn't it,' Susan said. 'A meeting of feminine minds in the drawing room! A plan that turned out to be short-lived!'

'How short-lived?'

'I believe the minutes didn't manage to reach double figures.'

'Then I'm going to need those alibis.'

'For my part, Inspector,' Susan continued, 'I remained in the drawing room the whole time – reading.'

'Could anyone corroborate this?'

'Fawcett brought me refreshment at one point, otherwise I'm afraid it's my word alone.'

'Collins.'

'Right you are, sir,' the sergeant replied, already one foot in front of the other.

'Lady de Trouville?'

'I?'

'I must insist,' Dunderdale replied, his patience beginning to slip from his control.

'Very well, then, Detective, I really don't understand why

you're getting into such a state about it! If you must know, Susan wanted to spend the time reading and Bertha sitting. It was simply a case of boredom and if it's a toss-up between boredom and an afternoon nap then I choose the nap.'

'*Meaning* you *don't* have an alibi,' Clara remarked.

'Of course I have an alibi!'

'Really! Who was it then?'

'Who what?'

'Who was it who shared your bed?'

'No one shared my bed! That's just like you to say such a thing!'

'Miss de Trouville, please allow me to ask the questions. Go ahead, Lady de Trouville, explain what you mean.'

'I mean my maid will provide you with my alibi.'

'She was in the room with you? The whole time?'

'Well, *no*. I only meant I told her I was going for a lie down.'

'She never entered your room at any time?'

'No – but then, I don't know, do I, if I was napping!'

'Yes, Collins?'

'Fawcett says he took a tray of refreshments into't drawing room at three and that Miss Markham were alone, readin' a book 'bout rice and steps…?' Susan resisted the urge to laugh at Fawcett's, or Collins's, description. 'He were certain o't time, he said, for he always organises afternoon tea at three. Shall I go find the lady's maid now, sir?'

'Thank you, Collins. *Mrs Taylor*, your turn?'

'Sorry?'

'Your alibi, please?'

'I'm not sure if I'll be of much help, Detective. My mind's all over the place with all of the day's worries!'

'And what worries would they be, Mrs Taylor?'

'Naturally, of the thought of Stephen – and Betsy,

of course – being alone on the moor with a murderer and spectre on the loose.'

'I see. If we could return to *you*, Mrs Taylor.'

'What about me?'

'For heaven's sake, Boots! The detective wants to know what you did when you left the drawing room? Where did you go?'

'There's no need to snap, Clara. I went up to see Rose in the nursery, Detective.'

'And the maid can attest to this?'

'Would she need to?'

'Yes.'

'Well, then, I didn't go up to the nursery,' Bertha answered in a hurry.

'But you just said so yourself, Mrs Taylor. You said you went up to see Miss Rose, in the nursery!'

'And I did. But I changed my mind when I got to the first floor.'

'Then what is it you *did* do?'

Bertha looked to Stephen for help. 'No use looking to me, old girl, I wasn't here! Just tell the detective and everything will be fine.'

'I locked myself in my room.'

'You *locked* yourself… *in* your room?'

'Yes. I sat on the window seat… to watch for Stephen's return.'

'How could you possibly watch out for our return when your room is at the front of the castle!' Clara ridiculed.

'Could anyone corroborate this, Mrs Taylor?'

'How would I know!'

'If you'll excuse me, sir?' Fawcett, in the process of adding Ava's cup and saucer to his tray, broke in. 'Joe McKinney told me he saw Mrs Taylor sitting at her bedroom window when he passed through the grounds. The time, to be precise, sir, would have been just before two o'clock.'

'Joe McKinney?' Dunderdale asked.

'Young Joe, the groom,' Stephen said. 'The head groom is also a "Joe".'

'Looks like you have your alibi, then, Mrs Taylor,' Dunderdale told her.

'Of course I do.'

At this point Sergeant Collins returned and said Lady de Trouville's maid had confirmed her lady *had* told her she was going for her afternoon nap but that she couldn't say any more for her lady always expressly forbids being disturbed during her 'sixth hour'. Thinking he'd much prefer the meeting of feminine minds, Gilbert Dunderdale bit down his lip.

Bringing an end to the questioning, Dunderdale called out to David, who was making a dash for the corridor. 'Two more things, Mr Rickard. Did your wife's footprints you spoke of become larger in size – *say* a man's size?'

'Yes,' David agreed, the small cut on his left brow already showing excellent signs of forming a scab.

'And the rumours – the non-financial ones we spoke of yesterday?'

'There's only the one.'

'Don't tell me, it concerns the kettle and the pot?'

'Then I won't tell you,' David said, already retracing his footsteps.

'I tell you what I'd like to do, right now,' Dunderdale said, when he was alone with Collins and Shaw, 'go up to the moor and take a look for myself. From what you said, Shaw, we could, between the three of us, easily track these footprints and see for ourselves!'

'Helm Wind won't allow it,' Shaw replied, now with the air of the expert, 'got right up now, it has.'

Dunderdale looked across to one of the large hall windows where the frozen snow was being ground against glass. 'If the Helm Wind really does carry rumours then I would expect it to etch out the name of our murderer on that window.'

'Sorry, sir?' both men replied.

'Nothing!'

'We could try tomorrow,' Collins suggested. 'There's a good chance footprints'll be there in morning – and Helm Wind will've passed by then.'

'Then it's settled. At first light.'

When dawn arrived, it cast the day's first light rays onto fresh snow, and as Smith chauffeured detective inspector and sergeant along the track towards the manor there was barely any evidence of his previous tyre tracks, let alone the ones from the evening before.

Dunderdale looked out the window, up to Cross Fell, and was met with a precarious blanket which threatened, if disturbed, to bring snow and snow... and more snow.

'It'll be deeper... up on't moor,' Collins told him.

'Damn and blast this weather!' was the response.

TEN

DUNDERDALE HOOKED HIS hat and coat on the stand behind the study door. 'It's the pagan story all over again.'

'It could've just been another walker, sir.'

'No, Shaw, if that were the case the walker would've been dressed for the outdoors same as everyone else, but our person of interest can't have been – can they?' Dunderdale asked both men.

'Because,' Collins began, 'if that were the case then Mrs Rickard's brain would've seen a walker but it didn't, it saw something different.'

'I'm going to speculate Mrs Rickard's catharsis related to her husband and youngest sister,' Dunderdale said.

'She couldn't stomach bein' close to 'em who'd betrayed her, that it, sir?' Shaw said.

'Same as our lass – no, nothing like that, I'd never betray her!' Collins divulged. 'I just meant if we've had a bit of a tiff she can't stand to be in same room as me.'

'Exactly,' Dunderdale said. 'Mrs Rickard's thoughts were busily concerned with her husband's infidelity so when her vision registers something in the distance, her mind processes exactly what the eye sees *not* what she thinks she's seeing, for that would mean she would have to be thinking about the pagan story and the spectre, and I think we can confidently say she wasn't.'

A bewildered look crossed Collins's face. 'So… if yer sayin' she described exactly what she saw then what she saw were the *spectre?*'

'Of course not!'

'You've lost me, sir.'

'What she saw, Sergeant, was someone who wanted her to believe she was seeing the spectre.'

'Someone with a… white dress pulled over their clothes…?' Shaw hesitated.

'And who could that someone be?' Dunderdale encouraged.

'The murderer, sir!'

'With the intention,' Collins added quickly, 'o' puttin' frighteners on Mrs Rickard. Bloody cruel if yer ask me…'

'Just like 'em that'd torture an animal afore slaughterin' it!' Shaw said.

'Bas—'

'Thank you, Collins,' Dunderdale interrupted. 'But, yes, a lot of trouble to go to before the act and all for the purpose of spelling out to Mrs Rickard her life was in imminent danger.'

'And you really think a woman'd do such a thing?' Shaw asked incredulously.

'Though I wouldn't rule out any sex at this stage, I never specified we were looking for a woman.'

'But…?'

'A man is perfectly capable of slipping a woman's dress over his garments.'

'A man… wearin' a woman's dress!' Shaw spoke with more incredulity.

'Spattered with red for effect!' Collins contributed.

'Finishing on that image, Shaw, I've a job for you.' Dunderdale passed a map of the estate across the desk. 'Mr Atkinson has arranged for a member of the outdoor staff to accompany you to the moor where you're to pinpoint on this map the exact locations of all noticeable physical changes within or close to the east boundary wall. First, though, find

207

Mr Rickard and ask him to mark a cross where he believes it was he discovered his wife. One more thing, Shaw… you're not to leave the place until you've searched the derelict farmhouse. Inside and out with particular focus on a white dress.'

'Yer've ruled out the husband then, sir?' Collins asked when Shaw departed.

'All of those within the walking party had opportunity – and Hera knows Mr Rickard's got the motive, what with the talk of his wife divorcing him—'

'By heck, sir, he's got a temper on him, that one!'

'As I was about to say, Collins… he fears he's losing his wife. *That* can make a man do desperate things *but* he's the one I can be sure isn't our attempted murderer.'

'Because o' Betsy. No one knows more than me that children make some o't best witnesses.'

'Not always, Sergeant, but yes, in the case of Miss Betsy I would agree with that statement. As regards Mrs Rickard, she's bloody lucky, that's what she is! I'm not proud of myself that she had to go through that ordeal but at least we now know with certainty she's not our murderer. In fact, Collins, I'm *more than* not proud of myself – I'm gravely disappointed; I should never have permitted liberty to trump safety!'

'Don't beat yerself up 'bout it, sir… Have yer wondered, sir, whether Mrs Rickard could've cooked whole thing up with Mr Atkinson, to try to throw us off the scent?'

'I'll grant you it's one hypothesis…'

'Thank yer, sir.'

'… though it's a bit of a wild one. If Mrs Rickard and Mr Atkinson are our culprits and it was organised for them to meet up on the moor in order to throw us off their scent, then they were tempting fate. Just think, Collins, if that were the case and he'd kept the pressure on too long…! *Besides*, Shaw's enquiries confirm Mr Atkinson's statement that he has alibis all over the estate.'

'Least we know for definite the murderer's motive is inheritance.'

'Which narrows the suspect list, but before we consider the sisters as our prime suspects, let's be positive we can unequivocally rule out Miss Markham. Forgetting the two hours needed to reach the farmhouse using the east track, we'll concentrate on the hour via the west track, meaning that although there would have been time for Miss Markham to travel up to the moor, there wouldn't have been the time for her to then hunt down Mrs Rickard, carry out the attack *and* return back in time for tea at fifteen hundred hours. Furthermore, Mr Rickard told us the attacker's footprints arrived *from* and fled *to* the north-east, meaning more time would need adding to her journey.'

'And cuttin' 'cross land makes the journey harder, what with it bein' off the beaten track.'

'Excellent point, Collins. Finally, the fact Miss Markham is a distant cousin with a greatly reduced possibility of her getting her hands on the inheritance means her motive is a weak one.'

'Not strictly true, sir.'

'Oh?'

'If it were her then granted she'd have to pop off a few more, but it's still doable, sir. Where is she now in line? Third?'

'Fifth.'

'Fifth?'

'Mrs Taylor, Miss Betsy' – Dunderdale counted off each finger – 'Miss Rose, Miss de Trouville *then* we reach Miss Markham. Mighty Ruler, Collins, it doesn't bear thinking about the young girls – like the Princes in the Tower!'

'Who would they be, sir?'

'Never mind.'

'So, we've ruled out Miss Susan Markham?'

'I'd say so.'

'Can't say I ever fancied her as the cold-blooded type, anyway.'

'That's because you're putting too much stock on a friendly character. Always remember, Collins, within each and every one of us lurks a potential murderer… only in some it's malevolently biding its time.'

'Original sin, sir?'

'I don't like to think of it in that way, Collins, as it predetermines we're born with evil in our hearts. I'm more inclined to believe nature has given us the tools to kill—'

'Like animals, sir?'

'We are animals, Collins. As I was about to say, nature also gave us free will to argue back against any such inclination. *Anyway*, returning to our list, we can rule Miss Markham out, as we can Lady de Trouville for the same temporal reason… *unless…*'

'She has an accomplice!'

'She does have a strong motive.'

'I thought there were no legal case for her to inherit, on account o't will sayin' only a blood heir could?'

'We understand that but she doesn't appear to. *Or*, possibly, she does know it and is still hoping to argue it out in a court of law. *Again*, there's no evidence of her and any potential accomplice.'

'The chief's nephew.'

'Are you doubting the word of your chief, Sergeant?'

'Right you are, sir.'

'Let's face it, Collins, we've nothing to point to in that regard.'

'Remember, though, sir, when yer interviewed her, she did threaten Mrs Rickard – something 'bout makin' sure she'd get the inheritance off her.'

'It wasn't an explicit threat, Collins.'

'It were *there*, sir.'

'Implicitly, one might say so, but it's tenuous.'

'Then we dismiss her, 'long with Miss Markham?'

'Hmm. Let's now consider the sisters, the top name being Mrs Taylor. If Mrs Taylor is our murderer then she's working with her husband for, whether she genuinely realises it or not, she does have an alibi *whereas* Mr Taylor has an advantage over his wife in that he was on the moor at the right time, *however…*'

'Constable Shaw, Mr Rickard, Betsy, Miss de Trouville and Mr Johnson were all witnesses he were over near the east wall before the fog moved in and when Mr Rickard appeared carryin' Mrs Rickard he were still there.'

'South-east of the crime scene, yes. And *yet* he does have a motive; upon Mrs Rickard's death, as Sir Henry's next heir-of-blood, Mrs Taylor would inherit a vast fortune,' Dunderdale said, thinking about all those numbers written down in ink.

'We also know he's often strapped for cash.'

'Temporary episodes, he would argue. And so now we arrive at the youngest sister, Miss Clara de Trouville. Similar story as Mr Taylor in that she and Mr Johnson were in much the same location before the fog moved in, as they were when Mr Rickard arrived carrying his wife. *Likewise*, she also has a strong motive.'

'There were two o' them, sir… many hands make light work.'

'You're thinking they did it together? Except we have Mr Rickard's statement stating there was only the one set of prints.'

'One set o' prints for Mr Johnson, sir. Miss de Trouville will've been one further up on't left, wearin' a white dress.'

'Interesting, Collins. I must admit I do have to entertain the idea Mr Johnson could have as much motive as Miss de Trouville.'

'Imagines himself as marryin' her?'

'An obvious supposition. Question is, did any of them – Miss de Trouville, Mr Johnson, Mr Taylor – have the time to leave their last known locations, travel further uphill than Mrs Rickard, cut across the moor south-west, locate her footprints, track her down, carry out the attack, travel back upland north-east then all the way back down again to arrive at the old farmhouse at the same time as Mr Rickard carrying Mrs Rickard?'

'Ten minutes, Mr Rickard said it took him to get down from scene o't crime to farmhouse. How much time have we to work with, sir?'

'The party left the manor at thirteen hundred, arrived at the old farmhouse at approximately fourteen hundred and Constable Shaw puts the time of the whole group coming back together again at fourteen hundred and forty hours.'

'Forty minutes. I'd say that's plenty enough time.'

'We have to factor in each time the attacker travelled north or north-east they were moving uphill *and* into a headwind – a Helm headwind at that! Conversely, as they travelled south or south-west the tailwind and downhill gradient will have offered some assistance. He or she might just make it, though *not* at a walking pace, and remember, it was you who spoke of it being harder terrain off the beaten track.'

'It were, sir,' Sergeant Collins acknowledged proudly.

'*And*, of course, this is reliant on the culprit being capable of navigating their way through dense fog to track down Mrs Rickard.'

'I'd say all three o' them are young enough and all look in good health to manage it, sir.'

'Then we'll agree not to rule any of them out. As for our murderer being someone from outside the family, I'm prepared to eat my Homburg if the motive turns out to be something other than the inheritance— *What is it*, Sergeant?'

'We've missed a possible alliance, sir. Youngest sister could be in league with Mr Rickard.'

'Ah, that! One problem, though, Mr Rickard has Miss Betsy for an alibi and Miss de Trouville has Mr Johnson. With regards to the latter, your hypothesis relies on Mr Johnson being an accomplice.'

'Again, doable, sir,' Collins replied, adopting the adjective Stephen had earlier used. 'The' could've promised him money.'

'He could have been financially induced, yes. Risky, though, even if plenty of lovers *have* made faithful killers by not giving one another away. Let us suppose you are correct and Mr Rickard and Miss de Trouville are crazily in love enough to consider removing the obstacle to their future…'

'That'd be Mrs Rickard – after all, it's now legal for a man to marry his dead wife's sister.'

'Correct, this would be a stroke of good luck, but once they bring in a third party the risk greatly increases. Plenty of individuals who've been party to murder have folded under interrogation, particularly when that individual is only a small cog in the machine. I would say Mr Rickard and Miss de Trouville both have above average intelligence and, having such common sense, I expect they would have been aware of this.'

'The' were stupid enough to have an affair – and to get found out,' Collins pointed out.

———

While they awaited Shaw's return, Dunderdale told Collins it wouldn't hurt to carry out another search of the castle. Collins asked if they were looking for a white dress spattered with some red substance to which Dunderdale confirmed they were, along with the dagger 'for this could be just the key to unlocking this investigation'.

Dunderdale commenced with the drawing room next door where, upon turning the door handle, he was at once hoodwinked by the voice of an angel.

'Ooh, I am sorry, sir,' the second housemaid said.

'I don't see why someone with a beautiful voice such as yours would deem it necessary to apologise, for you're likely to lift the spirits of even the most grief-stricken household.'

'It's an old one, sir – carol, that is. I must have something to keep me muddled thoughts occupied since I'm left alone. 'Course, by rights, I shouldn't still be cleanin' – supposed to be done early morning afore everyone's down but how can that be when I'm on me own! It's same every Christmastide with us both needed to deep clean ready for New Year that Ivy gets to laik in nursery! Then, I suppose that's right, I mean Ivy were here afore me so it's only right she gets more perks, eh. If I bide me time, Mum says, perks'll come me way soon enough. Anyway, sir, I were meanin' carol goes as far back as Sir Henry's sixteenth great-grandfather and a poem that were supposed to be 'bout Saint Nicholas and him savin' three kiddies. That's why I'm singin' it today, sir, what with today bein' Feast o' Holy Innocents.'

'Well, you'll receive no complaint from me! Tell me, what's your name?'

'Elizabeth, sir, though I prefer Lizzie. In't village the' call me Lizzie "Silver-Tone" – I'm in church choir, if yer see, eh.'

'I most certainly do see,' Dunderdale said, guessing the

other reason for her nickname being attributed to the colour of her hair. 'Now, Lizzie, is there anything you'd like to tell me regarding the murders of Sir Henry and Mr James Bowes?'

'I already told Mum I know nowt that'd put me in killer's mind – she sent me little brother round, twinin' on, she were, so he said, that she'd a mind to send for me to come home if she weren't so reliant on me wage.'

'So there's nothing you know that could help with my enquiries?'

'Nowt, sir. Now, I'm sorry but I must be 'bout me business else Mr Fawcett'll have something in his mind, eh.'

'Then I insist you continue with your carol for I too could do with some vigour injecting into my blood!'

Complying, the housemaid dusted ornately carved panels, curved window ledges and gilded portrait frames, her silver tones – '… *perdidit, dit, dit, perdidit, dit, dit, perdidit spolia princeps infernorum…*' – elevating the drawing room's cosy proportions while the inspector meticulously dismantled cushions from their seats, plants from their pots and drawers their bureau.

His search uncovering nothing, Dunderdale left Lizzie to her repetitive syllables and end rhymes and made his way across the hall.

'She shan't inherit his title… of that she can be sure,' Bertha told her company.

'Nobody would have inherited his title,' Clara corrected her.

'You've some strange laws in this land,' Chester remarked.

'There have to be standards…' Bertha retorted.

'Forgetting standards, Bertha and Clara are right,' Susan said. 'Even had James survived Henry – may his soul rest in peace! – he would have been found unworthy and so unable to have inherited the baronetcy. Women and bastards, the downtrodden of our society!'

'Steady on, Suzie,' Stephen laughed, 'do draw it mild!'

'Wouldn't you agree, Inspector?' Susan said to Dunderdale.

Refraining from making another comment regarding 'commoners', Dunderdale acknowledged Donnelly, who was standing outside the library door.

'Shouldn't you be resting, Mrs Rickard?' Dunderdale said, quickly closing the door to shield her from her family's conversation.

'On the contrary, Detective Inspector, I should be employed.'

'If you think so?'

'I do. I refuse to sit around and wallow in a state of self-pity and fear. I've given instruction for Tom to continue with the management of the estate, but I shan't make any decision about the inheritance until you find... *until* your enquiries are complete.' Ava turned a page of the opened ledger. '*And so*, remembering, as each New Year approached, Uncle's routine for checking the accounts, I thought a quick look at the books would offer me some employment.'

'Then while you do so, do you mind my inspecting the room?'

'Not at all.'

But Dunderdale left the room having found no hidden dress or dagger behind any row of books; Ava, similarly, struggling to find one discrepancy within Sir Henry's columns of figures.

Next door in the dining room, Turner was finishing off clearing away the breakfast items. When, upon Dunderdale's entrance, he proceeded to talk of snow, the detective inspector said he didn't wish to disturb him and would return later.

Moving up to the first floor, in the nursery Betsy deserted the construction of a Tudor house – leaving a mystified Rose, and equally perplexed Ivy, to battle with the placement of Lott's sturdy stone bricks – in order to interrogate the policeman over why he was on all fours like a dog, looking under her bed. Dunderdale replied he was in search of adult toys to which Betsy offered her assistance. Dunderdale explained these were the kind of toys only an adult would be able to see and when Betsy said *she'd* be able to see because her eyes always helped Martha to thread her cotton through her needle, he then added that these were the kind of toys that, if looked upon by a child, would immediately disappear. Although Betsy appeared to accept this explanation – it was the season of magic after all, she insisted on tailing Dunderdale, promising him that as soon as he instructed her to close her eyes with a 'NOW!' then she would do so.

Unfortunately, for both adult and child, there was no call for Dunderdale to shout any such command; nor would there have been any need for him to call out 'NOW!' had he permitted Betsy to shadow him on his remaining search, for in none of the rooms that he managed to gain access to – the list of rooms in his notebook ticked off accordingly – did he discover a white dress or a dagger.

He arrived back in the hall as Chester was commenting that he'd worked out what was missing from 'this joint' and that *that* something was a housekeeper. As Susan proceeded to provide Chester with the history of a power struggle between butler and housekeeper – in which butler had won out, subsequently scoring another point when successfully persuading his employer that the manor's requirements could be met without the housekeeper's replacement, Clara rose to meet David at the foot of the stairs.

Holding her cigarette holder seductively to her lips, she refused to double tap the polished stone instrument and, holding her nerve, looked up into David's face.

Relaxing, David reached into his pocket for his lighter.

Things are shifting, Dunderdale said to himself.

———

It had taken Constable Shaw almost four hours to return.

Dunderdale and Collins had just converged in the dining room – the former alerting the latter to the dining room not being on his list – when, as Collins was about to leave, Shaw walked in with a bowl of hot soup, compliments of Mrs Clarke.

'There you are, sir! Yer don't mind, do yer?'

'I don't, Constable, but Fawcett will so you'd better close that door behind you pronto!'

Hunkering down over his bowl of much-needed soup, Shaw said, 'Snow's gettin' heavier, sir. Looks like it's in for next couple o' days.'

'Never mind that! What have you discovered?'

Shaw pushed a weather-beaten map across the highly lacquered dining table. Unfolding the map, Dunderdale used the candelabras from the centre of the table to weigh down its corners and, to the sound of Shaw shovelling soup-dripping bread into his mouth, he studied the constable's heavily drawn crosses. Within moments he was drawing his sergeant's attention to a stile within the east boundary wall. 'See there, Collins… north-east of Mr Rickard's mark…'

'The stile' – Shaw reached into his trouser pocket – 'is where I found this…'

'I know I shouldn't be surprised, but I really never expected another!' Dunderdale took the black feather from Shaw and ran his fingers along its silky length.

'It were shoved under one o't stones, right next to where the stile cuts through the wall. Stuck out like a sore thumb, it were. Should've had more snow on it, is what I thought, but it didn't and I think it didn't because it had a bit o' shelter from't overhangin' coping stone 'bove it. If it'd been there a long time, more snow might've managed to get at it, but it looked to me, sir, like it'd only got a dustin' o' last night's snow on it.'

'You were right, sir,' Collins said, 'there's no escapin' Pearl's story.'

'It's not Miss Bell's story, Collins; granted, thanks to the Bell family, it enjoys posterity, but the story belongs to the de Trouville family. I'd say, this is an exact match for the feather found lying on Sir Henry's tongue and the one discovered within Mr Bowes's pocket.' Tapping the 'X' on the map – the word 'stile' scribbled crudely underneath – with the tip of the feather's shaft, Dunderdale pondered before saying, 'Would you say, Shaw, someone had tried to conceal it?'

'I would that, sir.'

Dunderdale traced the solid line on the map, that was the east boundary wall, down to the oblong filled with diagonal lines. 'And what of the old farmhouse?'

'Nothing, sir. No evidence, no garments, white or otherwise… and we scoured the whole place inside *and* out, as instructed.'

'And Collins and I have been scouring the castle. So far, no sign of any such white dress round here either.' Dunderdale pocketed the feather. 'You've done well today, Shaw – mind, it's not that you've redeemed yourself for you've nothing to prove; I take full responsibility for what befell Mrs Rickard yesterday.'

'Sir.'

'You any hunches then, sir?' Collins asked. 'A suspect?'

Shaw – a hunk of bread clamped in his mouth – awaited the answer from the lionised Detective Inspector Dunderdale of Manchester City Police.

'Without evidence, Collins, it's all circumstantial,' Dunderdale replied, refusing to commit himself. 'If only we could find the dagger used to slit the baronet's…' His voice petering off, Dunderdale regarded the blazing fire. 'Sergeant…'

'Sir?'

'Find me Fawcett.'

Fawcett's gaze was immediately drawn to Shaw sitting at the dining table with a bowl in front of him, then to the candelabras-cum-paperweights. 'Sir?'

'Tell me, Fawcett, were *all* of the chimneys cleared of daw nests in the autumn?'

'Yes, sir. *That is* the ones which were to be lit during the winter months. Sir Henry believes – beg your pardon, sir – Sir Henry believed in efficiency and did not wish to waste labour on clearing chimneys in which fires were never lit.'

'And which chimneys were these?'

'The library. The hall – on the side of the drawing room.'

'The library and the hall – closest to the drawing room. Any others?'

'The study.'

'The study – of course! Just why is that, Fawcett?'

'Although Sir Henry spent most of his time in there, he always swore by a cool room to keep the mind energised. Heat, he said, was likely to send one's mind to sleep.'

'Fair point, though I'd argue a freezing cold room is not conducive for writing either – likely to lock up the digits! And the first floor?'

'Knowing the guest list for Christmas, Sir Henry ordered

all bedroom chimneys to be cleared with the exception of two bedrooms that would be unused: the room between Miss Clara's and Miss Markham's rooms; and the one closest to Mr and Mrs Rickard's apartment in the east tower.'

'I make that five chimneys: library, one in the hall, study and two bedrooms. Any of these five have easy access?'

'With the exception of the kitchen, all chimneys are accessible via the ramparts. The apartment stacks are accessed through the east tower rampart, as is the study's stack; the unused bedroom closest to the east tower, which I just spoke of, is directly above the study so they share the same stack. Only the spiral staircase leads to this rampart. All other stacks are accessed via a door on the third floor. May I ask, sir, is one contemplating an inspection of said chimney stacks?'

'One is, Fawcett.'

'Then I would suggest extreme caution be taken, particularly with the east tower battlement,' Fawcett told him, Dunderdale wondering whether his tone had ever risen to convey an exclamation mark. 'It was a later addition with the crenellations merely a feature of low proportions and I don't need to remind you, sir, the conditions outside are treacherous.'

Shaw was left to finish his soup in peace while Collins followed Dunderdale out and down the corridor towards the east tower. Halting on the spiral staircase at the first floor, Dunderdale shouted down the landing to where Donnelly was now standing outside the Rickards' apartment door, a reminder for the constable to guard the lady with his life. Donnelly returned he would and Dunderdale, giving a nod, continued with Collins in tow.

Passing by Tom's apartment on the second floor, Dunderdale felt the steps weren't too demanding – considering he'd already climbed the staircase today – but by the time they reached the third floor he was already using the rope rail for support. Taking a breather outside Violet's apartment, Dunderdale contemplated first an inspection of the lower chimney stacks when a second wind came upon him, encouraging him onwards and upwards. At Sir Henry's apartment he paused to re-tie the short piece of rope, secured to and hanging from the rail, across the door – his earlier search of the baronet's apartment having resulted in no additional findings to Chief Constable Watson's own search.

Finally arriving at the top of the tower, Dunderdale struggled with the large key in the old door lock before then having to put all of his body weight behind him to inch the door open.

'Baby Jesus!' Collins exclaimed from a lower step.

'Just wait 'til you see the battlement – or, I should say, lack of!' Tightly gripping the door handle, Dunderdale stepped up and out onto the snow-covered rampart. 'Second thoughts, Collins,' he called over his shoulder, 'I'd better go this alone.'

According to Fawcett's description, Dunderdale was able to ascertain the stack almost within touching distance belonged to the study. The snow whipping round him, he made a step towards the chimney's rise that was only a little higher than the low crenellation; his shoe failing to gain purchase, he sensed gravity dragging him backwards and as he tried to readdress the balance, he overcompensated and was catapulted forwards; in that split moment Dunderdale didn't realise the quick reaction of his hands until he was immobilised on his knees in the snow with his arms hooked round the chimney stack. Holding on for what he believed to be a meaningful life, Gilbert Dunderdale watched his Homburg float down two storeys towards the third-floor roof.

'SIR!'

'STAY. WHERE. YOU. ARE! IT'S FINE, COLLINS… *I'M* FINE.'

Only a few feet away, tucked inside the tower's shell, Collins was gripped hold of the rope rail as he watched Dunderdale right himself. To reassure his aide, Dunderdale turned his head and, forcing a smile, breathed, 'Fawcett wasn't joking about the conditions being treacherous!'

Peering down into the stack, Dunderdale found the chimney to be bunged with snow. With the flakes settling onto his thinning hair, Dunderdale began industriously scooping away until the leather of his glove detected material that proved to be a twig. While un-weaving twig from twig, Dunderdale imagined he could hear lofty Latin echoes of Lizzie 'Silver-Tone's' contagious carol – *auditory remnants from my time in the drawing room*, he deduced since he'd locked the study behind him.

After the removal of a couple of handfuls of twigs, the day's weakened sun reflected a tiny ray of light. Dunderdale's initial logic was the object would turn out to be a stolen article pilfered and woven, without method, into this year's nest by an inquisitive daw. But, after carefully removing the object and holding it up in front of his face, Dunderdale turned again to Collins and this time the smile on his face was genuine. With even more care, he then extended an arm and deposited a blood-stained dagger into the paper bag Collins held out.

Not someone normally afflicted with a fear of heights, nevertheless the slip had unnerved Dunderdale and so he thanked all of the Greek gods and goddesses that there'd now be no need for him to have to travel the three sides of the tower in order to access the chimney stack feeding the apartments. For good measure, he was about to ask Artemis for a safe return to the stairs when something occurred to him.

Delving back into the chimney, he continued to dismantle the jackdaw nest and after stripping away another layer, there rested a second object – a glass bottle.

Eleven

'Whisky…? sir?'

The carol still reeling off within his eardrum, Dunderdale viewed the glass bottle sitting on its paper bag in the middle of the desk.

'Paris's not known for whisky, is it, though?' Collins continued.

'No, Collins, it's not.' No longer endowed with his inferior's eyesight, his spectacles perched on the end of his nose, Dunderdale leaned in close to the tiny label. 'Number Five… Channel? Chann-*ell*…? Paris. *And* where was it that I heard of "Number Five"…?'

'Lady de Trouville's perfume!'

'By Athena, you're right, Collins! And the word's *Cha-nel*! *Ch* as in *champagne*! *And*, if I'm not mistaken, it is perfume that Paris's known for.' Yet Dunderdale didn't think it looked like a perfume bottle. Lacking the generic ornamental fauna and flora mouldings, the glass bottle's form was made up of simple lines with an understated glass stopper sitting, he thought, oddly atop – Dunderdale experienced the urge to remove that stopper and to take a sniff of the empty vessel's innards but, following forensic protocol, he resisted. He supposed the perfume bottle's design was following the fashion of the day where women were no longer accentuating their bodily curves, whilst, paradoxically, exposing more of their flesh. 'I don't understand it,' he said, almost a mumble.

'It's the perfume bottle stolen from under the Christmas tree, sir,' Collins told him.

'Though I think you're right, that's not what I meant… Collins, I believe Lady de Trouville is still sitting in the hall, therefore, your job is to keep an eye on her – covertly, mind you! If she rises from her seat, you're to stop her. Use whatever excuse you can to keep her engaged – she's not to put so much as a toe on a stair tread!'

'Leave her to me, sir.'

As Dunderdale imagined, the lady of the manor's vanity had not allowed her to dispose of the empty perfume box that was standing proud in the centre of her dressing table. A plain biscuit-coloured box, its edges bordered with black and its seal broken. *So, this is modernity!* Dunderdale thought, realising its bottle would have stood out like a sore thumb amongst its ornate counterparts.

With a gloved hand, Dunderdale removed the glass bottle from its paper bag and lined it up, side-by-side, with the box: the heights, widths and depths were a match; the labels identical.

Content with the identification, Dunderdale was stowing the bottle back into its bag, readying to leave, when his attention was drawn to a thin red ribbon, barely an inch of it protruding from underneath one of the bottom drawers of Violet's dresser.

Removing the drawer, Dunderdale tracked the other end of the ribbon to where it was tied round one of two bunches of envelopes stowed in the cramped rear space of the drawer's shelf. Removing the bunches, Dunderdale saw the top visible envelopes were both addressed in an unrefined cursive hand to 'My Sweet Violet'. Each bundle was tied with a length of the dainty red ribbon, its tails ultra-long like those of the swallow, which he'd always regarded as a superfluous and pretentious addition – his friend Howard had laughed at that description before educating Gilbert that they were the male swallow's streamer feathers designed to attract the female.

Pausing to strain to listen and hearing no alarm call – the carol now irrigated clear from his ears – Dunderdale proceeded to skim through the first batch of letters. Written with mostly ill-formed characters, and some illegible words, each letter was dated prior to Violet having met Sir Henry – a meeting Dunderdale suspected to be not-so-chance. The contents were graphic in detail, of the shared love between 'Sweet Violet' and a man who always signed off with a 'P'; *one* Midsummer scene, upon it unwittingly materialising within his head, Gilbert Dunderdale found to be particularly revolting.

Stacking the envelopes back together, Dunderdale picked up the second bundle. Conscious of the time, he randomly removed an envelope and dated its letter to after the joining of hands of Violet and Sir Henry. P's style hadn't changed; heavily penned, the writing looked hurried, as though its author feared losing their train of thought. Just as hurriedly, Dunderdale read the lover's thoughts of the life they would have upon Sir Henry's demise: *Hold steadfast. The miser's years are numbered and his end will make you a rich widow – a very rich widow, my sweet, Sweet Violet.* The capitalised letters of her given banal name standing out on the page and symbolising P's love for his childhood friend. *Then it's true, Violet Olsen as was,* Dunderdale said to himself, *here is proof of your having enjoyed, and continuing to enjoy, sexual relations with the chief constable's nephew—!*

'THIS MUST BE A DIFFICULT TIME FOR YOU… *MY LADY*,' Collins warned his superior, his voice pouring in through the door which Dunderdale had left ajar – Collins must have found himself unable to deny the lady's toes.

'There's no need to shout,' Violet said.

'SORRY – *Sorry*, your ladyship.'

Dunderdale returned the letter to its envelope, slipped the envelope into its place, stacked the envelopes together and – his large fingers working with surprising dexterity – secured each batch with a delicate bow complete with its thin red swallow tail.

'I do thank you, Sergeant, for escorting me up to my room – it was a kind offer. All anyone else can think of is Ava! For fear of screaming, I have to say I've found it quite tedious… *Ava this, Ava that*… After all, it's not as though it's her husband that's been murdered…!'

The two batches of love letters bundled back into their nesting place – barely an inch of thin red ribbon once again trapped underneath a bottom drawer, Dunderdale made to close the door to the spiral staircase; hearing Violet's voice close in – '… I really do wonder if she planned it all… for sympathy…' – he was convinced his presence would be discovered. Collins, though, proved himself much better suited to playing detective than Dunderdale had given him credit for; as well as having already slowed their ascent, when the little landing came into view and he was confronted with the inspector through the open door, he abruptly halted with a 'MOTHER O' BABY JESUS!' and immediately began to massage a phantom cramp in his right leg.

'What's wrong with you!' Violet – not in sight – asked, her tone discourteous.

An impressed Dunderdale quietly closed the door and, from where he exited via the door adjacent to the staff staircase, he could see Collins still administering self-help.

'She's a foolish girl for havin' kept them,' Collins said when Dunderdale told him of his further discovery.

'It's not sentimentality that's guided this foolishness, either,' Dunderdale agreed, thinking of the perfume box.

'Shall I bring her back down, then, sir?'

'No, not yet, Collins. I'd first like to speak with her maid.'

Collins went to fetch Lady de Trouville's maid and Dunderdale waited, watching the door, his Homburg returned to the coat stand, courtesy of George, who'd led the rescue mission to retrieve it from the third-floor rampart.

'Ah, Mrs Carver, thank you for allowing me a moment of your time.'

'As long as it is a moment, Inspector, she's given me a list as long as your arm – that bell of hers doesn't stop ringing! D'you know,' she continued, forgetting her own urgency while Dunderdale carried out an eye measurement of what he'd always considered an average arm length, 'she's up there now – gone for a nap, already! She could learn something from Mrs Ava, she could. Had her life threatened, has Mrs Ava, but will you find her hiding and napping away? No, you won't. Like me, Mrs Ava's not afraid of real work.'

The maid's substitution of 'my lady' for less respectful pronouns was not lost on Dunderdale, as wasn't the fact May was evidently already seeking another lady to serve. 'Why I sent Sergeant Collins for you was to ask about Lady de Trouville's Christmas present posted to the manor.'

'That joke against her was nothing to do with me! And actually, when I think of it, the joke was more on me – fancy making me think I'd a present! Still, unlike some, *I* shan't complain.'

'I'd like to ask you about the packaging?'

'The packaging?'

'The outer packaging that the present arrived in. What did you do with it?'

'I must say, that's an odd question.'

'To which the answer is…?'

'Well, naturally, I threw it away.'

'*Where* did you throw it away?'

'Why, in the outside bin, naturally, along with the note.'

'Collins—'

'It won't be there,' May informed Collins, who was already making for the door. 'Each day, outdoor staff's tasked with sorting through the rubbish: most of it gets taken down to the village rubbish tip but things that can burn are burned.'

'Such as paper?'

'*Such as paper*. It'll be well and truly burned to ash by now… like the Christmas present wrappings.'

'Of course,' Dunderdale said, recalling the small plume of white smoke that had risen from the vicinity of the stable block when he and Collins had followed Harry James across the snow-covered lawn on Boxing Day. 'Then do you happen to remember the postmark?'

'No, I don't.'

'If you would take a moment to think… perhaps you remember glimpsing the place of posting?'

'I hardly think so. I was more interested, Inspector, in what I thought was my present inside the package!'

'That's lucky, Collins,' Dunderdale said when May left to polish *her* shoes.

'What is, sir?'

'You'd drawn the short straw.'

'Sir?'

'If they weren't partial to a bit of burning, then, right now, you'd be down at the village rubbish tip.'

'In that case, sir, I count myself very fortunate and thank the outdoor staff for their efficiency.'

'Except now we'll never know the place of posting!'

'Yer mean if it were posted in Carlisle?'

'Hmm.' Dunderdale reached for ink and paper and, after writing down a full page of instruction, he said, 'Right then, Collins, I'd say Shaw's had sufficient rest.'

One foot on a dining table chair in the servants' hall, an elbow on his knee and his chin rested in his hand, Shaw said something to which Lizzie giggled.

'You never told me,' Dunderdale said to Collins, 'that Shaw was such an entertaining man.'

Almost toppling the chair, Shaw stood up and straightened his uniform. 'Sir.'

'Elizabeth,' Fawcett said, curiously appearing from behind Dunderdale and Collins, 'is this you finished for the day?'

'No, Mr Fawcett.'

'I thought not. Off you go.'

'Yes, Mr Fawcett.' Rising from her seat, Lizzie departed, her rosy cheeks further reddening.

'Is there anything I can help with, sir?'

'No, thank you, Fawcett. And rest assured, we'll be out from under your feet in a moment.' Dunderdale turned to Shaw. 'I'm glad to see you're revived from the elements for I've another task for you.'

'Sir?'

Dunderdale set down two paper bags on the dining table. 'The contents of each of these bags require taking to Appleby Police Station – without delay. As I don't want the items in question exposed to the elements any more than they already have been, Smith's kindly going to take you. He'll meet you out front.'

'He's just at the stables,' Collins added, 'fillin' the motor up with benzole.'

'Sir.' Shaw reached for the bags.

'One moment, Shaw. There's also this letter for Chief Constable Watson – explaining.' Dunderdale refused to immediately relinquish said letter upon Shaw taking hold of it. 'When I say I'm entrusting you with a great responsibility, I think you can guess the contents within the bags. Know that back in Manchester I wouldn't trust just any old constable with the safekeeping of one of these bags, let alone two.'

'I understand, sir.'

'Good.' Dunderdale yielded the envelope. 'Then jump to it.'

Dunderdale and Collins followed Shaw through to the hall and while Shaw waited in the vestibule, Dunderdale and Collins looked out from one of the hall's great windows.

'I hope they do manage to get through,' Dunderdale worried.

'The' will. It's not too deep yet and roads will've been cleared in parts by locals. Well then, sir, hasn't today been a day o' discoveries! It's got to be the missin' dagger – hasn't it, sir?'

'The staining would suggest so.'

'I know hawthorn's often been used for handles as it's considered lucky but there's not many gruesome-lookin' handles like that one!'

'It *was* hideous,' Dunderdale agreed, thinking of the hawthorn, which looked to have been contorted into a rope effect, the inner twisting of dark grey bark that had blackened with age now scored with blood. 'At every turn in this investigation we come up against that damn pagan story!'

'Not so lucky for Sir Henry, that dagger weren't,' Collins continued. 'It were also said yer'd be protected under a hawthorn tree on account of its thorns… only to then go and plant it in hedges everywhere to keep the likes of us out!'

'Change, Collins, that's what it was, not to mention a different time. Don't fear, though, things are changing again.'

'So the' say, sir… so the' say.'

Dunderdale looked at his watch. 'What's keeping Smith?'

'He'll be round soon enough, sir,' Collins reassured him while buffing the silver buttons of his tunic with his black wool gloves. 'What a funny-lookin' perfume bottle that were! Remember me sayin' poison were a woman's weapon, sir? Well, perfume's also a woman's thing.'

'Yes, Sergeant, I can see where you're going with this' – the motor car rounded the corner – 'a woman bought the perfume and, if logic follows, then our murderer is also a woman, *except* men often buy their wives perfume.'

'*And* man, woman he's courtin', *and* – God forgive me for sayin' such a thing – men their lovers.'

'*Their lovers…*' Dunderdale repeated, '… *Collins*, after Shaw!'

———

It was New Year's Eve and while preparations were under way for the night's celebrations, Dunderdale – still waiting to hear the answers to his questions – was complaining to Collins. 'Just what the Zeus are they playing at!'

'I suppose the' do things different, sir.'

'There's only one way to find answers, Collins, and that's to get your backside off your cosy cushion and go ask!'

'I only meant the'll be busier, sir.'

'No busier than Manchester, Sergeant.'

'I suppose you'd know, sir.'

Settling down into the seat Sir Henry had for so long occupied, Dunderdale rubbed his hands together with intensity.

'You certain I can't ask Fawcett to get a fire goin', sir? I wouldn't mind some heat, myself – snow's brought a real bitter cold with it last few days.'

'It's a tempting proposition, Collins, but we'd better not. To light a fire would mean removing the daw's nest from the chimney and *that* would alert the murderer to our discovery.'

'Right you are, sir. I must say, I liked the word yer used when yer told Shaw to get right back here.'

'You mean when I told him he's to *hightail* it from Appleby Police Station to Crowthwaite Castle when the replies come in? I overheard Mr Johnson using the word when he was saying how he'd *hightailed* it out of the south.'

'*Hightail*… I like it.'

'Until Shaw does "hightail it", we can do no more except sit… and wait.' And, his vision concentrated on his hanging Homburg, Dunderdale began tapping out a pattern on his teeth with a fingernail. It was a restlessness Charles Collins had not witnessed in the week of his having known him.

Gilbert Dunderdale also recognised this disquietude. It was nothing new. He'd experienced the same feeling during previous investigations and it was always when he was close to uncovering his suspect. It was invariably the fitting together of the final components that brought on this state of unease and as there'd never been a case that had foiled him yet, he didn't know whether his nerves were likely to crumble should the reverse ever become true.

'Keep yer pecker up, sir. Yer'll hear back soon enough. At least yer've had reports back confirmin' yer found both murder weapons.'

'It's never just one man's work, Collins, but yes, we have that at least to be thankful for. The pathology reports are conclusive: the blade matches that which killed Sir Henry – its length and thickness consistent with the neck wound, while the staining has been confirmed as human blood – a match for Sir Henry's blood type...'

'You were hopin' for fingerprints, though, weren't yer, sir?'

'Yes, I was... *then again* it's usually a case of sod's law that the murderer wears gloves when carrying out the act *and* when disposing of the weapon. A lot of hard work is what's required in this line of work, Collins, but there's always got to be a tad of hope – without hope, there'd not be many of us doing this job! *Fortunately*, as we hoped, the perfume bottle does contain traces of arsenic trioxide; *unfortunately*, the murderer once again slipped on their gloves before they handled the bottle to administer the poison and when disposing of it in the chimney stack.'

'*And* when he or she put the poison in't bottle, sir. Do yer think this were done before it were sent out in't post?'

'Yes, I think it was.'

'A clever way to sneak it into't manor, it were! What I don't understand, though, is why go to the bother o' washin' the champagne glass but not the perfume bottle? Unless there weren't time – no, that don't make sense, either, for if the'd time to wash a glass then it were hardly much more time to also wash a bottle, now, were it!'

'Ah, Collins, you've just taken from the tips of my fingers the very piece of jigsaw I know to fit into one of three remaining blanks, *but*, like me, you're realising it to be a stubborn piece!'

Collins, doing a poor job of holding back a proud smile, decided to take his superior up on his offer and settled deeper into his seat to bide his time – listening to a rhythm on bone while he did so.

Struggling with his own instruction, the rhythm suddenly

ceased and, with a scrape of wood on stone, Dunderdale was up and pacing the study's square. A couple of laps later he paused at the bookshelves and after scrutinising book spines and the odd object he finally settled on a photograph, Collins appearing at his shoulder. Within a few moments, Dunderdale was off on another pace and Collins shuffled closer to the bookshelf.

The framed photograph was of a younger Sir Henry outdoors in winter, standing within a white landscape beside his kill – a white stag with a dark shadow on his breast. Collins counted twelve points to its antlers, like the white stag's head mounted high in the hall. Sir Henry was holding the rifle that had ended the animal's life with one hand, in the other his hip flask. Collins leaned in closer to follow the contour line that ran downhill to the dilapidated farmhouse in the distance, before following it back up again to Sir Henry.

'It seems sacrilege, doesn't it,' Dunderdale said, breaking in on Collins's grey matter activity, 'to kill something so pure. I've never been able to fathom why we think *this* for this animal other than the religious connotations surrounding its colour.'

'It's not that, sir…'

'Then what is it that's furrowed your brow, Sergeant?'

'I didn't get it before, sir, but I do now.'

'Didn't get *what*, Sergeant?'

'Something young Betsy said…'

A few minutes later, Dunderdale was pondering on Collin's recount. 'You remember my wondering *why* arsenic trioxide?'

'I do, sir. Smith were drivin' us to Appleby at the time.'

'Well, now I know.'

'Sir?'

'Historically, the substance has been called the "inheritance powder" – of course, I always knew this, but I'd been thinking about the motive from the wrong angle! I really do think there was never a choice for our murderer, concerning the poison – it always had to be arsenic trioxide. I congratulate you, Collins, you have just managed to fit the piece of jigsaw into its allotted place!'

'Are we there then, sir?'

'Not quite, Collins. Remember… I spoke of three blanks…?'

'Then yer still holdin' two pieces o' jigsaw in yer fingertips.'

'The replies I'm waiting on,' Dunderdale agreed.

'But can we prove what I just told yer, sir?'

'I'm not sure we can but that's not going to stop us from trying. Collins, fetch me Mr Johnson. *Then*,' Dunderdale added as Collins reached the door, 'there are two rooms which require searching for a particular item…'

Collins returned ten minutes later. He noted Chester once more seated cosily in the hall and when he opened the door to the study, he was met with Shaw, who had arrived only a moment before after 'hightailing it' from Appleby.

Dunderdale was busily scrutinising a document and when he raised his head, his eyes were flooded with adrenaline. 'Shaw, I want you and Donnelly to round up the family and guests along with Mr Atkinson and Fawcett. I'd like to see them all in the hall in *say*… fifteen minutes.'

'Yes, sir.'

Shaw left and Collins placed a paper bag on the desk in front of his superior.

'Collins's – Dunderdale, more interested in Shaw's delivery, slapped the document zealously with the back of his hand – 'all of the blanks are now filled in! We have our proof!'

TWELVE

'The natural order permits neither the lord nor the lady of the manor to invite a servant to take a seat in the family's private areas, sir,' Fawcett replied.

'As you wish,' Dunderdale said. 'Mr Atkinson?'

Tom joined Fawcett by the grand staircase. 'Thank you, Detective Inspector, but I too would prefer to stand.'

David garbled something into his whisky.

Dunderdale had chosen *his* place, standing in front of the Christmas tree, whose needles looked petrified, clinging to their branches, awaiting epiphany.

After double-checking Sergeant Collins and Constables Shaw and Donnelly had all exits covered, Dunderdale thanked everyone for joining him.

'Not before time,' Violet said from the seat closest to the fire, 'I've tonight to get ready for!'

'Life must go on.' Clara spoke flippantly, none of her hypocrisy audible.

'There's plenty of time,' Susan told Violet.

'I hope this means we'll be able to leave as soon as the passes are clear,' David mentioned.

'Oh, I do hope so, Stephen,' Bertha said.

'I'm sure it will mean that, old girl.'

'As I previously explained,' Dunderdale replied, 'no person here has been held against their will. *Now*, if we could begin... As with the story Miss Bell tells the new arrival to Crowthwaite, the unfolding of the murders which took place here at Crowthwaite Castle on Christmas Day begins with a "murder of crows". As you're all aware, for the pagans, the sacrifice was an offering to their gods and goddesses in return for a bountiful harvest and good health. Simply put, it was about survival. Many centuries later, the story diverged when Sir Henry de Trouville – third baronet, if I remember correctly – re-enacted the sacrifice. I can't speak for the then lord of the manor's motivations, and although one could argue his logic was his son's survival, when Miss Bell told me the story, I heard of one person's survival, not a whole tribe's… something entirely different. Mrs Rickard, recount for us, if you would, your family's motto.'

'*Per familia, divitiae et immortalitas affuo.*'

'In English, please, for a poor-learned man.'

Ava hesitated and Clara, sighing, said, 'Not even now when Uncle's dead can you bring yourself to deviate from the Latin! "Through family, wealth and immortality flow", Detective.'

'Thank you, Miss de Trouville. *Through family, wealth and immortality flow.* An archaic and materialistic outlook still being regurgitated in the twentieth century by the late Sir Henry. Gone is the story's moral of the collective community working together for survival; replaced with aristocracy's individualistic outlook, the de Trouville's story focuses on family wealth and succession. On self-preservation, if you'll pardon my candour. Likewise, the nature of the murders of Sir Henry and Mr Bowes was unconcerned with human sacrifice for the many. No. Its motivation was purely one of inheritance – of this there's no dispute. Mr Bowes was murdered because he was named as the sole beneficiary of the Crowthwaite Manor estate and we know this because Sir Henry's murder then immediately followed; further proof of the motive came only a couple of days later with the attack – no, we shall call it what it was – the *attempted murder* of Mrs Rickard.

'Last Wednesday, Sergeant Collins and I paid a visit to Miss Bell's home, "Crowdundle"; a charming cottage though it is, there's just no getting away from the crow, is there! I recall one particular moment in her story – not of the third baronet's reincarnation of the pagan "murder of crows" sacrifice, rather the longevity with the sacrifice being practised through the next few successions of the de Trouvilles when the father made a sacrifice of a murder of crows as an offering to the revived pagan gods in the hope it would guarantee a healthy line of male successors. And it did... until Sir Henry, tenth baronet.' Dunderdale, sensing the baronet's presence, glanced across the hall. 'I believe that *family – children* – lie at the heart of this investigation. *But* how can this be when Sir Henry had reached his twilight years having not sired a child? Leaving aside James Bowes, not one child was known to have been conceived throughout the term of Sir Henry's three marriages' – Violet crossed her legs – 'so it can't very well be *his* children at the heart of all this. Remind me, Collins, the strength of a father's emotions for his children. The exact words please.'

'"Give our lives".'

'What does it mean, Collins?'

'That us fathers would give our lives for our children.'

'*Give. Our. Lives.*' After a pause, Dunderdale added, 'Is that not so, Mr Taylor?'

'It is indeed, Detective.'

'I believe when you spoke the three words to Sergeant Collins, you spoke them with conviction. A conviction that one day you may very well end up sacrificing your own life for that of young Betsy and Rose – your reasoning, not mine.'

Stephen appeared confused.

'I imagine you were smart enough to realise the possibility you might one day pay the price for the taking of another's life… two lives, to be precise.'

'I say, now look here, one can't go around making such claims, and I'm not sure what good it will do you,' Stephen protested, while the face of every other person was looking upon either the accused or the accuser with just as much incredulity – Susan, the exception, was regarding Dunderdale with concentrated thought. 'Only a corrupt copper would be able to produce evidence against an innocent man and, if I've read you correctly, Detective, you're an honest man, though I'll grant you even an honest man is entitled to his mistakes.'

'I appreciate your concern for how I've conducted the investigation, as I do those previously expressed by Mr Rickard, for I've never wished for any human being to look upon the black cap, the same as I've always hoped those who contemplate murder would remember the value of life before it's too late. Unfortunately, Mrs Rickard's attacker had no such change of heart – her life was saved only by her husband's quick thinking. Fawcett,' Dunderdale added while giving Collins the nod, 'if you wouldn't mind clearing the coffee table.'

While they did as asked, Dunderdale – appreciating the fire's comforts – removed a pair of gloves from his pocket and proceeded to put them on; a long-drawn-out process as he filled the time by employing his forefinger in the action of diligently prodding the fabric between each finger until it made contact with the skin fold.

'Thank you, Collins,' he said when the sergeant set down four paper bags and an unfolded map of the estate on the coffee table. After directing his audience's attention to each walker's given positions on the map, Dunderdale pointed out the stile marked with Constable Shaw's cross and explained

241

how simple it would have been for any one of the walkers, using the fog as a shield, to follow the east boundary wall upland until they happened upon *that* stile, and then to turn left and follow a straight line downhill in a south-west direction where they could intersect a set of footprints in the snow. 'Mrs Rickard's footprints.'

'It's plausible,' David said, edging forward in his seat towards the map, 'but where's your proof?'

'We must give credit to Constable Shaw, not only for realising the stile in the wall higher upland to be a marker, but also for his discovery of this' – Dunderdale removed a feather from one of the paper bags – 'which was discovered partly concealed under a stone in the wall… next to the stile.'

'A stile and a feather – this is your evidence against Stephen!' Clara said disbelievingly.

'*The stile* is a physical change in the wall which I believe was a marker for the murderer to alter their direction of travel. If you care to take a look at the map, you will see it is north-east of the mark made by Mr Rickard of the location of his wife's attack, the location where he saw footprints travelling to and from the scene. *The feather* is evidence the attempted murder of your sister is linked with the murders of Sir Henry and Mr Bowes – the link being the pagan story and the feather being identical to the one found lying on Sir Henry's tongue and the one discovered in Mr Bowes's pocket. Three daw tail feathers. I believe the murderer planned to leave this feather about Mrs Rickard's body' – Ava's eyes only briefly closed – 'but when disturbed, fleeing, they realised it would be sheer stupidity to keep the feather on their person. And so they decided to discard it – not to the ground, though, but concealed within the wall where it could not be blown downwind along with them.'

'You *believe* a lot, Detective,' Clara replied, '*quite* a lot that I'm reminded of childhood tales.'

'What you say regarding the stile and feather may be true *but* – as Clara points out – neither is proof of *I* being the murderer!' Stephen protested.

'Of course not,' Bertha agreed.

'You're right, Mr Taylor, taken together these two objects are not sufficient evidence,' Dunderdale permitted and, pausing in his speech, he popped the feather back into its bag while Tom, now taking an interest in the proceedings, seated himself down on the stairs; Fawcett remained standing. 'I, therefore, suggest we travel further back… to Sir Henry's murder…'

'For which you have my alibi, as given to the chief constable – remember? I was sleeping by Bertha's side the whole night. What little night's sleep we had after James's tragic death, that is.'

'Yes, according to the alibis given, everyone within these castle walls was sleeping at the time of Sir Henry's murder,' Dunderdale said, delving into a second bag and removing its contents.

'Then it was the hunting dagger!' Stephen remarked with surprise.

'The irony,' David said.

'You recognise it, Mr Taylor?' Dunderdale asked.

'None better. The amount of times I've seen it mounted inside the gun cabinet when retrieving Winnie – though it's usually clean and polished.'

'Is that—?'

'*Blood*, my lady? It most certainly is. Your husband's, to be precise.'

Violet's rose-rouged cheeks frosted over; Bertha looked anywhere but; Tom bowed his head.

'If asked, Sergeant Collins would recall my hopes of finding the dagger used in the murder of Sir Henry. He would tell you how I hoped the dagger could be the key to our solving the investigation. Alack, although containing traces of blood matching that of Sir Henry's blood group, no fingerprints were to be found. The last clean and polish you gave it, Fawcett, was exceptional!'

The slight rise of Fawcett's shoulder communicated an inconvenience and Dunderdale reached for a third paper bag.

'Why have you my gloves?' Stephen asked when its contents were removed.

'Excellent, Mr Taylor, you have identified this pair of black leather gloves to be your property and, when I send them off to the laboratory, I'm confident traces of blood matching that of Sir Henry's blood type will be discovered upon them – within the seams, would be my guess.'

The whole room now looked to Stephen.

'I doubt that very much and if you do happen to find that to be the case then the only explanation could be the murderer used my gloves in order to incriminate me!'

'A reply I've heard one too many times! Sometimes, I must admit, the accused is telling the truth.' Closely inspecting each glove, Dunderdale added, 'I imagine you cleaned them the best you could and that you dared not risk disposing of them as their absence would be noticeable when venturing outdoors.'

'Some other person may have had the need to clean them, but not I!'

'No?' Dunderdale placed the gloves down carefully on top of their bag and reached for the final paper bag, removing and centring its item on top of the map.

'Chanel Number Five!' Violet exclaimed, making a grab for the bottle.

'Please refrain from touching the evidence, my lady.'

'Evidence for what?' Violet said. 'Larceny—? Just a minute… there's no perfume left!'

'How hilarious,' Clara laughed.

'So it was you!'

'*That* would rely on my being interested in you and I'm not remotely so.'

'To steal a present is one thing, but then for you to go and empty the whole of the perfume away – *how cruel!*'

'How many more times, I know nothing of your damn perfume! Though, I must say, whoever did do it knows it to be a necessary evil – the thought of such a marvel to have been wasted on your skin!'

Violet's jaw dropped, but she'd have to learn to fight her own corner for neither Ava nor Susan issued any rebuke, both having agreed to use silence as the best weapon to blunt the sharpness of Clara's tongue.

'This' – David jabbed his finger towards the bottle – '*this* is what the fuss has been all about! It doesn't even look like a perfume bottle! But then I suppose that's because it signifies a new world order being sold as liberation. Pity the women aren't smarter…'

'Now is not the time for facetiousness,' Susan reminded him.

'I'm being perfectly serious… the fairer sex, they're lapping it up.' And looking across to his wife he asked whether she'd be making a purchase. Ava cocked her weapon of silence. '*Anyway,*' David was addressing Dunderdale again, 'do make up your mind who the accused is: first it was Stephen, now you're saying it's Clara!'

'I wish everyone would stop saying I stole the damned perfume!'

'Clara ain't no thief,' Chester said.

'We're not dealing with a thief, Mr Johnson. *If* we could return to the perfume bottle, I'd like to tell you about its discovery.'

'Then do get on with it,' David said.

'It was discovered, Mr Rickard, hidden amongst a daw's nest, in a chimney… along with the dagger.'

'Why would Violet's perfume be hidden with the dagger used to murder Henry?' Susan asked.

'The simple answer is the bottle contains traces of arsenic trioxide.'

The accusatory stares of those present split evenly between Violet and Clara, the latter appealing to her brother-in-law, 'David, darling, why do you look at me in that way…? You don't believe—!'

'You say,' Susan broke in, 'the dagger and bottle were discovered in a chimney – which one?'

'The study. Do you know, I've asked myself, why *this* chimney? Aside from the obvious of *a)* it being one of the most secluded chimneys, *and b)* the increased possibility of its daw nest not having been removed, I think the answer is something of a disturbing joke. One might say, the final insult to Sir Henry's memory.'

'Are you talking of the chimney stack at the top of the east tower?' Clara said in an attempt to deflect suspicion away from herself.

'I'm not the only one in the east tower!'

'No. You're not,' David agreed, turning his head slightly until Tom was within his peripheral vision.

'Anyone,' Dunderdale spoke authoritatively, 'I repeat, *anyone* could have accessed the east tower rampart. *Now*, if you'll recall my hopes of discovering a set of fingerprints on the dagger having being dashed, what I'd not realised was although a murder weapon would offer my biggest clue, it wouldn't be the dagger. Sergeant Collins's initial thought was the bottle had housed whisky. It was at this time, when we were pondering over the bottle's use, that Collins remembered the missing perfume. I have to agree with my lady, it was indeed a cruel joke… to take a Christmas present and leave the recipient with only the wrappings…'

'I'm glad someone appreciates how upsetting it's been!' Violet said.

'In reality, though, this bottle shouldn't exist. That's correct, isn't it…' Dunderdale gave a dramatic pause while taking in each and every person, then, resting his vision, he said, 'Miss de Trouville?'

'I knew it!' Violet shrieked, overpowering Clara's denial.

'*What* do you know?' Bertha asked Violet, clearly confused. 'That Clara stole your perfume or that she's the murderer?'

'Take care your *boots* don't trip you up, sister.'

'As you yourself are aware, Mrs Taylor,' Dunderdale said, cutting off Violet's accusation of thief *and* murderer, 'your younger sister understands the perfume not yet to be on the market—'

'I'm sure I'm aware of no such thing!'

'After making their enquiries,' Dunderdale continued, ignoring the denial, 'Scotland Yard have confirmed what you both understood to be correct: they could find no perfume named Chanel Number Five – or *Chanel Numéro Sink*, if you prefer—'

'*Cinq*,' Clara pronounced, 'rhymes with "sank", Detective, as in "I *sank* to the darkest depths in despair!"'

'I thank you, Miss Clara de Trouville, for your eloquence,' Dunderdale returned. 'Scotland Yard could find no perfume named *Chanel Numéro Cinq* available for purchase *anywhere* in London. It would appear the perfume is not due for release until late next year.'

'That can't be – it's right there!' Violet said emphatically.

'Yes, my lady, it is,' Dunderdale concurred.

'Will you stop speaking in riddles!' David said, clearly irritated.

'I apologise, Mr Rickard, and ask for your forbearance. You see, the whole story concerning the perfume was a riddle within itself. The boxed bottle that arrived at the manor wrapped for the season and packaged for the post never contained any perfume…'

'But it must have!'

'No, my lady, what I say is correct: the bottle contained no trace of perfume. Prior to poison being added, the bottle was empty… and had been for well over a year.'

'Just when I thought we were making progress.' David rose to pour himself a refill.

'The origin of this empty perfume bottle,' Dunderdale began, projecting his voice for David's benefit, 'concerns a young lady from London who, like Lady de Trouville, heard of the creation of a perfume by the designer, Miss Gabrielle Chanel…'

'"Coco" Chanel,' Clara enlightened him.

'Are we to be told the name of this young lady and her connection with Crowthwaite Manor?' David asked, seating himself back down.

'All in good time, Mr Rickard. First, I'd like to introduce another lady, an older lady who, on the fifth of May, nineteen twenty-one, was fortunate to have been invited to Miss *Coco* Chanel's launch party. I say fortunate, because it was at this party in Paris that Miss Chanel made a gift of her perfume to a select few of her high-society friends. Our older lady, however, chose not to sample her perfume, instead making it known during her London circuit the following year she could perhaps be induced to part with her "precious" gift…'

'For a nominal fee, no doubt,' David said. 'I suppose this is where the younger lady comes in?'

'It is, Mr Rickard. The young lady in question had a wealthy "benefactor" who secured the winning bid. What I've just relayed to you was told to Scotland Yard during their enquiries, the young lady adding how she'd loved the fragrance so much that she'd doused her skin, clothes and even bedding with it. Reluctant to be parted with this symbol of fashion and wealth, the lady kept the empty bottle boxed and neatly presented on her dressing table. I saw a similar display,' Dunderdale added, singling out Violet, 'only a few days ago.'

'The young lady's not *me*!'

'A few *months* ago,' Dunderdale continued, leaving Violet reeling, 'the lady in question was paid a final visit by her benefactor. Afterwards, when he'd left, she noticed the box, along with empty perfume bottle had disappeared. *This* is how a perfume bottle which should not exist stands before us and *why* it is devoid of said perfume.'

'If you're saying Violet brought the empty perfume bottle and box with her when she moved into the manor, why did she then send it to herself through the post?' Clara asked.

'I didn't!'

'She didn't.'

'But she is the young lady who you talk of?'

'No, I'm not!'

'No, she's not.'

David's grip of his glass tightened. 'I'd say now's a good time for you to reveal the name of the young woman.'

'Her name is Miss Lydia Shelton.'

'Then—'

'Her benefactor was Mr Taylor... your brother-in-law.'

'Stephen, what do they mean?' Bertha asked.

'If I did buy an expensive bottle of perfume that doesn't prove this is the same bottle!' Stephen hastened. 'What you need to realise about Lydia, Detective, is she's vindictive... She resents that I came to my senses.'

'Miss Shelton said she would be willing to take the stand to testify to the fact that you gifted her a bottle of *Chanel Numéro Cinq*.'

'It still doesn't prove this is the same perfume bottle!'

'Miss Shelton's testimony will state how she'd ended her relationship with you and her surprise when you later turned up on her doorstep, claiming the reason being you felt the relationship had ended on bad terms. She told the detective, she would swear to it being only after this visit when the box and its contents were missing. According to the detective, she's still kicking up quite a fuss about it, to this day accusing you, Mr Taylor, of "pilfering" – so much of a fuss, the detective felt compelled to ask if she'd like to press charges to which she answered what was the point when it was empty.'

'You do know how to pick them... You truly are a fool!'

'Clara, sister, this is no joking matter! You do realise this is not just about some stupid perfume – the detective is trying to set me up as a murderer!'

Ava rose from her seat and Stephen, his tone rising, accused Clara: 'Look what you've gone and done! Ava now fears to sit beside me!'

'I'm *accusing* you of murder, Mr Taylor, there's a huge difference,' Dunderdale distinguished as Ava joined him by the Christmas tree, taking the vacant storyteller's chair. 'I do wonder if the idea of concealing the poison within the perfume bottle first entered your head when your unsuspecting wife told you of Sir Henry's request for Miss de Trouville to purchase the perfume for his wife? Mr Atkinson, do you happen to remember the date when your employer asked you to write the letter?'

'Not the exact date but it was after the wedding, in September.'

'I told Bertha of the request when we met for lunch on the last Friday,' Clara mentioned, 'which, if I remember correctly, was the twenty-eighth.'

'Miss Shelton told Scotland Yard the date of Mr Taylor's final visit to her flat was Saturday the twenty-ninth.'

'Stephen? Stephen, who is this Miss Shelton?' Bertha cried.

'Oh, for heaven's sake, Boots, Lydia Shelton is Stephen's mistress!' Clara sighed in exasperation.

Bertha, her complexion now matching that of her older sister, appealed for her husband's denial.

'I'm sorry, Bertha,' he disappointed her, 'I'm afraid what Clara says is true, though Lydia's no longer any claim to the title. Don't look like that, old girl! Come now, you know the survival of marriage sometimes demands the strains and pressures, only a husband can experience, be relieved through other means.'

Bertha muttered this wasn't the place for such discussion, but she really did wish he had spoken to her of *these* strains and pressures.

'Really, Boots, d'you expect us to believe you knew nothing of the affair? You truly are infuriating! For myself, when the rumour reached my ear, I let it waft on by. After all, I'm nobody's wife... if I were, I would know how to keep my man.'

251

The two sisters held one another's stare... until the younger sister's lids folded, and when Stephen reached for his wife's hand, Bertha gave him the cold shoulder – fingers and thumbs poised, ready to untie a shoelace.

'Anyhow, Detective,' Stephen said, regathering himself, 'I'm afraid you're jumping the gun. The fact I've admitted to an adulterous relationship with a woman to whom I gifted perfume, does not equate to evidence of *I* having poisoned James.'

'That's right,' Bertha agreed – having just publicly witnessed the label of 'adulterer' attached to her husband, she refused to also tag him with 'murderer' – 'Stephen was standing beside myself and Clara and Chester during Uncle's toast. James, when he was poisoned, was at the other side of the hall... *over there*... with David.'

'Though I'm unsure as to why you wish to point out my proximity to the poisoned victim, Bertha,' David said, 'she is correct, Inspector, when she says Stephen did not come in close contact with James, nor James with him, during the toast.'

'Whilst being open to correction, there is one more part of the story I've yet to relate: Mr Bowes did not ingest the poison during the champagne toast.' Dunderdale gave everyone a moment to digest this little fact. 'I must admit, when I read the pathologist's report that said the perfume bottle was unwashed, I was relieved, but I was also intrigued as to why the murderer went to the trouble of washing clean the champagne glass but not the perfume bottle. Not until Sergeant Collins related to me a story Miss Betsy had told him, did I understand. You see the murderer hoped to deflect the time of Mr Bowes's murder. The murderer wanted us to believe a fabrication that Mr Bowes was poisoned during the toast. I also think that by not washing the bottle, in the event of it ever being discovered, it was hoped it would incriminate Lady

Violet de Trouville.' Dunderdale waved down Violet's complaint as unnecessary. 'Do you have anything to tell us, Mr Taylor, of how the poison was administered to Mr Bowes?'

'Of course I don't!'

'Then I would ask all of you here in this room to look upon the bottle before you and tell me what you see?'

'My empty perfume bottle!' Violet retorted.

'Avant-garde claptrap,' David said.

'As I know it's a perfume bottle, that's all I'm able to see,' Clara said.

'I see what Sergeant Collins saw,' Susan said, 'a whisky bottle.'

'Susan, you're right!' Chester said.

'Or a...?' Dunderdale encouraged Susan and Chester to expand.

'Hip flask,' David answered.

'A *hip flask*. What I neglected to tell you all earlier is the bottle also contains traces of whisky...' Dunderdale's pause was punctuated with echoes of 'whisky?' 'A whisky-arsenic trioxide mixture, if you like... I believe, Mr Taylor' – Dunderdale was now brandishing Stephen's leather gloves in the air – 'you were wearing your gloves when you handed Mr Bowes a nip of whisky on return from midnight Mass.'

'That I can agree with. After all, it's no mystery it was freezing!'

'Earlier, I asked Sergeant Collins to search Mr Bowes's room to check if he too owned a pair of gloves. They lie up there still... along with other garments which the young man will never wear again. Now I *have* my confirmation, it stands to reason Mr Bowes will have been wearing his gloves when attending midnight Mass and this explains why neither his, nor your fingerprints, Mr Taylor, were found on the perfume bottle.'

'What does he mean?' Bertha said.

'I think we're about to find out, old girl.'

'So that's how it was done!' Susan said.

Chester was in deep thought.

Ava, reliving a reflection of the last days of James's life in the glossy dark green of the holly sitting on the high mantelpiece, recoiled from David's sudden outburst – 'THEN IT WAS *YOU* WHO ATTACKED AVA!'

'Thank you, Constable Donnelly, for assisting Mr Rickard in the retaking of his seat,' Dunderdale said.

'I don't understand,' Violet said, 'what has my perfume bottle to do with Stephen's hip flask?'

'You truly are a most stupid woman – have you been listening to nothing!' Clara said, and this time Susan really could not justify admonishing her, even if she'd wanted to. 'The detective thinks Stephen used your damn perfume bottle to sneak arsenic *whatever-you-call-it* into the manor!'

'More than that, Miss de Trouville, I *know* Mr Taylor offered Mr Bowes a nip from that very perfume bottle.'

Chester shook his head. 'That ain't how it happened – it can't be! Sir, I told you already, I saw Stephen with my own eyes, nippin' at his own liquor, right before James.'

'Yes, you did, Mr Johnson. When I called you into the study a short while ago, you confirmed what I suspected: that you saw Mr Taylor take a nip *and then* you saw Mr Bowes take a nip. However, when I pressed you to recount accurately what you saw, you said when little Betsy alerted you to her father keeping out the cold, Mr Taylor then offered you a nip while in the process of stowing his hip flask into his pocket. That's when, you declining, Mr Bowes said he would accept – at which point Mr Taylor again removed the hip flask from his pocket.'

'That's what I've been tryin' to tell you! Sir, after Stephen had a good nip, I saw him lick the dribble from his chin!'

'That's right, Chester, my friend!' Stephen said.

'I agree that's exactly what you recounted to me, Mr Johnson. You also said the three of you were at the back of the group at this point?'

'That's right.'

'And when I asked if Mr Taylor pulled Mr Bowes to one side you replied…?'

'Into the shadows, makin' me think the prohibition had crossed the Atlantic.'

'Then I will tell you the reason for Mr Taylor pulling Mr Bowes into the shadows was to reduce the latter's visibility, for what then transpired was, rather than removing his hip flask from its pocket, Mr Taylor reached into his other pocket and removed the perfume bottle. Both men wearing gloves, Mr Bowes's touch would not have been able to discern between glass and metal. In freezing conditions, with the snow falling down around them, his lips would have equally failed to register the difference. Arsenic trioxide being odourless and tasteless, it too would have remained undetected. There were only three elements which could have registered with Mr Bowes; the size and shape are two of these but, as we've just established, the *Chanel Numéro Cinq* bottle could easily be mistaken for a hip flask.' Dunderdale turned to Stephen. 'The third element is the stopper. Therefore, I assume you first removed the glass stopper before passing Mr Bowes his death?'

His mind ticking over, Chester looked from Dunderdale to Stephen.

'I never offered James a nip – he *asked* for one. It was only then that I passed him the only hip flask on me – mine! The same one *I* had drunk from, like Chester says!'

'I'll admit it's genius. How could anyone accuse you of poisoning Mr Bowes when you, yourself, partook of the same drink!'

'*Genius* if that's what did happen, but I say to you all' – Stephen was now submitting his plea to his jury – 'as God is my witness, it's a work of fiction!'

Swallowing Stephen's infidelity – the shoelace still firmly intact with a pristine little bow – Bertha was the first of the 'twelve' to issue a verdict. 'Of course it is,' she said, taking her husband's hand.

'What the hell woulda happened if I'd have accepted?' Chester demanded unexpectedly, having switched to the prosecutor's side.

'I imagine, Mr Johnson,' Dunderdale said when Stephen refused to answer, 'had you taken Mr Taylor up on his offer then he would have passed you *his* hip flask.'

'Is that right, huh…? Or would I have been just some luckless fool?'

'Chester… darling,' Clara said soothingly, 'we don't yet know this *is* what happened.'

'The evidence has been set down before us, Clara,' Susan argued, 'a perfume bottle containing traces of whisky *and* poison.'

Clara shook her head. 'Not "Meek-and-Mild" Stephen! David…?'

David was glaring at Stephen.

'No,' Clara persisted, 'I can't believe it's one of us. It has to be Violet!'

'How could you!' Violet squealed.

'It must be, Detective – Violet and a lover you've yet to learn of!'

'Your aunt's conscience, Miss de Trouville, is clear of murder.'

Catching everyone unaware, David launched his empty glass across the room; the crystal rebounded off Stephen's temple before disappearing behind the settee to crash onto the stone floor.

'Fawcett, if you wouldn't mind,' Dunderdale said as Donnelly and Collins restrained David.

'Why?' Ava spoke for only the second time.

'You must believe me, dearest Ava,' Stephen answered, massaging his right temple, 'the sweetest sister-in-law a man could wish for – it wasn't me!'

'Why?' Ava repeated.

'What your sister-in-law wishes to know, Mr Taylor, is why did you need the inheritance? Whilst interviewing your wife, she told myself and Sergeant Collins you're a very wealthy man.'

Stephen looked to the staircase – a bump above his right eye already rising – and Dunderdale wondered if he was thinking of Betsy and Rose, tucked away in the nursery, insulated from the horrors of real life.

'Taylor's Shipping, Mrs Rickard,' Dunderdale volunteered when Stephen was not forthcoming, 'is on the brink of liquidation.'

'Who told you that!' Stephen demanded as Bertha blurted out 'Don't be absurd!' and others gasped.

'It's not true that just before Christmas the bank issued you with a foreclosure notice?' Dunderdale challenged.

'Stephen?'

'LIQUIDATION!' David's anger had morphed into a form of derangement. 'Administration would be bad enough,' he laughed to the sound of broken crystal being swept into a dustpan, 'but LIQUIDATION!'

'You may well be surprised, Mr Rickard; after all, you

related to me you did not take seriously the rumours circulating in your gentleman's club. Nor did *Sir Henry* suspect, not even when you, Mr Taylor, asked him for a loan on the night of your arrival – although I imagine you never enlightened him to the small print. In the end, it mattered little, for you'd already planned for murder. Your meticulous planning confirms this – that you had no faith in Sir Henry agreeing to any further loans. It would have come as no surprise to you when he turned down your request, especially considering you would have been asking for a substantial amount, to put you back in the black – not to mention the repayment of his last loan still outstanding to this day.'

'Stephen!'

'You lost your money,' Violet screeched, 'so you thought you'd take mine!'

'My dear,' Susan spoke softly, but resolutely, 'it's not *your* money.'

'For my part,' Dunderdale continued over Violet's rerun of her being Henry's widow, 'I struggle to understand how one person could single-handedly lose the entire wealth of a family business that has enjoyed success for over a century… Alas, I am but a simple man! *Mrs Taylor*, I regret to inform you that since inheriting Taylor's Shipping, your husband has made bad after bad investment and as a result has had to take out a number of loans from a number of parties – the collateral for one of these loans being your family home.'

'STEPHEN…? Tell him he's misinformed!'

'Don't worry, old girl, everything the detective's said is all circumstantial… nothing more,' Stephen replied, evading his wife's real concern.

'Too much circumstance, is what I'll argue! Mrs Taylor, I have it on good authority – Scotland Yard authority – the current financial state of Taylor's Shipping is as I have just related. *And so* we come back full circle to those three small words… "Give our lives". Your aim, Mr Taylor, was to provide for your children but you misinterpreted what it means to be the provider for one's family and because of this you failed. Your *sin* was murdering with the intention of saving your children from financial disgrace; from a fall from the wealth which, in their young lives, they'd already become accustomed to. Mr Taylor, do you agree this to be your motivation?'

'The meaning of the words when I spoke them was and is the same as when spoken by any decent, loving father – that we love our children.'

Dunderdale nodded. 'Have it your way.'

'What do you mean?' Bertha wanted to know. 'Stephen, what does he mean?'

'He means,' Susan said to Bertha, 'Stephen was given the chance to explain how it was he became a murderer.'

'YOU… FUCKING… DEVIOUS… BASTARD!' David's final launch – his hands outstretched like claws – was thwarted by Donnelly and Collins, who, having remained at his shoulder, soon had him pressed back into his cushioned seat.

With a shake of his head, Dunderdale warned Tom, who'd also risen with the intention of doling out a bit of his own justice.

Tom re-seated himself.

'Detective, are you *really* sure?' Clara asked with a solemnity Dunderdale had not before witnessed about her.

'HE'S SURE,' David growled, straining at his bonds.

'Clara,' Chester said, 'I saw many injustices back in the USA… it looks like this ain't one of 'em.'

'Two final questions, Mr Taylor. First, how did you come by the knowledge of Mr Bowes being Sir Henry's heir?'

'That would be the time when Atkins read to us Henry's last will and testament… on Boxing Day.'

'No, Mr Taylor, you gained access to Sir Henry's last will and testament – how, I don't know, but access it you did! It's the codicil which you first heard of at the reading of the will. The two feathers taken from a culled daw in the forest are proof of this – that *two* murders were planned for.'

'So that's what you were referring to when you badgered me about an excursion into the forest!' Clara said, astonished. 'You really did consider me to be a murderess…!'

'It's not a pleasant feeling, is it,' Stephen said, the curve of his lips belying the sentiment.

'Much more pleasant than experiencing being poisoned or having your throat cut,' Dunderdale replied. 'To venture out deep into the forest to locate two daw tail feathers was not incidental but a symbolic act to provide a direct link with the pagan story, otherwise it would have been simple to take them from any one of the six feathered items stored in the attic – as you did when you needed easy access to a feather for a walk you knew, only too well, Mr Taylor, would be suggested by another member of the family. Which brings me to my final question. How did you recreate the spectre? Come now, Mr Taylor, there's no need to look so gormless! The spectre Mrs Rickard witnessed on the moor – did you employ someone?'

'To do what, *Dunderhead*?'

'Ah! There's the man I've been seeking!' Dunderdale returned the accused's smile. 'Did you, Mr Taylor, employ someone to wander round the moor wearing a white dress to put the fear of God into Mrs Rickard?'

'Again, you have me at a loss.'

Thirteen

'WHAT MADE YER first suspect him?' Collins asked as Shaw and Donnelly led a handcuffed Mr Stephen Taylor out to the waiting motor car.

'Remember when you said to me, Collins, how children make excellent witnesses?'

'I do, sir. You said "not always".'

'Then you'll remember I conceded Miss Betsy to be a reliable witness. Well, it was *she* who provided me with my biggest clue as to her father being the murderer, though she – may Hera bless her – has no idea and I wish for her to remain ignorant of the fact.'

'I understand, sir.'

'The clue, Collins, was Miss Betsy hearing her father repeat her name on the foggy moor. She called him "silly" for this concern and no one would have thought it odd for a loving father to panic so. I know I didn't! But along with this thought, I had the image of a murderer attempting to make himself heard in order to establish his alibi. There was no reason why Mr Taylor could not hear his daughter's reply if she could hear his call for they were on the same latitude – we know this for we have Shaw's account of Mr Taylor and Mr Rickard arriving at the farmhouse at the same time. I regarded it as odd that, for a man who had a great deal of experience of walking this moorland in all weathers, Mr Taylor did not move away from the east boundary wall when searching for his child. He created the alibi of a continued interest in the stag after it had jumped the wall to make us think he remained rooted there until the realisation of Miss Betsy being lost in the fog, but in actual fact, he only waited there until the fog thickened. After his business of murder was interrupted, he returned to the same area and only *then* did he begin shouting Miss Betsy's name – quite a delay between the fog setting in and the loving father calling out for his daughter, wouldn't you agree? The time it took him to cover more ground than Mr Rickard was cancelled out by the additional time it took Mr Rickard to carry his wife back to the farmhouse.

'Before we left that day, remembering my prime suspect's game of hide-and-seek, when I sent you to find Smith for our lift back to Appleby, I popped back up to the attic to see whether a feather was missing from any of the cloaks or masks… *Lo and behold* a feather was missing from one of the cloaks – its neighbouring feather dislodged – and yet, we know that after the murders of Mr Bowes and Sir Henry, all items were fully intact. It was because of this missing feather that I wasn't surprised when Shaw found a black feather on the moorland – surprised, yes, that Shaw had discovered one, but not surprised one existed for the purpose of leaving upon Mrs Rickard's body.'

'Remarkable, sir!' the sergeant congratulated the inspector.

'I told you, Collins, it's never one man's work. Your linking of Miss Betsy's story of her father not liking the cold with how the arsenic trioxide could have been administered to Mr Bowes was instrumental in the cracking of this case.'

Collins's countenance was beaming. 'I suddenly realised, sir, little Betsy were really sayin' to me – when she told me Mr Johnson liked the cold, like her – that her dad'd offered Mr Johnson a nip o't strong stuff and that he'd refused. I then got to wonderin', what if Mr Bowes were also offered a nip but *he* accepted, *and* what if it were given to him in't perfume bottle – after all, I did think from't start it looked like a whisky bottle o' some sort!'

'Then,' Dunderdale added, 'when I asked if there was anything else that had been discussed between you and the Taylors, you told me of a father declaring he would give his life for his children.'

'Do yer think he were givin' away a clue?'

'If he was it was inadvertently.'

'But do yer think you've enough to convict him – he didn't seem to think so?'

'I'm confident *we* do, Collins.' Dunderdale drew the sergeant deeper into the cold corner, further away from where the family was still convened near the fire where they were mulling over the recent developments. 'The reply from Scotland Yard finished by saying there'd been some suspicion surrounding the death of Mr Taylor's late father.'

'The' don't think he'd something to do with it!' Collins whispered, shocked.

'Looks like they did and they will again once the chief constable puts a call through to them that Mr Stephen Taylor has been arrested on two accounts of murder and one of attempted murder.'

'Then the'll open up an investigation?'

'Yes, Collins, I think they will…'

———

'Isn't it said a wife usually knows these things,' Clara said to Chester and Susan.

'Bertha's not your "usual" wife,' Susan replied softly, conscious of being overheard by the not-so-usual wife, who was sitting in oblivion beside the seat cushion still warm from her husband's touch.

As he was promising to do Stephen harm before Shaw and Donnelly had the chance to cart him off, Ava had stood before her husband, her hands on his arms, and looking up into his face, she'd told him to let the King's justice deal with him. David, agreeing, had cleaved to this open show of tenderness – the hope which had abandoned him returned.

Reading in his blue eyes the beginnings of a thaw, Ava now moved across to comfort Bertha, who, an ally by her side, demanded, 'What are you all whispering about?'

Violet said the obvious. 'Clara's mocking you.'

'I was wondering, Boots,' Clara said, 'if our sister would be willing to settle the affair of our inheritance.'

'Not now,' Susan said.

'Yes, *now*,' Bertha replied, turning on her ally. 'Ava, you've just heard I'm left with nothing… my husband gone, along with his business, and the house – *my house, Ava!*'

'You really want to talk about this now?' Ava challenged her siblings.

'Yes, *now*,' Bertha repeated as Susan sat back and waited. 'Because, Ava, I realise I *do* have something: I have my third inheritance.'

'Boots is right…'

'Stop calling me that!'

'… the inheritance must be split equally between the three of us. From what you've always told me of father, he would have fought for that.'

'We don't know what father would have wanted,' Ava corrected Clara. 'Furthermore, Uncle inherited the estate and the family wealth, not Father.'

'Don't be a bitch!'

'CLARA.'

'No, David, it's about time she realised the world does not begin and end with "Ava".'

'The inheritance is not about *me*, it's about Uncle's wishes concerning Crowthwaite Manor and its future.'

'But it is about you! If the stars were to fall from the sky, our heaven would be gone but you'd be sitting there... with a lap full of diamonds!'

'You can all argue as much as you like,' Violet said, 'but you forget *I* am Henry's widow and *I* will fight for what's mine!'

'There's going to be no splitting of any estate!' Ava blurted out; Dunderdale, still deep in shadow, smiled. '*THERE!*'

'And this is your final word?' Clara said.

'It is.'

'Boots, are you just going to sit there and say nothing?'

'Looks like you'll have to marry, after all,' Bertha replied.

'And you, *Boots*, will be free to marry once again,' Clara countered, 'once your husband swings from the gallows.'

'DON'T CALL ME BY THAT NAME!'

'Ava, I won't beg,' Clara said, determined. 'Uncle's gone, leaving me with no yearly income. Therefore, I *must* have my inheritance.'

'Ava,' Bertha began, tightening the bow, 'pity me. Don't turn your back on your faithful sister, not now. Not when Stephen has just been accused of murder. Not when I'm left with nothing... *PLEASE... AVA?*'

'I won't let sororal emotions be my guide.'

'Ava, I'll be left homeless!'

'Of course I won't see you and the girls out on the streets. I will honour the family code, but it will be a sober generosity that will guide my decisions. Clara, it is time you claim responsibility for your life... you will have options—'

'OPTIONS! What kind of options can the woman who abandoned love for wealth offer? No, thank you, Ava, I will take no lecture from you.'

'Then don't infer instruction, but advice… from a sister who cares for you,' Ava added, her last words freezing Clara's rebut. 'It is now you'll realise just how generous Uncle was in permitting your yearly allowance in perpetuity.'

'Generous! The bastard cut it off before Stephen murdered him—'

'Don't say those words!' Bertha railed.

'Why not, they're accurate! *Ava*, had Uncle not sent instruction to Atkins to cut off my allowance, you'd have no choice but to honour his previous commitments. I don't see why I should suffer my loss of income when Uncle's bad humour was caused by Violet!'

'It was caused by nothing of the sort!' Violet asserted. 'You know full well Henry was angry with you for chasing after David!'

'I suppose you would know all about *chasing after David*!'

'Come now, girls, show some decorum,' Susan said, breaking her pact with Ava and silencing David.

'I've *still* to decide which raven you are, Susan. As for Uncle, I feel no loss for him – DO YOU HEAR THAT? I MISS YOU NOT AND I HOPE YOU DROWN IN AN ETERNITY OF HELL'S FIERY WATERS, YOU TIGHT-FISTED BASTARD!'

Dunderdale looked up to the portrait, half expecting it to respond.

'For all Uncle's faults,' Ava told Clara, 'he still indulged you. Yes, you can laugh! I know you won't acknowledge what I'm about to say, for you saw a tyrant, but Uncle did take his family duties and responsibilities seriously. For you, that meant a yearly allowance which more than permitted you to live a frivolous and meaningless lifestyle… one in which you thought only of pleasure.'

'Easy to condemn when one is content with a dull life!'

'I will not make Uncle's mistakes,' Ava continued. 'I will make my commitment to you, that as your eldest sister, I too will not neglect my family duties and responsibilities.'

'Then you will split the inheritance three ways?' Bertha asked expectantly.

'I will not.'

'But you just said!'

'I have already said I will see neither you nor my nieces without a home. Now, I offer to help Clara settle into a new life where I hope she will discover her true self – if she'll take my advice?'

'Here's my own advice to you, dearest sister… take care the money doesn't bastardise you like it did Uncle.'

Chester followed Clara up the stairs; Bertha, saying she must have a lie down, was not far behind them.

When David rose to join his wife, Susan gestured to Violet they should make themselves scarce.

'Come on,' Dunderdale said to Collins, 'it's time we said our goodbyes.'

The two policemen caught up with Violet as she headed for the east tower. 'My lady, we'll be saying our farewells.'

Violet, not slowing her pace, looked over her shoulder. 'Goodbye.'

'Not so much as a thank you for you keepin' quiet 'bout her affair with Peter Barnes! Do yer know, sir, I don't think she were worried 'bout bein' given three years.'

'I think you're right, the young lady's weekly visits to Carlisle would have put a cuckoo in the nest, sooner or later.

Once you begin living a lie, Collins, it's hard to find your way back to the truth.' With one hand paused on the kitchen door, Dunderdale added, 'If there's one thing I would say to you, it would be to always remember this.'

'I doubt we'll ever see him again, eh,' the first kitchen maid said.

'Here comes the inspector that found him out!' the second kitchen maid replied.

'We've come to say goodbye,' Dunderdale told Mrs Clarke.

'Yer not stayin' for tonight's celebrations?' the first kitchen maid queried.

'What better way to see in New Year than with the family who've much to thank yer for,' Mrs Clarke agreed.

'I thank you for the offer but ask that you accept my apologies. I've already accepted an invitation to spend the remainder of this year and the opening of the next with the chief constable and his wife. Mrs Watson was quite insistent I join their celebrations.'

'She puts on a good spread, she does… yer'll not be disappointed. There'll be plenty o' guests, too, if I know Mrs Watson!'

'Hmm,' Dunderdale replied.

''Tis a pity,' the first kitchen maid complained, 'us 'bout to make wassail… to toast in twenty-four.'

'Mrs Watson'll have wassail,' Mrs Clarke told her protégé.

'She'll not have a silver wassail bowl like ours! Drink won't be nowt like our wassail, neither. We're sousin' our apples in mulled mead,' the young maid told Dunderdale, 'and we'll be spicin' with sugar, ginger, cinnamon and nutmeg – mind, there's more ingredients, but that's a secret, eh,' she added, tapping her nose.

'Will *he* be spendin' New Year in a cell – *Mr Taylor?*' the second kitchen maid asked, the name a whisper – Stephen already a taboo subject.

'He will,' Dunderdale confirmed.

'Divn't be botherin' the inspector nae more 'bout that matter!' Mrs Clarke interrupted, and the maid's mouth closed again.

'Well, we shan't keep you,' Dunderdale said, and after exchanges of 'Happy New Year!', Mrs Clarke called out 'Washail!' to which Dunderdale turned back round to reply 'Drinchail!'

'I'll certainly toast yer tonight, Inspector, and wish "yer be healthy" for now, cos o' you, the castle can settle back down into itself and I just know Mrs Ava's goin' to be a mistress to rival any other!'

'A cook and two kitchen maids for one baronet and his wife,' Collins criticised as he closed the kitchen door, Lizzie quickly passing by with a bucket in hand.

'Goodbye, Lizzie "Silver-Tone"!' Dunderdale called out.

'Goodbye, sir! Goodbye, Sergeant!'

'Yes, it does seem excessive, Collins,' Dunderdale said, referring to the sergeant's criticism. 'Though I suppose there's all the staff who also need feeding... including the outdoor staff.'

'Never thought of it like that.'

'And now Mrs Rickard's inherited, who knows what the future will hold for Crowthwaite Manor— Hang fire, Collins...' Dunderdale said upon hearing voices.

'What do yer think twenty-four'll bring, Mr Fawcett?'

'Not another year like this one, I'm hoping, Mr Turner.'

'*If New Year's Eve night-wind blows south,*' George began, '*It betokeneth warmth and growth; If west, much milk, and fish in the sea; If north, cold and storms there will be; If east, the trees will bear much fruit; If north-east, flee it, man and brute!*'

'Fawcett. Mr Turner,' Dunderdale said as the two servants rounded the corner from the laundry room, 'we're about to leave.'

'Then a Happy New Year to yer, Inspector,' George said.

'Sir,' Fawcett said in farewell and when Dunderdale doffed his hat the makings of a smile lined the butler's face.

Susan had returned to the hall and was alone with Ava; there was no sign of David. After more farewells and a bit of banter between Susan and Dunderdale and Ava's gratitude for a job well done, Susan told the policemen a motor car had arrived for them, 'sent from Appleby'.

'Then now we *do* leave, Collins. Miss Markham.'

Susan shook his hand.

'I'll walk you out,' Ava insisted.

Dunderdale, about to follow, halted. 'You've had the other fire lit!'

Ava smiled.

Dunderdale looked up to Sir Henry's portrait and noticed the light from the second fire had cast some colour into the baronet's cheeks.

'What is it?' Ava asked.

'For one moment, I imagined a speck of humanity.'

'It was rarely on view; nevertheless, it was there.'

Collins was already seated in the waiting motor car as Dunderdale and Ava stepped out into the dusk, their shoes creating fresh prints in the snow while Dunderdale's coat flapped east towards the forest.

'Be true to yourself,' he told her, immediately feeling a hypocrite.

'I will,' she assured him.

'Then all that's left to be said is "goodbye".'

'Goodbye, Detective Inspector.'

One foot inside the motor car, Dunderdale turned back. 'From here on in, every winter solstice, make sure Ivy brings in the she-holly ahead of the he-holly.'

'What about together… side by side?'

'That would work,' Gilbert Dunderdale agreed and, with a final smile, climbed in.

Epilogue

'Fawcett.'

'Madam,' the butler greeted his employer in the corridor. 'I have, this moment, delivered a letter into Mrs Taylor's hands.'

'You mean…?' Ava asked.

'I couldn't possibly say.'

Ava, dressed for riding, entered the dining room and found her sister had finally descended to breakfast.

'I can't read it…' Bertha said.

Ava took a deep breath. 'Would you like me to read it for you?'

Bertha pushed the envelope across the table. 'I don't wish to know.'

Ava tore open the envelope and, removing the letter, her eyes began to scan from left to right.

'Oh, just read it out!'

Pulling out a chair, Ava returned to the top of the page and read, 'Bertha, old girl…'

My appeals having failed, this morning as I awaited the opening of my cell door for the final time, I was suddenly overcome with a compulsion to ask for pen and paper, so I could write you my last words. I know that you, Bertha – the most loyal of wives – will pass this truth on to our girls when they are old

*enough to understand. You see, old girl, I realise I
must confess the sin of murder.*

*Being bound by the laws of human nature, I
would have much preferred to continue saying all
of what Dunderdale accused was a lie; yet I know, as
my existence approaches its end, I must admit that
I, Stephen Taylor, father and husband – having been
in such despair over the loss of our family's wealth,
the fear for our girls' futures – did murder Henry
and James... and that, had David not been madly
in love with his wife, would have murdered sweet
Ava too.*

Ava closed her eyes to give thanks to David.

*Where Dunderdale was wrong was that James's
death was never planned for. Knowing, as did we all,
Henry took secretive nips on the journey back from
midnight Mass (never the journey to, the hypocrite
not wanting liquor on his breath while under God's
roof), it was he who was to be poisoned. I'd planned
to substitute his hip flask for the perfume bottle on
Christmas Eve – and I would have, had the thought
not occurred to me on our train journey down that I
should check the contents of his will.*

*The old fool made it easy, too easy for me. All it
took was to borrow the spare study key from the estate
office and hide in a dark corner, biding my time until*

Henry arrived to open his safe, lighting up its combination as he did so. I almost put a stop to the whole business when I read James was his son, the one to inherit. But what was a man to do, old girl, when he stood to lose everything, including the futures he'd promised to his two young daughters? No, James's life could not be saved; Henry's last will and testament sealed his fate – our girls' lives trumped his.

A third of the inheritance would have sufficed – it should have only ever been Henry. Then only Henry and James, but once I understood the careful wording of the will, I knew that Atkins was Henry's man and he would do all in his power to ensure only one person be permitted to inherit the entire fortune. And so, I resolved myself to only Henry and James and Ava.

Poor James! It wasn't a dignified death – I acknowledge this; when it was to be Henry's death it was perfectly justified, after all he was despised by so many and a man who's so despised has no worth and his ending matters not. For James, I am heartily sorry the death was an excruciating one, though it did allow for Henry to die like the sacrificial virgin and I recognise this tied in much more neatly with his family's legacy.

Don't judge me too harshly, old girl, for your uncle's death. Surely, as a mother, you can see it was only too easy to slit the throat of a man who didn't know the true meaning of the word 'family'.

'… Are you sure you wish me to go on?'

'I hardly think it could get any worse.'

> Truly, when I think of his Christmas toast, all I hear is a man so consumed with his own immortality that I believe if he could have achieved it without an heir, he would never have married.
>
> Don't be alarmed, old girl, when I tell you, you won't be the first to read this letter. After its first reading a copy will have been made and I'm glad for it, for Dunderdale will be appreciative of the following facts. As you will know, Scotland Yard could find nothing in their investigation of my father's death. It is Time which is to blame for their failure to find murder. I lay bare my soul to you, Bertha Taylor — from my cold confines where, any moment, the key will turn in the lock, to tell you I still believe it to have been an act of mercy, his mind not being what it ought to have been. A son's final act.

'No!' Bertha cried.

'If you can bear it,' Ava told her, referring to their hearing Stephen's 'truths', 'then so can I.'

Taking her sister's hand, Bertha nodded.

> As for Ava's apparition, I know nothing. However, I have been thinking a great deal of the spectre and I've come to the conclusion we're to believe she gave her life to the wrong god. I, on the other hand, may

have committed a greater sin and in doing so must have promised mine to the devil. Which brings me back to my reason for my truth: in writing to you to confess my sins in full, I renege on the contract made and deliver myself back into God's hands. I hope by writing this truth, God will be merciful, and I hope that our girls – my Besty Betsy and dearest Rose – will one day be able to forgive me...

... their ever-loving father.

'... At least now you know,' Ava said, tightening their bond.

Bertha blinked, moistening each cheek which had been a desert for more than a year.

'You left this on the desk,' Tom told Ava as he entered the dining room brandishing an envelope in her writing; his other arm cradling a newborn.

'It's from Stephen...' Ava said when Tom realised the scene he'd happened upon, '... written two days ago.'

'On the day of...?'

'Yes,' Ava replied as Betsy's excited voice came down the grand staircase.

The baby gave a cry, its voice still a bleat. 'There, little man... Daddy's here.'

After hugging Bertha – telling her sister how proud she was of her and promising they were through the worst – Ava softly stroked a lock of white-blonde hair from the baby's forehead before kissing him on top of his head.

Her head bowed, Tom leaned into Ava and, his lips lightly touching her neck, whispered, 'I love you, Mrs Atkinson.'

Turning her head up to her husband's face, Ava's eyes

spoke her reply as Betsy stormed into the dining room – her nanny trailing after her with Rose in tow.

'Aunt Ava, I'm ready for my hack.'

'*Hack*, I thought you said it would only be a short ride down to the village! Ava, it's only been ten weeks!'

'I'm fine… I'll *be* fine.'

'We'll be fine, Uncle Tom,' Betsy corrected.

Tom regarded his new family. 'So we will, Betsy… so we will.'

———

The white stripe of Ava's chestnut Anglo-Arab bobbed in tune to its springing step, its nostrils flaring and its tail carried high.

'Later,' Ava told the mare, patting the arched neck.

'Aunt Ava's not allowed to give you your head, you silly mare,' Betsy agreed, her little pony trying to match the horse's stride. 'Young Joe will take you out later – won't he, Aunt Ava?'

Smiling down on her niece, Ava noticed the dust being kicked up by the eight hooves. George's forecast was right – *again*, she thought. The ground that was often saturated was rapidly drying out.

As they followed the track westwards along Cross Fell's contour, Ava recalled David's withered words, courtesy of Clara's paraphrasing… *No, WE shan't be visiting this summer, nor any other time, for that matter. I may have considered your invitation, but David's adamant he won't ever set eyes on you again while you carry the name of another man.*

Shaking herself from the memory, Ava halted to pass the time of day with one of her tenants – Betsy showing off her new plaited reins that matched the little plaits in her pony's mane.

The reins were also presented to Bert while he held Ava's horse, Ava popping into Crowthwaite's village store to say hello to the postmistress and hand over an invitation for posting.

At The Black Feather, Pearl called out from the doorway, a male traveller by her side: 'How's little Harry doin'?'

'Still doesn't say much,' Ava joked.

'Just like his father!'

As the two women laughed, a jackdaw flew above their heads heading north-east, a twig in its beak.

The beginnings of the next layer for another clutch of eggs.

D.M. Austin lives with her husband and their teenage son in their home county of Yorkshire. As a mature student, D.M. Austin studied Primary Teaching for two years and Education Studies for the final third year at York St John University before graduating with First Class honours. *A Christmas Murder of Crows* is D.M. Austin's debut novel, introducing Inspector Gilbert Dunderdale as a Golden Age detective. When not writing, D.M. Austin can be found hill walking, mountain biking, drawing or snuggled in her reading corner reading fiction and non-fiction across a range of genres.

Printed in Great Britain
by Amazon

13256619R00169